ᎭMANDA
CADABRA
AND THE CELLAR OF SECRETS

HOLLY BELL

Other titles by Holly Bell

Amanda Cadabra and The Hidey-Hole Truth
(The Amanda Cadabra Cozy Mysteries Book 1)

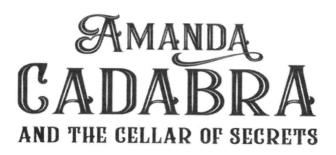

AMANDA CADABRA
AND THE CELLAR OF SECRETS

HOLLY BELL

To Pravin and Philippa

And above all, watch with glittering eyes

the whole world around you

because the greatest secrets are hidden

in the most unlikely places.

Those who don't believe in magic

will never find it.

Roald Dahl

CONTENTS

THE VILLAGE OF SUNKEN MADLEY AND THE

KEY

1. Amanda's House
2. Sunken Madley Manor
3. The Sinner's Rue Pub
4. The Library
5. St Ursula-without-Barnet

6. Medical Centre
7. Priory Ruins
8. Playing Fields
9 The Snout and Trough Pub
10. Post Office/Corner Shop

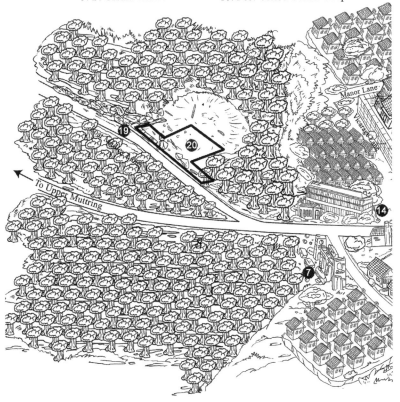

ANNEXE OF *LOST MADLEY*

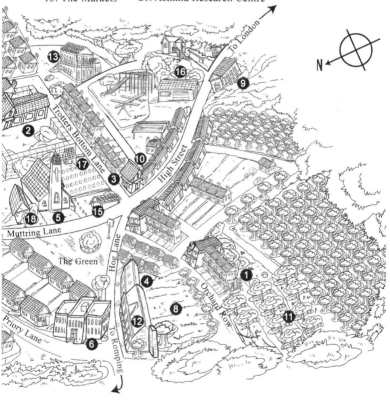

KEY

1. The Apple Cart Pub
2. George's House
3. The Shelter

THE VILLAGE OF LITTLE MADLEY

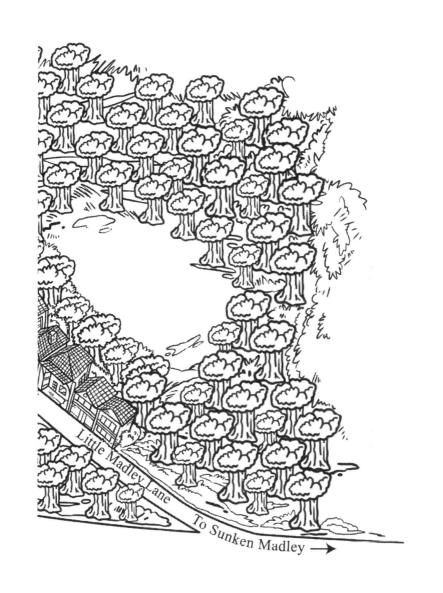

Introduction

Please note that to enhance the reader's experience of Amanda's world, this British-set story, by a British author, uses British English spelling, vocabulary, grammar and usage, and includes local and foreign accents, dialects and a magical language that vary from different versions of English as it is written and spoken in other parts of our wonderful, diverse world.

Chapter 1

❧

WHY AMANDA FOUND THE BODY

Call a doctor or search for clues? Amanda Cadabra took the few vital seconds to make the decision.

But then, she had never been impulsive.

* * * * *

'Mrs Cadabra, with the best will in the world from you and your husband, your granddaughter could not have had a normal childhood.'

In response, the lady seated with regal posture on the chintz sofa, inhaled, and raised an eyebrow, rendering her larger violet eye even more magnified than usual. Her piercing glare demanded an explanation. Detective Sergeant Thomas Trelawney of the Devon and Cornwall Police was not easily intimidated, as Vic 'The Headbanger' Hardy could have told anyone brave enough to have asked him.

However, on this, his first visit, to 26 Orchard Row, Sunken Madley, Trelawney needed to make some kind of connection with Senara, Perran, and their beloved granddaughter and adoptee Amanda. These three were, after all, the only witnesses to the day of the incident, 28 years ago, that he was here to continue investigating.

'Here' was a village that had grown up out of the rural landscape over a period of 800 years. It lay 13 miles to the north of the Houses of Parliament, and three miles south of the border of Hertfordshire. Herts, as the abbreviation is styled, was home to Jane Austen's Emma and the seat of the burgeoning aircraft industry in the last century. Since those days, the county boundaries had been moved so that Sunken Madley was now, technically, on the outskirts of Greater London.

Nevertheless, Sunken Madley still was, in spirit, a country village, off the beaten track, hidden by the encircling trees. It was distinguished only by its orchard of Hormead Pearmain apples, and fine stained-glass windows, adorning the medieval church of St Ursula-without-Barnet. Of particular interest to students of the art, was the composition of the saint and the little bear with the bag of apples.

A gust of wind cast a pink handful of cherry blossom against the living room window as Trelawney's hazel eyes returned Mrs Cadabra's gaze politely but unwaveringly. He said mildly, 'In other words, Amanda wouldn't always have been able to play in the fields, run up and down the garden, maybe eat anything she wanted, like the other children here could.'

'One couldn't expect you to know this, Sergeant, not having any of your own,' Mrs Cadabra pronounced with sympathetic condescension, 'but,' and she took a loose hairpin from her white victory roll, 'children ... adapt.' She speared the accessory back into her coiffure to signal that the subject was closed.

Trelawney hadn't finished. He thrived on puzzles, bringing

order to chaos, and justice to the wronged. However, above these assets, his soon-to-be-retired boss, Chief Inspector Hogarth, trusted his seasoned judgment, especially of when to operate with a light touch.

He swivelled his tall, slim, grey-suited form towards Perran, who smiled kindly and said, with his gentle Cornish-flavoured voice, 'I know what you mean, Sergeant. But Amanda was always a very special little one. Since she was a bian, a baby, she spent her fair share of nights in the local hospital when we didn't know if she'd pull through. We did our best to help her, but in the end, she learned the hard way that her choices had consequences.'

'Did that make Amanda fearful? Wary?'

'Oh no, Sergeant, just careful, wise even, beyond her years. Though in others she's young for her age. But, as Senara said, she got used to things, like carrying her inhaler, avoiding certain food, watching the pollen count. Amanda always says, 'It isn't terminal, after all, it's just asthma.'

* * * * *

It was asthma that had brought Amanda Cadabra to this moment, this room … this body.

She felt for a pulse.

* * * * *

It had all happened a great deal sooner than anyone in the village could have expected. Even Dr Sharma, who was in the know, when she told Amanda about the new allergy clinic, had said that it was months away.

Amanda had dropped in, to collect a repeat prescription for her asthma inhaler, on her way to see about a furniture restoration job. An eager trainee from infancy, Amanda had taken over her grandfather's business.

Asthma and furniture restoration were unlikely bedfellows, with the toxic chemicals, dust, and hard physical labour. This had niggled Trelawney from the first time he had read the case file three years ago.

Amanda's secret levitation skills enabled her to cope covertly but ably. Trelawney, however, was a long way from even contemplating this possibility. And even if he had been able to, it would have been only with extreme scepticism and inexplicable discomfort.

Still, Amanda took sensible precautions and always had her inhaler handy. Dr Sharma was a respected and gifted physician, and between her own magic and the general practitioner's medicine, the asthma was under reasonable control.

However, there was no denying that Amanda's chest momentarily tightened when Neeta Sharma had told her *where* they were going to build an allergy research centre.

Chapter 2

❧

LORDS, AND SHOCK AT THE BUFFET

The news came from a new and unexpected source. And Amanda would never have heard it, if she had succumbed to her natural social reticence.

In spite of his 'word of a cricketer' promise, Middlesex batsman and new Sunken Madley VIP and eye candy… cancelled.

Ten days ago, at the end of the most complicated, challenging and eventful weekend of her life unravelling the mysteries, ghosts and potential scandal of the Manor, the celebrity cricket hero Ryan Ford had made Amanda a promise. He was to share details of a secret entrance to Sunken Madley Manor and to treat Amanda to dinner at the Snout and Trough. However, golden-haired, fit, tanned and handsome eligible bachelor (as a dozen villagers had taken pains to impress on Amanda) was about to make a regretful phone call.

Amanda had walked into the workshop at 9 o'clock on an alternately sunny and showery morning. Pushing a strand of her long mouse-brown hair back into her practical plait, she locked herself in, went to her bench, slotted her iPod into the player and set it to play.

She sang along as she looked for her close-work glasses. Not the clear lens ones that she used to hide her eyes from Normals after she'd been using magic. In terms of maintaining secrecy, it was an unfortunate by-product of Amanda's use of her mystical abilities that it caused the islands of golden brown pigment in the sea of her blue eyes to expand, resulting in a colour change, noticeable to the extra observant.

Amanda picked up a hacksaw, marked up a length of white ash and made a notch deep enough to hold the blade.

'*Ahiewske!*' she bade the hacksaw, and it began a rhythmic to and fro in time to the music.

She was about to get the cabinet scraper and the nail remover going when her mobile phone rang. Amanda turned off the music and answered.

It was Ryan Ford.

'I'm *incredibly* sorry, Amanda. Believe me, if there was *any* way I could be there, I would. *Please*, say you understand.'

'Of course,' she answered politely, subduing her disappointment.

'I do hope that means you'll still be using the tickets?'

He had previously peace-offered them to atone for giving Amanda an uncomfortable moment on his first outing for the Sunken Madley cricket team.

'All right. Sure,' Amanda agreed reluctantly.

'Can't *wait* to see you. Jake, our left-arm bowler and a great pal, is having his birthday bash after the match in the Nursery Pavilion. I've told him all about you, and he *insists* I invite you. You *will* come, won't you?' Ryan entreated.

Amanda recoiled. Social functions weren't her thing at all. 'Look I'd rather leave it. I won't know anyone —'

'You'll know *me*! And you'll have your best friend with you. And you don't have to stay long. Please?' he said appealingly.

He's told his friend all about me? thought Amanda. That's going a bit fast, isn't it? What she said aloud was,

'Very well. I mean, thank you, that's very kind.'

'Thank *you*, Amanda. See you Saturday.'

'Goodbye.' She tapped off the call.

Amanda's jury was still out on Ryan Ford. She never seemed to experience the same emotion for more than five minutes when she was around him. Amanda was, by turns, charmed, alarmed, incensed or suspicious. No wonder Gordon French, the local team umpire and retired head of Sunken Madley School, had cautioned her regarding Ryan.

Nevertheless, so it was, the following Saturday morning, at a quarter past nine, Amanda Cadabra was walking to the car belonging to her next-door neighbour and best friend Claire. Claire Ruggieri, several years older than Amanda but her number one fan, was, in her own words, 'a media slave'.

Claire of the chocolate brown hair and eyes was well connected, vivacious and usually at work. It was Claire who, years ago, had brought sheltered and retiring Amanda out of her village shell and into the bright light of London nightlife, to dancing and even romance of a cautious and discreet kind.

To none of the men labelled 'unsuitable' by Granny and Grandpa, and which was borne out in every case, did Amanda consider, for so much as a moment, confiding her magical gifts. Indeed, neither had she told Claire, much as she loved her.

If her best friend acquired any information about Amanda that needed to be kept secret, Amanda dared not trust Claire to keep her own counsel. She could all too easily blurt it out, to the wrong person, to *any* person. And in the media, there would be an ear for the unusual, the newsworthy. If it reached the wrong people, the risk to Amanda would be very real.

Claire was a Normal. Granny had impressed on Amanda, from the very beginning, that Normals and Magic were an uncomfortable and even dangerous combination.

As Claire locked her front door and turned towards her lime green Audi Sportback, she spotted him, leisurely approaching, a walking collection of furry stormclouds studded with two livid yellow eyes.

'Come to say goodbye?' asked Claire, hopefully.

But Tempest planted himself next to the rear passenger door, and looked up at her with disgruntled impatience.

Tempest was Amanda's familiar; a reincarnated cat, courtesy of some very rare and potent spell-weaving by Granny and Grandpa, when Amanda was 15 years old. His contempt for the human species was unbounded and evident, with the exception of Amanda whom he regarded as his special ward. Only from her would he accept endearments and verbal teasing. There were one or two select persons whom he tolerated and allowed to give him treats. Claire was one of them.

Amanda intervened, offering diplomatically, 'Would you like to warm up the car while I get His Highness's blanket?'

'I have a choice?' asked Claire, helplessly.

'Well,' Amanda considered, 'you can, *A*: not let him in and have the accusatory stare seared on your mind for the duration of the day. *B*: you can let him in and find a lot of cat hairs over your upholstery. *C*: you can let me protect the seat before you grant him the access that he considers to be his divine right.'

'Hm,' agreed Claire.

'You know what he's like,' Amanda said, apologetically.

'I do. As every householder and shop owner in this village knows: he's wherever he wants to be. Look at him.'

Tempest was offering his profile for her admiration.

'True,' acknowledged Amanda, with a rueful smile. 'Do you mind, Claire?'

'No, it's OK,' she acquiesced good-naturedly.

'I expect he thinks we should be honoured!' Tempest was pleased to see that Amanda saw it that way. He always chose to disregard her unseemly mirth whenever he assumed his place on one of the passenger seats of her car.

Amanda was back in seconds with a square of fake fur with a tiger's head on it, which she arranged on the back seat. She stood back, and Tempest minced in and settled himself in chauffeured splendour behind the driver. It never failed to amuse her, and she laughed as they set off.

The country lane to Sunken Madley runs south to meet the A1000 that goes to Barnet. From there, over some 10 miles, the road slopes down towards the heart of London.

Amanda, Claire and Tempest followed it as far as East Finchley where they turned off along The Bishop's Avenue, alias Billionaire's Row. At its pinnacle, they went right and through the narrow gap by The Spaniard's Inn, haunt of notorious highwayman Dick Turpin. Thence they drove through Hampstead to St John's Wood and parked near the underground station. They disembarked and walked south towards Lord's Cricket ground, home of the MCC, Marylebone County Cricket club, where the game has been played for over two hundred years.

Tempest decided to make his own way there and attend to any business he might have along the way.

'How has the furniture restoration business been going since Perran passed on?' asked Claire, as they approached their destination.

'Fine,' Amanda replied sunnily, 'Grandpa trained me well and prepared me to take over.'

'Getting plenty of customers?'

'Oh, yes. More from the village than before, actually.'

'I'll bet.'

'Why?'

'People in Sunken Madley care for you. You'll always be little Amanda to them. And they see you as all alone now both your grandparents are gone.'

'You may have a point. They've got even keener to marry me off.'

'They equate having "a good man" around with being safe and secure,' said Claire.

'I suppose they mean well. Even if it is a bit stifling.'

'Tell me about it. When I go to family events I'm still called Piccola, even by people younger, and shorter, than I am. I see it as affectionate.'

'Fair enough,' conceded Amanda with a smile.

They found their seats and settled in well before the Five-

Minute Bell called the players to the field.

It was a close-run match, but, thanks to the Middlesex captain, the home team won the day, and he was awarded Man of the Match. Ryan came in for his share of the glory, having partnered his skipper to get his crucial century, in other words, 100 runs. It was their 119 partnership that had pipped the opposing team to the post.

The final applause pattered away, and, variously joyful and disappointed, the members of the crowd gathered their belongings to head for refreshments or the return home. The ladies took their time.

'Let's give Ryan a while to change before we turn up. Or he won't be there yet, and I'll feel completely out of place,' said Amanda. Even so, as, by degrees, they approached the Nursery Pavilion, Amanda's nerve began to fail her. 'Oh, couldn't we just go home, Claire? I can text him and convey my apologies. I doubt he'll notice my absence.'

'Screw your courage to the sticking place, *mon ami*,' said Claire. 'I think he *will* notice your absence and you have given your word.'

'True, I have,' admitted Amanda. She took a deep breath and straightened her back, a gesture that anyone who knew Senara, her grandmother, would instantly have recognised. Amanda glanced down at her ensemble. She was becomingly arrayed in a new dress that Claire had given her, sheer, self-patterned, soft gold semi-transparent fabric over a layer of cream silk.

No one would have guessed that, below the fitted bodice and beneath the flowing skirt, snug in her stocking top, was a very particular IKEA pencil. The most powerful of all her magical tools, this was, in fact, her Pocket-wand, Dr Bertil Bergstrom's patent invention, and Amanda knew better than to leave her house without it.

The Nursery Pavilion was distinguished by a glass wall of sliding panels that gave onto a narrow terrace at the edge of the cricket field. At this moment, it was a-throng with fashionable elegance and sporting excellence. Round tables gowned in spotless white damask, were laid with fine dining ware and crystal for the guests, who were seated or standing, chatting animatedly.

Amanda spotted Ryan at the centre of the knot of admirers. The captain's arm was around his shoulders as they were professionally photographed for magazines and selfied for social networking sites.

'He's busy,' stated Amanda, with a certain amount of relief.

'Come on, let's eat,' suggested Claire. 'The food here'll be good.' They approached one of the buffet tables and began helping themselves to the delicacies on offer.

Abruptly, Amanda gasped.

'What's wrong?' asked Claire in consternation.

'Oh, I wish he wouldn't *do* that!' exclaimed Amanda. Claire looked towards Ryan. But he was not the source of Amanda's irritation.

Tempest had somehow insinuated himself into the Pavilion, and was ensconced under the buffet table, lying in wait for his harem of two to attend to his nutritional preferences. As Amanda had stood pondering the gourmet choices, he had shot out a paw to make sudden and startling contact with her foot.

Amanda knowingly scanned the array for her familiar's favourite. She scooped up a helping of caviar in a lettuce leaf. Pretending to attend to her shoe, she knelt and laid it in front of Tempest, who acknowledged her graciously.

'Not that you deserve it, Brat Cat,' she whispered.

Claire found a mini salmon roulade and got it under the table on the ruse of dropping her napkin then bobbing briefly to retrieve it from the floor.

'Behave!' Amanda adjured her familiar.

'Behave? I always behave,' replied a familiar voice. Ryan had succeeded in detaching himself from his fans, and had navigated the room to Amanda's side.

'Oh, I meant —'

'You made it! How can I thank you? May I assume I'm forgiven?' he said winningly.

'Good game,' commented Claire, weighing up his penitent act and noting that Amanda was ignoring the question of forgiveness.

'Well, hello,' said Ryan, recognising her. 'So *you're* Amanda's best friend?'

'The very same,' acknowledged Claire, with her professional, media smile.

'Delighted to see you,' said Ryan, courteously. 'Did you both enjoy the match?'

'Yes, and you acquitted yourself admirably,' Amanda praised him.

'Thank you. I wasn't expecting quite this level of excitement.' He moved closer to Amanda and lowered his voice. 'I'd hoped we'd get more of an opportunity to chat.'

Ryan inhaled sharply as he felt a hand on his shoulder. As he looked, it slid around his neck, and a tall, faultlessly coiffured and made-up brunette undulated into his arm and seemed to coil around him, putting Amanda vividly in mind of the Serpent around the Tree of Knowledge in the Garden of Eden.

Chapter 3

✦

DADDY'S LITTLE PROJECT

'Darling Ry-Ry,' the Serpent in brunette guise sighed huskily. 'It's been for*ever*.'

'Oh hello,' he answered, less than enthused but civil. He seemed unable to disengage himself politely. 'I didn't see you.'

'And I could see *no* one here but you.' The woman was pointedly ignoring Claire and Amanda who began to take the opportunity to sidle away.

Ryan, still unable to break free from the scented embrace, cleared his throat and performed the introductions.

'Amanda, Claire, this is Samantha. We … er —'

'Are old friends,' she said, looking into his eyes with a sultry smile and touching his neck with an ice-pink taloned finger. Ryan gently removed her hand and said,

'Amanda and Claire are from my village, two of my especially valued neighbours,'

Amanda refrained from mentioning that he had only just found out that Claire was one of them

'Oh, I know!' said Samantha, her attention momentarily

distracted from Ryan. 'Mad Sinking.'

'Sunken Madley,' corrected Amanda.

'Yes, Daddy's little project,' she purred.

Amanda was taken aback.

'Excuse me?'

'It's all I hear about from him. He's raring to go. They're sticking the poles in and measuring and things on Monday. I expect you'll all turn out for the occasion.'

'What?' queried Amanda, frowning in confusion.

'Not sure I'll be there. Mud and wellies. Not really my bag,' she said, looking down at the Chanel purse dangling at her hip.

Amanda was bewildered. There were no building works scheduled in the village. 'Excuse me, but … what are you talking about?'

'The lab? The clinic research centre thing. I'm sure it's at Mad Whatever.'

Light dawned. 'You mean the projected asthma research centre at Lost Madley?'

'Yes, of course,' replied Samantha, barely escaping adding 'duh'.

'But that isn't for *months*,' objected Amanda. 'What about planning permission?'

'Oh, Daddy's got *that*,' Samantha uttered dismissively with a wave of her fingers. 'Yes, and without local backhanders if *that's* what you're thinking. It's not like anyone wants the land for anything. No rare species there, just a lot of rubble and earth.'

Amanda felt rocked. It was all too quick, too soon, and somehow … too wrong. Not the clinic. The place … *That* place. And now it seemed there was no time … no way to stop it. 'You say they're marking out the foundations the day after tomorrow?'

'Yes. Why? What does it matter? You look like you've seen a ghost. Here, have some champagne.'

Claire looked at her friend in surprise and concern.

In seconds, the voices around Amanda faded, as though she were under water. The sensation she'd had in Dr Sharma's office, the day her GP, her General Practitioner, had told her about the site, came back in tripled intensity.

Lost Madley. An annexe of her village, separated by a couple of hundred yards, in the forest. Some houses, a small pub and a shop. Bombed during the 1940s, houses levelled, fatalities and casualties, the fortunes of war sweeping clean the board. The survivors were re-housed, it was never rebuilt. No one spoke of it. The birds did not sing there, and the trees were thin.

She had seen it once, long ago. Only once. The memory chilled her.

Now, standing in the Nursery Pavilion of Lord's cricket ground on this bright June day, for a split second, the hamlet swam before her eyes as it had been before the bombs fell. The single lane, the old pub with the small-paned window of the bar, a young man and woman .... Suddenly it dissolved and was gone.

Amanda came back to the present at the sound of Ryan's anxious voice in her ear. She took a deep breath and forced a smile.

'It's nothing. Just surprised. Too much champagne,' she jested, although she had yet to sample so much as a sip.

'We'll leave you to recover,' said the Serpent, still coiled around Mr Ford. 'Ry-Ry, Daddy will be *devastated* not to have been here to see you, but Sir Michael is very anxious to meet the hero of the match.' She inclined her head in the direction of one of the club's most influential sponsors.

'But …,' objected Ryan, 'Ok, I'll be right th—'

'Sir Michael is *waiting*, darling. Do come along.'

Samantha maneuvered him inexorably away as he called back to Amanda and Claire, 'Thank you for making it here. I'll call you. Do enjoy yoursel…'

Claire rolled her eyes. Amanda nodded her head and smiled at her friend. 'Yes, now that we're here, let's do just that.'

They gathered delicacies into three napkins, and looked at one another conspiratorially.

'And now…' They nodded and said simultaneously, 'We

have another appointment.'

'With darling Pierce-y!' declared Claire, affectedly, in a passable imitation of Samantha.

'Indeed. I have a treat for us,' Amanda confided 'Pierce Brosnan in *Goldeneye*. Special Edition.'

Claire's eyes lit up. 'Oh, marvelous!'

Their light-hearted exchange considerably restored Amanda, after the shock of Samantha's announcement, and her brief flashback to a past she had never known.

'Come dahhhling!' said Claire and they linked arms and exited laughing into the late afternoon sunshine. 'Don't take any notice of Samantha.'

'You know her?' asked Amanda. 'She acted like she'd never seen you before.'

'Oh, I just assume it's all fake. Maybe she isn't like that at all. Actually, I don't think she's ever had the chance to find out *what* she's like. Between wealthy, divorced parents bidding exorbitant stakes for her affection, Sam's had her every whim catered to. She's never had to even *think* for herself. She's probably just copying her equally clueless friends.' Claire sounded to Amanda like she was trying to convince herself.

They reached the Audi to find Tempest curled up asleep on the newly parked, still-warm, bonnet of a red and black Mini Cooper S. He unwound himself, dropped lithely to the ground, and took a leisurely stroll in through the back passenger door of Claire's car that Amanda was holding open for him. He reflected that his witch was a good little thing and did have her uses after all.

Amanda settled herself and fastened her seatbelt.

As they emerged from the underground depths of the car park, into the street with its trees and open sky, her mind returned to the Pavilion. In spite of the cloudless afternoon, a shadow crossed her mind. She stared unseeing through the windscreen at the passing London plane trees, and said, half to herself,

'It must be a mistake. They can't possibly be starting tomorrow. Samantha must have been winding me up ..., surely?'

Chapter 4

❧

MONDAY MORNING

By Monday morning, Amanda had decided that she didn't believe, or, at least, didn't *want* to believe, Samantha's tale. The work on the asthma research centre couldn't possibly be commencing in Lost Madley that day.

Amanda resolutely walked up the path by the early fruiting cherry tree. She glanced up to see how the crop was growing, while fledgeling starlings on the grass tried to hurry off on inexpert wings. She entered her workshop and had barely begun to lock herself in, when the doorbell rang.

It was Joan the postlady holding a sheaf of letters and a packet easily small enough to have fitted through the letterbox. That meant only one thing: Joan had News.

'Good morning, Joan.'

'Morning, love. Well.' She paused for dramatic effect. 'They've started!'

'They?' queried Amanda.

'You know … the works.'

'The works?'

'The building in Lost Madley,' explained Joan.

'You *know* about that?' asked Amanda, in surprise.

'Course, I do. *Every*one knows.'

'How come?'

'Oo, these things get around you know. And he did come and ask,' Joan said with typical vagueness.

'Who did?'

'That Damian with the car.'

'Sorry?'

'He came and explained. In the pub.'

Amanda's sleep had been restless and ridden by unremembered dreams for the last two nights, and she wasn't feeling at her best and brightest. 'You've lost me.'

'Damian from the building, the research centre project,' said Joan patiently. 'He came in the pub and talked about it and what he wanted to do and his poor mum and, of course, no one had any objections. Though some said, who knows what's still down there, poor things. And best not to disturb the dead, but as far as we were concerned it was all fine with us, and good luck to him. And. of course, we all thought of you, and wouldn't it be a marvel if they had a cure for you, love, bless your heart.'

Amanda followed Joan's rambling monologue as best she could and extracted the essential information, saying, 'So, you knew they were starting today.'

'Oh yes, and those of us who can are off to have a look. You want to get a move on, dear, if you want to see the start, though I dare say they'll be there all day. I'll be along when I finish my rounds, you can be sure. Most exciting thing that's happened round here since the new church roof!'

Amanda wasn't sure what to say. Or, indeed, what to do.

'Well ... Joan. Thank you for bringing me up to speed.'

'That's all right. Mind how you go. See you in a bit!'

And she was off down the path with Amanda standing

rooted to the spot as Joan closed the gate and waved. Amanda felt Tempest rubbing comfortingly around her ankles and looked down.

'What do you think about all that?'

He looked at her intently.

'You, think we should go and take a gander, don't you?'

He blinked slowly once, for 'yes'.

'All right. Let me just add another coat of lacquer to that side table and it can be drying while we're out.'

It was soon done. Amanda shed her overalls, replaced them with jeans and yellow top, grabbed her jacket and went out to the British racing green Vauxhall Astra. Emblazoned in gold lettering down the sides was: Cadabra Restoration and Repairs

It had been bequeathed to her by Grandpa, together with the business.

Curiously enough, today, neither of her grandparents was to be found. Grandpa hadn't been in the workshop and Granny hadn't been around the house or garden. It wasn't exactly unusual. Since they'd transferred to the spirit plane they had come and gone with not much explanation, but it did seem like a curious coincidence.

'Where are they?' Amanda said rhetorically to Tempest. He clearly either knew and wasn't saying, or neither knew nor cared, especially in the case of Granny with whom he shared a mutual antipathy. To him she was still as solid, real and unpleasant as ever. He considered the inability of most humans to perceive either her or Perran as a singular mark of their species' inferiority.

Amanda noticed that Tempest had chosen to sit on the front passenger seat. Probably so he could remark on the standard of her driving and tell her where to park.

She drove to the end of Orchard Row and turned left into Hog Lane, then left again round the green into Muttring

Lane, which led north to the next village of Upper Muttring. However, as soon as she had passed the last house in Sunken Madley, Amanda took what was little more than a mud track leading off into the trees, to the right of the road. She slowed the Astra to a crawl, and the lane gave way to thinning silver birches that showed the ruins-cum-building site to the right.

This was the first time Amanda had been up close and personal to Lost Madley, and she was glad to have Tempest with her. He meowed, and she pulled off the track and parked.

Chapter 5

❧

PEGGING OUT

As Amanda approached on foot, she saw various villagers on the left of the track and strangers on the right of it whom she assumed were part of the construction crew. Most wore hi-visibility jackets of neon yellow and hard hats. They seemed to be organising themselves into teams. One or two kept glancing along the road as though watching for someone.

The silver birches were spindly here and even though it was summer not one of them bore a living leaf. Tall, spritely 90-something Miss de Havillande of The Grange was there with her great friend and contemporary, the petite, fairy-like Miss Armstrong-Witworth. Miss de Havillande's terrier was exploiting the comparatively abundant proximity of trees.

Amanda looked around for Tempest who was passing the time attempting to intimidate Churchill, by advancing by degrees into his space. But Churchill was too elderly and oblivious to be perturbed. Since the day Tempest had defended him against an overexcited visiting Chihuahua, he had refused to be convinced by Tempest's fake guerrilla incursions.

Mr Hanley-Page, of Vintage Vehicles at the other end of the village, stood a little distance from them and was the first to spot the newcomer.

'Hello there, Amanda.'

She looked towards the source of the voice to see the dapper septuagenarian. What he lacked in height he made up for in style, and today was sporting a light linen suit topped with a straw boater. He waved his omnipresent cigar and tipped his hat, showing receding silver-grey hair and unshading his bright grey eyes. He stubbed out the smouldering Cuban roll, aware that it would do her asthma no favours.

'Hello, Mr Hanley-Page. No Rolls Royce out for the occasion?'

'No, I'm saving the Phantom for the great inauguration. And seeing that, as far as we're concerned, it's being built in your honour, I'll take you for a spin in it afterwards, if you're game.'

'Thank you,' answered Amanda, aware that this was no small boon.

'I see you brought the motor. Still serving you well?'

'Oh yes, Grandpa left me well provided for.'

'So, what do you think of all this then?' he asked, with a sweep his hand.

'There's not much to see yet,' Amanda observed.

'Well, they're about to start pegging out.'

'What does that mean, please?'

'It means measuring and laying markers to show where the foundations will be dug. D'you see that tall, beige tripod with what looks like a camera on the top?'

'Yes,' she said, following the line of his pointing arm.

'That's a laser station. That'll give a straight line for the pegs, or posts. They'll want to sink the posts down as far as the foundations will be dug. Probably about a yard, or a meter as they say these days.'

Amanda watched the men standing around and continuing to glance along the lane. 'Why aren't they starting?'

'I expect they're waiting for — ah …'

Up the track, with the sound of a low breath, came a bright red Jaguar I-PACE driven by a man of middle years wearing sunglasses. As the vehicle passed, Amanda could see that the luxurious interior was handsomely upholstered in cream. He stopped near the builders and got out. He was of slightly below average height, with a pleasant, round, boyish face, thinning, short, light brown hair, and clad in a leather jacket that matched the seats of his car.

'Flash Harry,' muttered Mr Hanley-Page disapprovingly.

One of the group of builders advanced to greet the Jaguar driver, who took off his shades revealing dark brown, attractively engaging but rather anxious eyes. They were set under brows and nose that were perfectly straight, and counterbalanced by a circular, dimple-like well in his chin.

'Damian, we were just waiting for you.'

'Peter,' said cream leather enthusiastically, 'great to see you. Well, this is the big day!'

Amanda remembered something that Joan had said. 'Ah, so that's the Damian who came and talked to people in the pub about this project?'

'I wasn't there,' said Mr Hanley-Page stiffly.

'You don't object, though?'

'No. No, I'm all for asthma research. It's just where they've chosen to build it. But what happened here was before my time.'

'Who is Peter, do you suppose?'

'The project supervisor most likely. He'll be in charge of the marking out.'

Suddenly Damian turned to the villagers, and, with a well-modulated speaking voice, announced,

'Good morning, neighbours. I'd like to thank you for turning up to be here for the first day of our project. Please feel free to ask any questions about the proceedings. The site office and some facilities will be arriving soon, and then we can offer you tea and coffee. In the meantime, let's enjoy the launch!'

'Watching other people work, in other words,' said Mr Hanley-Page.

Amanda observed how the laser station was used. It was too early to see the extent of the building and her attention wandered around the site, over to the villagers along the track leading north away from the site, then back towards the workers.

And that was when she saw him. She'd registered him only vaguely before, assuming he was part of Damian's work crew. But now she observed him with attention for the first time.

He stood at a little distance from the builders and was watching them intently. There was something different about him. No hard hat for one thing. But the way he was dressed ... He was the only non-villager wearing a suit-style jacket. Brown over a white shirt and tie, and there was something odd about his trousers. What was it? Turn-ups? No, that wasn't particularly strange ... it was ... it was .... Or was it something else about his clothes? Her eyes rose over his tie to his face. He was looking straight at her with a sort of interested, even pleased, air.

'Barry!'

Amanda's attention was abruptly pulled back to the site, as one of the workers called out for assistance. His tall peg had hit an obstruction, and he needed someone to hold it while he banged it in. But all of the others were busy with other pegs and sightings. Damian took a few strides to his car, stripping off his leather jacket, slung it onto the back seat and was quickly in place to help. It could be seen that he wore sensible boots, jeans and work shirt.

'Hm,' grunted Mr Hanley-Page. 'Seems he's not quite so useless as I thought.' He turned to Amanda. 'So ... when do you start at The Grange?'

'The Grange?'

'Yes, Miss de Havillande has some work for you. Hasn't she told you?'

'Erm ... no. Did she tell *you*? I thought you weren't on speaking terms.'

'Oh, between you and me that's just banter. Keeps us both on our toes, don't you know. That's classified, mind you!'

Which means, thought Amanda, that only three-quarters of the village knows rather than all of it.

It seemed there was not much to be seen that day and she did have work to do.

'Well, I must be off. Thank you for the tutorial, Mr Hanley-Page. Goodbye.'

'Goodbye, dear. See you tomorrow.'

Amanda looked around for her erstwhile passenger. 'Tempest! Coming?'

Her familiar had had enough of attempting to tease Churchill, and accompanied her back to the car. It was bright day but the sunlight between the thin trees was wan and feeble.

Amanda took a last look around for the strange man. But he was gone.

That night his image swam in and out of her unsettling dreams.

·

Chapter 6

꧁

SUNKEN MADLEY

Stand upon the granite heights of the Scottish city of Edinburgh, *Dùn Èideann* in the old tongue, and you will see the Roman road sweep left to the east. Follow it south as it keeps well away from the perilous Pennines, gives safe passage through the Yorkshire moors, stays west of the treacherous fenlands, and finds its way to the gentler climes of Londinium, now London.

But the capital of England is not our destination. For, some dozen miles north of the Tower of London, a lane switches back off the highway, and up into the village of Sunken Madley. Its name is a shame buried so deep, none but the very few have had the memory passed down to them. Even fewer remain who honour the magical legacy of the spring that rises now only as a pleasant note in a yellowing guidebook.

Here to the west of the lane and at the end of the village, where the Hormead Pearmain apple orchards take back the land from the houses, is a cottage. It was the home, passed down from teacher to apprentice over centuries, of the wisewoman of the village. Though few now carry that knowledge. To the rest, it is simply number 26 Orchard Row.

The last occupant ends her days without having found one worthy of receiving The Knowing, and the link seems broken. But not quite. Here comes a young couple, newly eloped, a Romeo and Juliet, fleeing the long feuds of their families, seeking and finding peace: she of the long chestnut locks and aristocratic bearing, he tall, kindly, of a clan of farmers but with the soul of a knight.

Time passes, their children grow and leave, and now there is a baby playing with the daisies in the back lawn. Now you see her, now you don't … until …. she makes a final return. She is three years old, and this is home. She toddles up the path from the back of the house, between the vegetable beds and the fruit trees to the door of the workshop. The knight, her grandfather, opens to her.

The couple adopts her, and she becomes Amanda Cadabra, both legal daughter and natural granddaughter to Perran and Senara.

Three years pass before her magical nature shows itself. And now her apprenticeship begins. From Granny, she learns to focus, develop and deploy her powers with simple toys. Granny brings out *Wicc'huldol Galdorwrd Nha Koomwrtdreno Aon*. This long-hidden primer grimoire of her Cardiubarn ancestors comes into the light of the dining room, the darker enchantments having been sealed by Perran. At the end of each lesson Granny closes the book, and reminds her little granddaughter, 'You may read it, but no trying any spells on your own. Do you understand?'

'Yes, Granny.'

'And above all, even if your grandfather or I am present, never ..,'

'… use magic on a living thing,' Amanda finishes off.

Amanda has a retentive memory. Often when Granny introduces a new enchantment, Amanda has already learned it. However, she soon discovers that theory is very different from practice.

'It takes more than memory or more than words to execute a spell accurately,' said Granny as she cleaned up on the day of the rising incantation. Certain enchantments can make bread rise, dough rise, and cakes rise if very carefully managed. Amanda had to wear a dust mask while mixing the flour with salt, yeast, oil and water. The fine dust could bring on one of her asthma attacks. On this occasion, her culinary efforts had not been successful, and it was clear that the unintended result was going to be flatbread rather than the split tin she was aiming for.

'It hasn't worked,' Amanda said to Granny, who was observing from the kitchen sink where she was washing up.

'What are you going to do?' Senara asked casually.

'I could try a spell,' Amanda answered optimistically.

'Go on then,' said Granny, calmly.

Amanda looked from the oven to the table and back, sending her mouse-brown ponytail dancing from side to side. There was a loaf in each location. Two things to magic. She was going to need double power. And they hadn't risen at all so it would require extra on top of that.

'I think I'll need the wand,' she said decisively.

'All right,' said Senara, 'you know where it is, dear.' Amanda trotted into the dining room and brought the slender rod back with her. She positioned herself carefully at an apex to the oven and table. Flicking the wand from one to the other in a swift movement, she pronounced loudly.

'*Dahas, aereval!*'

The bread in the oven erupted and the mass of dough on the table exploded all over the Amanda, Senara, the kitchen table, chairs, floor and even made it to the kitchen door.

'Oops!' cried Amanda. 'I'm sorry, Granny.'

'That's all right, Ammy,' said Senara placidly beginning the clearing up process.

'Should I have just thrown it away and started again instead of resorting to a spell?' asked Amanda, reaching for the roll of kitchen paper towels.

'There's no harm in using a little magic in baking. Making something with love is, after all, a form of magic. It gives more delight and nourishment than food made without it. A meal made with hatred and bitterness, by the same token can poison the person who eats it, or, at least, give them an upset stomach. It is all the same energy. Like electricity. You can use it constructively or destructively. What counts is the intent.'

'I didn't intend to destroy the kitchen,' explained Amanda.

'Of course not, dear. But you only thought through the logistics. A spell is more than language, more than an intellectual process. It is about feeling your way to what you want to achieve. You will learn that with time and practice.'

'You're very wise, Granny,' the little girl observed.

Senara smiled down at her granddaughter and Amanda remembered Granny's lesson.

From Grandpa she learns the Cadabra ways with wood, from carpentry to furniture restoration, handed down through generations.

As her magical skills increase, she grows increasingly frustrated with Perran's insistence on learning her trade without them.

However, thanks to the wisdom of Ms Amelia Reading, her grandparents' greatest friend and fellow witch and Amanda's confidante-in-chief, Amanda survives the magic fever. She receives The Hat, and, finally, at the age of 13, the Cadabra's hereditary spellbook: *Forrag Seothe Macungreanz A Aclowundre* - For the Making of Wonderful Things.

It is a landmark in Amanda's mystic career. The next day, at her eager request, training begins.

'Magic,' said Perran, as he sat opposite his granddaughter, both of them atop high stools so they might lean on his workbench and sip their cups of Earl Grey tea at intervals, 'is different to what Normals think.'

Amanda had no idea what Normals thought about magic. Or anything else much for that matter. She tilted her head enquiringly, swaying her plaits, the orange ribbons catching in the lapels of her green boiler suit.

He continued. 'It is less frightening, more difficult and a greater responsibility than they imagine.'

Grandpa had never said much about magic before. Amelia had told her that he was every inch the equal of Granny in his knowledge and expertise, and had once accomplished a legendary deed.

'Now Lesson 1. I mentioned this yesterday: security. What does magic leave?'

Amanda thought, not even sure that she understood the question. Seeing her puzzled expression, Perran supplied the response.

'It leaves a trace, a sort of … smell. Most would say it tastes of tin and smells of sandalwood. So,' — Grandpa took her over to a workmate — 'here we have solder, made of ….'

Amanda knew the answer to this. 'Tin.'

'Good, Ammy. We put the soldering iron next to the solder. And in the incense burner over here on the windowsill …?'

'…sandalwood?'

'Yes, it clears the air, the energy.'

'I get it, Grandpa, people will see these things, and it will explain the … the trace.'

'Exactly. So you can start working with magic then, can you?'

'I suppose so?'

'Not yet, pet. First …,' said, Grandpa getting up and going to the back doors of the workshop. Amanda followed him out to the back gate. 'We check the lock on this.' Perran led her back in. 'We check these back doors are bolted'.

Amanda went ahead of him to the front door, saying, 'and we check that this is locked?'

'That's right. The window pane in it is frosted so as long as you're not weaving spells right behind it, you're fine. There are no sight lines from any of the windows to the neighbours' windows or gardens.'

Amanda nodded.

'The three checks are …?' Grandpa asked.

'Back gate, back doors, front door.'

'Good girl. And there endeth the lesson for Day One.'

The next day, when Amanda came into the workshop, Grandpa said, 'Now for the next question. He took a two-by-two length of pine and clamped it into the vice attached to the bench. Perran put out a range of hammers from a light, delicate one she'd first used as a four-year-old to his most massive mallet. He placed a line of nails from half-an-inch to four-inches long beside them. They sat down with their beginning-of-day mugs of tea at the bench.

Grandpa asked, 'What's the Wicc'yeth for hammer, hit?'

'*Frapka,*' answered Amanda without hesitation.

'Very good, Ammy. Now. See this medium hammer here, lass? Imagine there are three weights you can apply to a hammer blow: light, medium and heavy.'

'Yes,' Amanda said slowly.

'How many medium taps would it take to hammer this one-inch nail into this piece of mature pine?'

Amanda looked blank. 'I don't know.'

'Right. And if you don't know then the magic won't, the hammer won't. When you tell that hammer, *frapka*, you need to have in your mind, how heavy the stroke, the number of impacts, the resistance of the wood. Different sorts of pine, of different states of maturity, and that goes especially for oak, will need more taps or pressure.'

'I see,' said Amanda. 'It's a lot more complicated than I imagined.'

'Now do you understand why I made you wait to use spells in the workshop? Why you had to learn everything the Normal's way?'

'Yes, Grandpa,' she said nodding. 'I do. Why didn't you tell me this before?'

'Would it have made you any less frustrated, love?'

She laughed ruefully. 'No, Grandpa, no it wouldn't. You know me too well!'

'All right, then. Shall we start?'

'Yes,' Amanda said eagerly.

'Let's begin with some gentle taps of this hammer and count together. Are you ready?'

'Yes, Grandpa.'

'Raise the hammer off the bench.'

That was well within the scope of her levitation skills. She didn't even need the words, she just had to intend it. Without touching it, Amanda floated the tool and made it hover with the head touching the nail.

'Gently, then, Ammy. Say the spell.'

'*Frapka ynentel.*'

Nearly twenty years later and it was automatic. It took little spell power to simultaneously have brushes stirring glue and paint, a saw sawing, a hammer rapping, a plane planing as she sang along to her iPod.

Amanda had never had to tax her magical capacity.

But the time was coming.

Chapter 7

❧

THOMAS BEGINS TO REMEMBER

Being the person who finds the body never looks good. That thought darted into Amanda's mind.

The security guard on reception had seen her come in. Even told her that the doctor was expecting her. He would suppose she was meeting him right now. If Amanda delayed too long, then later the police would ask questions about why it took her so much time to raise the alarm.

She glanced around. It looked like an accident. But what if it wasn't?

* * * * *

Detective Inspector Thomas Trelawney slept well. Usually. One of the first lessons his mentor Chief Inspector Michael Hogarth had taught him was to leave work at the station door, and he had taken it, as he had everything Hogarth taught him, to heart.

Hogarth had been more than his boss, he had been his guide, counsellor, and, to some extent his confidant. Over the 14 years that they had worked together, they had become friends. Now that his chief had retired, the latter relationship was coming to the fore.

Hogarth's cottage was in the village of Mornan Bay, only four miles from the police station at the small coastal town of Parhayle. Thomas picked up a take-away dinner for them at least once a week, and so it was not difficult for Mike to note a change in his protégé, however subtle.

Thomas looked tired.

It has started the weekend he'd dropped in to see Amanda Cadabra at Sunken Madley Manor where she was working. Or was it the Monday after? Hogarth regarded him speculatively. He took an intuitive guess. If he was right, then something he'd been waiting for had begun.

'How are things?' he enquired, as they sat down with trays on their laps, unwrapping their repasts.

'Yours should be the adana kofte,' said Thomas, as Mike unwound the white paper from his dinner. Thomas had dropped in at their favourite kebab shop on the way. His was chicken shish with chilli sauce. They opened their cartons of rice and salad.

'Yup. Thanks, Thomas.'

They ate in silence for a few moments before Hogarth asked about the station news.

'Oh, quiet days with paperwork, interspersed with a flood of activity,' Thomas replied.

'Constable Nancarrow getting over her crush on you yet?'

Thomas blushed but grinned. 'I'm rather hoping she'll transfer her affections to the new detective sergeant.'

'Oh yes, I heard. No new chief inspector for you. You're going to carry the can with the aid of the constables and detective sergeant.'

'The word is that the station is too small, and there's too little crime to justify the pay grade of your replacement,' said Thomas.

'So you'll be the Man in Charge. Well, you're certainly up to the job.'

'Thank you, Mike. If I am, it's down to you teaching me the ropes for the last 15 years at least.'

'I had the aptest of pupils, Sherlock.'

They finished their food and sat with mugs of tea. Thomas looked meditatively into the small fire. Mike's voice interrupted his musings.

'Mind if I make an observation?'

'Go ahead,' responded Thomas curiously.

'The detective habit is hard to break,' Hogarth said whimsically.

Thomas looked a question.

'You look tired.'

'Oh well ... work ....'

'You have the tired look of the sleepless.'

Thomas knew that it would be a relief to tell Hogarth. 'Nothing escapes you, does it?'

'Start at the beginning,' Hogarth invited him.

Thomas took a deep breath and began. 'Ever since the appointment with Amanda Cadabra when I told her about the report, I've had mornings where I've woken up unsettled, and then, this past week, I've had a couple of disturbing dreams. Except they're more than the fabrications of a mind sorting the wheat from the chaff.'

'What about?'

'Well ... I'm in a house. Except it's more like a mansion. It's big and old, big rooms, a wooden floor. My feet make a noise when I walk. And yet, I'm closer to the ground, child-height. There's a smell. That smell. My father's there and some other people. Men, in suits, black suits. And a woman, a grand old woman. They keep asking my father about me. He's afraid. I'm not sure if it's for me or for himself. They keep asking him about me. "Can he ....?" But I can't hear what they're asking. And there's a name ...'

'A name?'

'Yes. It sounds like a spring, bouncing or a coil. If only I could remember and yet ... and yet I don't want to ... and yet I feel I must ... oh, it makes no sense.' He raked his hands through his short dark blond hair. He put aside his tray, got up abruptly and went to the window. 'I was fine before ...'

Hogarth could see Thomas was uncharacteristically irritated. He finished the sentence for his younger friend, 'Before Miss Cadabra cut up your peace?'

'Yes!'

'I can assure you on one point. It has never been intentional on her part to disturb it.' He paused. 'Would you say these are dreams or surfacing memories?'

'I have few memories from before I was 10 years old. That's always worked perfectly well for me ... and now ....'

'What do you think it is that you're remembering?' Hogarth prompted gently.

'It's *them*, isn't? My father's lot. That's the family pile I was in. The ancestral hall of the .... the what? My father is a Trelawney but his mother ... the name ....' He came back to his seat. 'You know, don't you?'

'It's surfacing in your memory,' replied Hogarth, noncommittally.

'Why now?'

'It's time, and you're ready.'

'What has all of this got to do with the Cadabras?' asked Thomas.

'If I'm not mistaken, Amanda Cadabra too is beginning to remember. You have to get there by yourself and so does she. But I will say only this: the keys to this case, this 28-year-old case of the death of Amanda's family, what sent them over a cliff to a crash that wasn't the cause of death, and much more besides, lie in your memory and in hers. But neither of you must force it.'

'Why not? What about, oh, hypnosis or regression or something?'

'Because you do not take a crowbar to Pandora's Box, my lad. Now don't worry. Now you've put it into words, you'll most likely find that it doesn't trouble you for a while. Let it come as and when it's ready. Remember, it's in the past, and the past can't harm you unless you let it. You're not that little boy any more.'

At least, thought Hogarth, for the most part. The best of that eager, bright child was still there. But there was more than enough grown man to protect him.

'You're not surprised are you, Mike?'

'No,' admitted Hogarth.

'In fact, something tells me that you've been waiting for this.'

'Very shrewd, Thomas. You never disappoint me, lad.'

'Are you going to tell me how long you've been waiting?'

Hogarth grunted. 'You've got me there.' How much to say? he asked himself.

'Everything is happening at the right time. I have faith in you. And in Amanda too, as a matter of fact.' He waited. 'Do you want to talk about it further?'

'No, no, I don't think I need to,' Thomas responded after a moment's thought. 'I suppose you're saying that there are some things I need to remember, and I will, all in good time, and the process needn't be traumatic,' he concluded optimistically, already reviving and looking more rested.

And yet, thought Hogarth, it is not going to be easy … But his feet are on the path now … and there is no turning back.

'I'll get us some more tea,' said Thomas cheerfully. He took the mugs out to the kitchen.

Hogarth sat and looked into the fire. The thin branches and a low flickering flame was just for decoration and comfort. It was a bright evening outside, sunny yet with dense, tense air. A summer storm was gathering.

.

Chapter 8

❧

THE PROFITEER

Amanda had stayed away for the rest of the pegging out. The strange man visited her mind every so often. But she had work to do.

The church lych gate had suffered from the impact of Iskender Demir's van when its driver was preoccupied with the theft of food from his kebab shop. Jane, the rector, didn't want to involve the insurance companies and put his premium up, so the three of them were working out it between them.

Iskender covered most of the cost, Jane insisted on being allowed to chip in, and Amanda said she already had just the right pieces of wood and materials, and would donate her time. All she needed was Iskender to lend his strong arms to lifting the gate off and later back onto the hinges, and to deliver it to her and collect it in his van.

Amanda replaced the broken spars and repaired the carving. She gave the gate a long overdue clean and several coats of wax. With Iskender's might and Amanda's guidance, it was now back in place.

'Thank you, ladies; you have both been very kind. I am sorry again, Jane.'

'These things happen, Iskender. Now don't you give it another thought. The thefts have stopped, and that's what counts.'

'Come and collect some dinner from the restaurant, on the house.'

'Thank you, Iskender.'

'You too, Amanda.'

'Thank you, I will.'

'See you both soon.'

They waved as he crossed the road back to the restaurant.

'You know,' said Jane, 'Nalini Sharma had some things go missing from the corner shop. But that's stopped too.'

Amanda could have taken credit for the cessation of the pilfering, but that was a private matter between her and the affair of Sunken Madley Manor.

'Hm,' she replied.

'Well, thank you, dear. The gate was more than ready for a facelift. Should be good for at least a decade or two. Heaven knows the last time it had any attention. Probably not since the time of —'

'Churchill! Heel!' The imperative addressed to her meandering terrier heralded the arrival of the indefatigable Miss de Havillande of The Grange, Sunken Madley's oldest and most distinguished resident.

'Jaaaane! Amandaaaaa!'

'Miss de Havillande,' responded Amanda.

'How are you, Cynthia?' asked the rector, kindly.

'Never mind that. This is clearly the hand of Providence that I should find the two of you here.'

The rector braced herself for an inevitable complaint.

'Jane. As carer of the souls of this parish, whether on two or four feet, there is a Matter that I must bring to your attention!'

The rector exuded an appropriate air of seriousness, and Miss de Havillande continued,

'Amanda, this concerns you. I have observed, and have witness testimony, that any establishment that services Your Cat with treats is completely free of rodents, foxes or any form of unwelcome incursion.'

Amanda was about to say that that seemed fair but thought better of it.

'On the other hand,' Miss de Havillande continued inexorably, 'any place that refuses his demands is over-run, infested, and their gardens used as little short of a latrine.'

'Oh dear,' began Amanda, but Miss de Havillande cut her short.

'In summary, it is clear to me that Don Tempestioni is running a protection rrrracket!'

Amanda and Jane folded their lips and struggled to maintain a serious expression. Jane outdid herself, nodding gravely and declaring,

'That would indeed be a reprehensible offence, Cynthia.'

'I will speak to him,' offered Amanda. Though she was well aware that she could no more prevent Tempest from doing anything than part the waters of Sunken Madley Pond.

'I hope you will do so, Amanda. And don't tell me that he is only one of the Lower Creatures and would not understand. I don't believe that for an instant. Jane, I hope that you too will address him on this matter.'

'Of course, Cynthia, I will do so. He is a not infrequent visitor to St Ursula. In fact, about that, Amanda — not that I want to pour oil on the fire — but do you think you could ask him *not* to drink out of the font before a christening? It was very embarrassing on Sunday. The couple walked in and saw him lapping away, and I had to empty it and refill it. I thought they'd cancel!'

'Yes, of course,' said Amanda apologetically. 'It's just that being ... er ... blessed, he considers it a better grade of water and therefore ... er, worthy — I mean ... yes, he has a somewhat overdeveloped sense of entitlement perhaps —'

'Yes,' intervened Miss de Havillande judicially, 'well, enough said on that score. I shall leave it with both of you. Meanwhile. I have some work for you, Amanda, dear. Some bits and pieces. They're breaking ground tomorrow. It's considered something of an occasion. Shall we meet there and you can come back to The Grange. How would that be?'

Amanda wavered. She did have a queue of jobs from other customers.

Abruptly, Granny and Grandpa appeared, flanking Miss de Havillande. Amanda tried not to look at them, but, instead, up to the right as though thinking.

'The other jobs can wait, love,' said Grandpa.

'Nothing that can't be postponed for dear Miss de Havillande,' added Granny.

Amanda inhaled, looked back at the illustrious owner of The Grange, smiled and spoke.

'Of course, Miss de Havillande.'

'That's right,' said Grandpa and disappeared.

'Quite right, dear,' said Granny, and vanished.

Chapter 9

❧

BREAKING GROUND, AND THE PORTRAIT

The site was now marked out. It was to be a long building, constructed partly over Lost Madley, with the central mass extending forward, beyond the trees and into the neighbouring wood-enclosed pasture.

The builders had removed the silver birches within the perimeter, but these had grown to no more than sapling height, were leaveless and came out as easily as spring onions.

The portable office and lavatories had been delivered and were in place. The diggers had been unloaded and were ready to scoop out the trenches for the footings. Damian had arrived in his red Jaguar, cast off his leather jacket and was leaning on a spade, waiting for The Moment.

A vehicle was heard coming up the track. A silver Volkswagen Touran hove into view. A man in jeans and black leather jacket, got out. He was about Damian's age with at least an extra four inches to his height, but carrying more weight. His hair was dark brown and straight. Arching brows and a long chin did not distract from the careworn expression of a man with an ambitious spouse, three demanding teenage children, an unnecessarily large mortgage and overextended credit.

Robin smiled at his friend. 'The big day.' He looked around at the villagers who were watching with interest. 'Very well done, Damian, creating such goodwill. You have a real gift for it.'

'Thanks. But we wouldn't be here today without your organisational skills.'

'We make a good team,' said Robin. 'Well, go on, man,' he added, clapping his friend on the back. 'Make the break.'

Robin held up his phone, camera video button ready, as Damian went to the trench-to-be and checked with the supervisor that he was correctly positioned. The blade of the spade slid into the clay, and gathered a load that was tossed aside, to applause from the crew and audience.

Amanda scanned to see who was present. And there he was again. Standing nearer to the builders than the villagers. The man in the jacket and strange trousers. Again he met her eyes. Amanda had made up her mind to approach him. She took a step …

'Amandaaaa! Over here, dear.' Miss de Havillande was beckoning with a raised gloved hand and a ringing call.

Compliantly, Amanda crossed the mulchy ground to Miss de Havillande's side. The elderly lady looked at her face with concern.

'Are you all right, my dear? You're looking a little pale.'

'I am well, thank you, Miss de Havillande.'

'Not overworking are you, dear?'

'No, the work is coming in steadily. It's just that I haven't been sleeping as well as usual.'

'Valerian. That's the thing for sleep. I have some in the garden. We'll pick some together. Shall we go?'

'Yes, yes, of course, Miss de Havillande.'

Amanda took a quick look back as they moved off. But again, the man was nowhere to be seen.

'The dining room table is in desperate need of attention. Some of my parties do get a little lively, and the furniture is not always given its due consideration.'

Miss de Havillande and Miss Armstrong-Witworth's parties were legendary. They were held at Christmas and sometimes Easter and Halloween too. The ladies were fond of fancy dress, dancing, and Venetian balls, so the occasions were little short of spectacular.

The magnificent chandelier would be taken down and cleaned. Amanda was repairing the links in one of the lesser ones, the day that Trelawney had made one of his irritatingly impromptu visits.

Miss de Havillande graciously accepted a lift from Amanda, and they had turned toward the car when they were hailed.

"Miss de Havillande?"

They turned to see Damian Gibbs striding towards them.

'Mr Gibbs,' Miss de Havillande greeted him graciously. 'Congratulations on breaking ground.'

'Thank you, ma'am,' he said with a slight bow.

She acknowledged his salute and said, 'May I present my dear friend, Amanda Cadabra.'

Abruptly, he straightened up, stuck for an appropriate response. This was a common reaction to her name.

'How do you do, Mr Gibbs,' said Amanda, to break the pause, extending her hand in a friendly manner.

'Hello, Amanda. Damian,' he responded lamely, shaking it.

'Amanda,' Miss de Havillande continued, 'is our resident furniture restorer and an excellent carpenter. I know that you have your own crew, but if you need any fine work attended to then may I suggest that you call upon Amanda's expertise.'

'Oh, but ... yes ... sure. Well, now. A lady carpenter ... that certainly is a ... a cool combination,' he said hooking his thumbs into his belt, and nodding. 'Right, well, ... come by any time. You'll be very welcome, I'm sure.'

The ladies thanked him, and they departed, leaving Damian, unusually, on the back foot.

Miss de Havillande chuckled, as they made for Amanda's

car. 'I expect most male desk workers feel a little threatened by a young woman, whose profession engages her in physical work in a branch of construction.'

'It happens. But he's doing a good deed with the Centre,' responded Amanda on a positive note, while privately putting Damian down as a bit of poser.

Miss de Havillande insisted on travelling beside Churchill in the back of the car. Tempest took up his place on the front passenger seat, every so often turning around to subdue Churchill with The Look.

They took the track to join Muttring Lane then drove south past the Priory ruins on the right, then the church on the left, turning left again by the pub into Trotters Bottom. Finally, they took a right through the open great gates, and parked in the driveway of Miss de Havillande's residence.

The Grange had an even older pedigree than the 400-year-old Tudor Sunken Madley Manor. Its residents accurately referred to it as 'a great barn of a place'. For that was precisely what the first structure had been: a storage facility for the millennium-old Benedictine priory on the edge of the village. The priory itself had now lain in ruins for some 500 years, but was a favourite remote vantage point and picnic spot for Amanda and Tempest.

The Grange, by contrast, had been built, burned down, rebuilt, blown down, rebuilt, fallen down, rebuilt, shot down, and finally remodelled and remodelled until it had reached its stately Georgian stone-faced structure. This was pleasantly symmetrical, rising over three floors including the ground floor, with a multitude of sash windows and a modestly pillared porch.

'Come in, Amanda. Yes, He can come too, only, do you hear me, young man?' Cynthia addressed Tempest, 'No harrying Churchill or Pushkin and no harassing Natasha!'

Pushkin was a timid Siberian long-haired, golden tabby and Natasha a Nevskaya Maskaradnaya, a cream, even longer haired cat with a light brown head and tail. She enjoyed blowing hot and cold on Tempest, gazing at him alluringly with sapphire eyes then rejecting his advances in no uncertain terms, when he employed a variety of ways of disturbing her peace. The felines' human was Gwendolen Armstrong-Witworth.

'See that you stay away from both of them!' continued Miss de Havillande, waving an admonitory finger.

Tempest assumed an air of wounded innocence.

'Don't play off your airs and graces on me. Off with you to the kitchen. Moffat will see that you get something ... Oh, dear no, he'll still be out ...'

'Miss Cynthia?' came the voice of the ladies' elderly retainer and general factotum. White-haired and insistently attired in a black suit with tails, he was the de facto master of the estate.

'Oh, Moffat, will you see to —'

'— Hm,' grunted Moffat disapprovingly. He nodded and led the way, muttering 'Varmint!'

Amanda had helped Grandpa to restore one or two pieces for the ladies and had been to The Grange for the occasional party. She had long yearned for a proper look at the house. It featured an elegantly sweeping main staircase and a decent sized ballroom that she had only ever seen crowded with people.

'Would you like a cup of tea first, after all the excitement, or are you eager for a little tour?'

'A little tour first, if I may,' replied Amanda.

'Of course, my dear, and by that time perhaps Gwendolen will have finished her stint in the garden and can join us.'

Amanda didn't know Miss Armstrong-Witworth very well. She always seemed like a shy daisy beside the vibrant rose of her companion.

'Well, now. Let me take you into the dining room first so that you can see the damage.

After Amanda had made a thorough inspection of the table, and they had discussed how best to proceed, they returned to the hall.

'We'll take the stairs to the long gallery, and that'll be enough for now,' said Miss de Havillande. 'I'd think you'd be more than ready for tea then.'

'Yes, that will be fine,' agreed Amanda.

'Now ... there are a number of paintings whose frames have suffered neglect over the years, and are fit to fall apart. Let's start here. Would you like a look at the bannister. I expect it could do with some attention too.'

Amanda regarded the practically polish-free, dented surface, and the damaged spindles.

'I must say, Miss de Havillande, this rail would be spectacular with the right care. It would gleam.'

'Noted. Now, here is the first of the artworks.' She gestured to the wall and a half-length portrait of a woman, dark with age-discoloured varnish. The deep, ornately carved wooden frame was gaping at the seams.

'This is my great-great-Aunt Sarah,' explained Miss de Havilland. 'A thought occurs to me. Have you done any restoration of paintings?'

That drew Amanda's attention to the picture itself. She gazed at the canvas. Suddenly she had the sensation of being underwater. Miss de Havillande's voice sounded distant and muffled. Her vision fizzed and darkened ...

Notwithstanding her age, Miss de Havillande still had her strength and could move quickly.

She caught Amanda before she hit the floor.

Chapter 10

✑

AUNT AMELIA

At 7 o'clock that evening, a 1955, brown and cream, R-Type Bentley drove into Sunken Madley, the low, evening sunshine glinting on its winged bonnet ornament.

It was the green apple of Dennis Hanley-Page's eye, and one he yearned to possess. For 23 years he had been trying to persuade Ms Amelia Reading to part with it, for steadily increasing sums of money. He had even proposed to her three times.

'Yes, Dennis,' she had replied, with amused tolerance, 'I know that it has absolutely nothing to do with —'

'Alas,' he mourned, 'you know me too well, Amelia.' He brightened. 'You see how well suited we are. Dammit, you're a woman after my own heart. Never met a lady who knew as much about classic cars as I do. You know, I do believe, I'd propose to you even if you didn't own the most beautiful motorcar between here and the National Motor Museum at Beaulieu. What d'you say? Shall we make a match of it?'

'I don't know what you'd say if I agreed! But I'll say the same thing that I always say! No, Dennis. I had that car from my uncle, he entrusted it to me, and we will not be parted nor united with your collection. You are, however, welcome to admire from afar. Which deep down you know suits you far better, Dennis,' Amelia added knowingly.

'Dear lady, you strike another blow to my heart,' he said with mock sorrow, a hand to his chest

'I'm sure you'll recover,' said Amelia encouragingly. 'Especially if you give up the cigars.'

'What? Am I to be permitted no solace?'

'Your solace can be dwelling on your élite collection that's worth millions and is the envy of three counties.'

He puffed out his chest.

'True true ... and it could all be yours ...'

She laughed outright and shook her head.

Amelia turned left into Orchard Row with perfectly judged speed, and drew up, with both offside wheels an inch from the pavement, outside number 26. She rose elegantly from the driver's seat, drawing her peach, ankle length, vintage summer coat free of the door. Her thick, short, dark chestnut bob, echoing the warm brown of her eyes, was ruffled by the breeze as she entered the gate and walked up the path as the door opened. Amanda welcomed her in.

'Hello, sweetie. You needn't have got up. I could have used my key.'

'It's all right, Aunt Amelia, I'm feeling much better now. I expect Mr Hanley-Page knows you've arrived.'

'I think he's got a proximity alarm that sounds when it detects Priscilla.'

Amelia saw that Amanda had been curled up on the sofa with a blanket, and bade her sit down again as she left for the kitchen. Ms Reading presently returned with mugs, and took a flask out of her ubiquitous black velvet holdall, of which Amanda had made a copy in her teens. It contained hot chocolate spiced with a little chilli, and made with coconut milk and cream.

'Here you are, Ammy. This should perk you up.' She

waited while Amanda took a couple of reviving sips. 'Now …
what happened?'

'Well … I was at Miss de Havillande's. She asked me to go
back with her and look at some jobs. And Granny and Grandpa,
who I hadn't seen for a couple of days, suddenly appeared and
told me to bump her to the front of the queue, so I knew it was
important. But of course, I didn't know why, because they still
never tell me anything!'

'Yes, I know, sweetie,' said Amelia, understandingly.

'Anyway … I'd looked at the dining table and the bannister,
and then Miss de Havillande started showing me the portraits.
She wants the loose frames repaired. And then she asked me about
cleaning the canvasses themselves. So, for the first time, I actually
looked at the painting and then … all at once, everything went
muffled and foggy and … black …. The next thing I knew, I was
waking up on the drawing-room sofa, and Miss de Havillande and
Miss Armstrong-Witworth and Moffat and Tempest were there.
No one made a fuss; Moffat brought me some hot sweet tea and
biscuits, and after a while, I felt better, and Miss de Havillande
said, we'll carry on another day and drove me home in the Astra.'

'I see …. Hm. Interesting. Let's go back to the painting.
You're standing in front of it and …'

'I was looking at the surface … and I noticed … let's see
… it was a woman. She had a … wait … yes … I had a flashback.
Or maybe a vision or daydream, I don't know … suddenly I
was floating — no, well anyway, I wasn't standing — and I was
looking at a painting, only it was a *different* painting … and that
was all. Then just now …'

'Yes?' prompted Amelia

'About half an hour ago, I was having a nap, and I had a
dream. The same thing, only this time there was a voice, talking
close to me …. And then there was that episode at Lords —'

'When you saw Lost Madley in the past?'

'Yes, and now this build on that place. The first time Dr
Patel told me about it, it gave me the shivers and now …. And

the man on the site. It's just happening so quickly. Everything is happening so quickly!'

Amelia looked at Amanda compassionately, then spoke gently, 'What did you expect? You crossed the Rubicon, sweetie.'

Amanda turned from consternation to puzzlement. 'What do you mean, Aunt Amelia?'

'You told me yourself. What happened at the Manor and in the Wood. The spells. For the first time, you used spells on a living thing, and a human at that. And more than once ...'

'But ... but ... you all said —'

'Oh yes, my dear, you did very well indeed. We are all immensely proud of you. But magic has consequences. Every spell has a residual effect, just as every action has a reaction. It might be a smell or a colour change in the eyes, like yours, or a ... billowing in space and time ... but it will happen. There is no silencer for a wand. Magic is part of nature, just as much as gravity, and it cannot escape its laws.'

Amanda was shocked. 'What have I done?'

'No more than any of us would have done, and perhaps we might not have been as quick thinking or done as much as good. We would only have been more aware of what might come after.'

Amanda sat and thought, looking into her hot chocolate. 'Granny said something,' she recalled. 'after all that business at the Manor ... when she reappeared .... she gave me some Golden Rules. And one of them was to be sensitive to the side effects of a spell, however small and to remember it. And the strange thing is that in the Wood I did feel something, and again in the Manor. But it was so slight, and I was too distracted to ....' She looked up at Amelia. 'Do you remember when I was about 12 years old, and I asked you if someone was looking for me?'

'Yes, I do, and I looked, and no one was.'

'Well ... now?'

Amelia looked into the west with inner far-seeing eyes. 'I'm not sure if they are looking. It is more that someone has been reminded of your existence.'

'I see. And somehow all of this is connected with the flashbacks?' asked Amanda.

Amelia took a crystal ball from her bag. It looked like a golden firework exploding over a silver beach, floating in a globe of water. 'I believe so,' Amelia answered, looking into the orb.

Amanda looked serious. 'It is one of the ripples from the stones I threw into the pool, the effects of the magic I used on living things?'

'Yes, so it would seem. But the waters may calm. And we need not assume that the pool is just full of piranha!' said Amelia smiling, 'Oh, and the upside is ... I think you may be getting a welcome visit sooner than you expected.'

'From a tall, dark, handsome stranger from over the sea?' asked Amanda teasingly.

'Tall yes, dark no, handsome ... yes, ... and he will be crossing water. Hmm ...,' replied Amelia, with an impish smile.

Amanda relaxed and grinned. 'Oh, Aunt Amelia, I do love you. Somehow you always make things seem all right again.'

'Well, that's what I'm here for, sweetie!'

Chapter 11

୧୬

IMPULSIVE

Amanda had never been impulsive. That is, more accurately, not since she was six years old.

It was the year that the first sign of her magical nature had clearly shown itself. The year of The Day of the Mustard Spoon, when reaching for the tiny implement she had moved it without making contact of any kind.

Training began, and within weeks she was able to slide and roll various objects in different directions at different speeds.

It was summer. A Sunday. And Grandpa and Granny had taken her to watch the cricket. Afterwards, they had made a detour to the playground near The Grange.

It was on the way back that it happened. Amanda, remarkably, in the opinion of some Sunken Madleyists, was not lonely, certainly not for the companionship of the other village children. She enjoyed the company of her grandparents and certain villagers. Sometimes, Amanda helped Joan the postlady deliver letters along Orchard Row, or, while Granny ran her errands, she would sit with Mrs Sharma's mother, enraptured, hearing tales of India. She would help Mr Jackson next door with the garden, or stay with the rector and offer her thoughts as Jane wrote the next Sunday sermon, which, being for a multi-faith and non-faith community, was basically variations on: be nice to each other.

Nevertheless, Amanda had been reading stories that contained children who did have friends of their own age, and wondered if she was letting the side down by not having made any.

Amanda had done the school experiment at the age of three, at nursery. This was a success, in that it yielded a definite and clear result: it was not the place for Amanda, home was where she would thrive educationally, and that was very soon borne out.

Senara and Perran were excellent educators, or facilitators, as they thought of themselves, serving the enquiring and sponge-like mind of their little granddaughter, as it hopped from one passion to another. However, Amanda had heard them asked by the neighbours 'what about socialisation?' and she knew that meant 'friends who were children'.

As they approached the High Street, an older child, Jade Kemp, crossing the road, lost control of her ball. It bounded along straight into the path of a car. Amanda, quick as a flash, let go of her grandparents' hands and swiftly moved in closer to alter the course of the ball with a spell. Being six years old, her judgement of speed was undeveloped, especially of a car driven by the village's (in the words of Miss de Havillande) demon driver. The car skidded to a halt with a screech of tyres, in front of Amanda, as Grandpa scooped her up. He gave a wave of apology to Mr Hanley Page, who was at the wheel of his Aston Martin DB5.

'Is she all right?' the driver asked anxiously.

'Yes, yes,' soothed Perran.

'No harm done, then.'

'Not to your tyres, I hope, Dennis,' said Perran, checking the offside ones.

'No, they're fine, I'm sure. Mind yourself on the roads, young Amanda,' he called as he drove on. Jade meanwhile had snatched up her toy, and, with a scowl, shouted, 'Leave my ball alone!' before running off towards Hog Lane.

Amanda's breathing became short from the stress of the near miss and the child's hostility in the face of her good intentions. They took her home, and, once she was calmed and had used her inhaler, Granny went off to the kitchen, and Grandpa, with Amanda on his lap, asked her gently what she was intending to do back there.

'I thought I could just change the direction of the ball, and then the car wouldn't squash it, and then she'd be grateful and like me, and I could make a friend,' Amanda explained with simple logic. 'I just needed to be a lot closer to make the spell work. I didn't know it was Mr Hanley-Page.'

'Well, that was a generous impulse,' commended Grandpa. 'It might be difficult at your age, but you need to think carefully before you act, about everything; as you do about running or going in the garden when there's a lot of pollen or eating things that might not be good for you.'

Granny came in with the tea tray and took up the thread.

'And imagine if the child had seen you change the direction of the ball or heard you saying your spell? What if Mr Hanley-Page hadn't seen you in time? I don't want to sound harsh, but this is serious, dear. Remember what has happened today. Remember that impulsiveness can get you killed.'

Amanda nodded gravely.

'Now, would you like some trifle? Something sweet to help with the shock?'

Her dimples reappeared as she nodded again, this time enthusiastically.

That was the day she stopped doing two things, one of them was trying to make friends by pleasing people; the other was to act on the spur of the moment.

Impulsiveness can get you killed.

* * * * *

What Amanda lacked in impulsiveness, she made up for in quick thinking.'

She looked up at the lab door. There was no key. She spoke to it:

'*Luxera.*'

The bolt slid into place.

Amanda took out her phone.

Chapter 12

✑

TALL, NOT DARK, AND HANDSOME, CROSSING THE WATER

'That sounds like Ryan,' Amanda said to Tempest, as she prepared to go out that morning. 'Except he isn't crossing water. Unless he's going the swim the village pond.'

Aunt Amelia's words had Amanda, in spite of herself, on the lookout. Tall, not dark, and therefore fair, surely, and handsome, and crossing water. Hmm.

And so it was that she planned to join the other interested members of the village at the site for The Pouring. Miss de Havillande had insisted that Amanda spend a few days at home and, besides, there was no hurry for the jobs to be done. Amanda was relieved to be able to clear her backlog and work through her queue of customers before beginning at The Grange.

The sun was out, the air was dry, and the pollen count was low.

Amanda had an errand at the post office first, sending an antique wooden toy that she'd repaired back to its owner. The corner shop door rang as she entered but the willowy form of Mrs

Sharma, who, with her husband, co-owned the establishment and at least two or three others in the village, was already present behind the counter. Amanda greeted her with pleasure.

'Hello, Amanda. What are you sending off today?'

'It's a wooden toy.'

'Will you need insurance for that?'

'I don't think it's that valuable, to be honest.'

As Mrs Sharma weighed the parcel, she asked, 'How is your young man?'

'I don't have a young man.' Amanda replied patiently.

'It's not working out then? Early days. Give it time.'

'Erm … whom do you mean, exactly, Aunty?' asked Amanda curiously, lapsing back into her childhood name for Mrs Sharma.

'Ryan Ford, of course. Although you may be right. That's £4.35. I'm not sure he is the best choice for you.'

Amanda breathed a sigh of relief, as she handed over the money. 'I trust your judgement, Mrs Sharma.'

'You should still call me Aunty, Amanda. I still watch out for you and you are not too old to take my advice, I am pleased to see.'

Amanda laughed. 'I don't think I will ever be too old to need good advice.'

'Well, you don't need to make any snap decisions. Many new people will be coming to work at the Centre.'

'Did you know they were going to start on it so soon?'

'But, yes, of course. It was in the papers: City Millionaire Spearheads Memorial Centre for Asthma. Plus it is the most exciting thing to happen in Sunken Madley since the new church roof.'

Ding!

A man in paint-stained overalls entered. Amanda registered medium height, black hair and an averagely attractive face. No correspondence there then.

'Mrs Sharma, we're ready to start. Did you want to do a last check, click a photo or anything?'

'No, no, thank you, please go ahead.'

Amanda looked at him as he left, wondering what was afoot.

Mrs Sharma said, 'Mr Blackaby is retiring. He has no one he wants to pass the business on to, so he is just selling the goodwill and client list to Upper Muttring Felicitous Funerals. I am not sure Yash and I were right to rent it out for that purpose. It always cast a pall over that end of the village.'

'How many years ago was that?' asked Amanda.

'Oh, at least thirty. But now it will be a — '

Ding! The shop door opened and Sylvia came in. ''Ello Nalini. Amanda, you'd best get a move on, dearie, or you'll miss the fun up at Lost Madley!' she adjured her young friend.

'You're quite right, Sylvia. Thank you, Aunty!'

'You're welcome. And don't worry. The right man will appear for you, you will see.'

Amanda made a hasty departure before any more attempts at matchmaking by her seniors could ensue.

The audience of locals at the site included three classes shepherded by curious teachers from Sunken Madley School to witness the discharge of concrete from the rotating tanks. It was to flow into the prepared frame to form the floor of the Centre. Among the students was Amanda's favourite teenager, Ruth Reiser, who took advantage of her instructor's distraction to intercept Amanda as soon as she arrived at the site.

'Hi Ruth, how's the book on alchemy?'

'Good, thanks. Just had to get away from those girls. They *live* in Facebook.'

'And where do you live?' asked Amanda, sympathetically.

'Medieval Europe? In my head, anyway.'

'Why don't you join a Medieval history group on Facebook, then you'd have something in common with your classmates?'

Ruth looked doubtful.

'I promise that that wouldn't mean you were selling out,'

Amanda reassured her. 'You might even make some interesting friends.'

That brought forth a smile from Ruth. '*Sensible* would be a start,' she said.

'I'm not sure how sensible the Dark Ages were. Actually, there's probably a medieval magic group, they might have a discussion on alchemy.'

'Ruth!' came a teacher's voice.

'Gotta go. Thanks for the tips, Amanda.'

'Well, Amanda,' said a deep, resonant voice above her head.

She looked around and up, to see the face of Gordon French, the retired headmaster of Sunken Madley School. They were on friendly terms even though Amanda had been home-educated. He had always kept an eye out for her welfare around the village.

'Hello, Mr French.' Amanda leaned around him to see if his lady was there. And spotted her a few yards away. 'How are things going?'

He beamed. 'Very well, very well indeed. And what do you think of all of this? I assume you will be attending the Centre when it's ready.'

'I shall, yes,' confirmed Amanda.

'Well, as you can see,' said Mr French, lowering his voice significantly, 'it means the influx of a lot of strangers. And as I've said to you before, you can't be too careful with people who are not Village.'

'Yes, Mr French, but the builders won't be here for long. They're not going to be new residents.'

'I wasn't referring to the crew, Amanda, who seem like a good set of fellows, but to the scientists and the other people who will be working at the Centre.'

'I understand, Mr French. Yes, I will be mindful of what you have said to me.'

'Good. Well, I'll be getting back to er ….'

'You do that, Mr French, and thank you for your concern,

and for coming over to talk to me.'

'Not at all.' And he made his stately progress back to his lady's side. Amanda reflected, watching him, he's tall and, I suppose, he might be thought of as handsome. But he's dark, spoken for and he's much too old for me. No. She needed to take a good look at the …

'Hello, Amanda.' This time the tones were gentler and more hesitant. She turned again to look up into the visage of Jonathan Sheppard, the epitome of the tall, dark and handsome hero out of a romance novel, if he were not a little on the slenderer, more delicate side.

'Hello, Jonathan,' Amanda greeted him with a smile. 'How are things at the library?'

'Oh, wonderful. I do enjoy it very much indeed. It's a sort of second home, you know.'

'I think Mrs Pagely's adopted you since you became her assistant.'

'She's very kind. In fact, I am here at her request.' He held up a Nikon camera. 'She knows I like photography and asked me to take some photographs for the Community Board on the library wall. Mrs Pagely says this is the most exciting thing to happen in Sunken Madley since the new church roof, and we should make a feature of it.'

'What a good idea. And it's a chance for the village to appreciate your photography skills.'

'Yes, Mrs Pagely said that,' he agreed with shining eyes.

'I'm sure you'll do an excellent job,' Amanda said encouragingly. 'I look forward to seeing them.'

'Thank you, Amanda.' And off he went, in search of angles.

Finally, Amanda had the chance to take a look around to scope out any possible candidates on the site for meeting Amelia's appealing description. One or two of the crew were tall and attractive, but neither of them appealed to her. Of course, there was always the strange man …, but, no, he was more of medium height.

She had walked over to reassure Miss de Havillande that she was not forgotten when Damian approached the ladies with his friend Robin in tow.

Amanda watched them walk up. Damian? … no … short …. His friend? No, too old ….

'Miss de Havillande, Amanda, hi. I just wanted to introduce my best buddy, Robin Streeter, the organisation's mastermind behind a lot of this project, hey Robin?' he said, clapping his pal on the shoulder.

'Hello, Miss … er … ?' said Robin, with more formal politeness than Damian.

'Cadabra,' Amanda answered in a friendly tone.

He raised his eyebrows registering surprise but made a gallant recovery. 'A magical name, but I expect you hear that all the time,' he said gracefully.

She smiled and said, 'Yes, rather a lot but I'll take it in the spirit intended.'

'Good,' he said with a pleased expression.

Damian chimed in. 'I'll leave you in Robin's capable hands, ladies. I just need to have a word with the supervisor before kickoff.'

Robin turned back to the Miss de Havillande and Amanda.

'Is there anything you'd like to know about the proceedings?'

'Actually, yes,' said Amanda, ever curious. 'What was the machine I saw leaving the village, when I was coming out of the corner shop the other day?'

'Can you describe it?'

'Let me see. It was on the back of a lorry. It had caterpillar tracks and a cab on top of them, and attached to it was what looked like a tall crane arm.'

Robin nodded recognition. 'That's a pile rig. The ground here is full of cavities and spaces because of the remains of Lost Madley that, out of respect, we didn't want to disturb. So the part of the lab that's being built over it is on stilts.'

'Stilts?'

'Yes. Made of concrete. But you can't drive concrete into the ground because it will crack. Or even if it's reinforced the pounding could cause a cave-in down there. The pile rig is a drill that makes a deep hole for a metal cylinder that is pushed in behind it. That gets filled with concrete. The metal cylinder might be removed afterwards but, either way, hey presto, you have a pile or pillar.'

'I see. And they're at intervals in the trench for the foundations, all around the perimeter of the site?'

'That's right. Then we join them together at the top to create a platform. That's what the pouring is about today: pouring the concrete floor. Or looked at another way, the concrete roof on top of the pillars like an ancient Greek temple.'

'Aha, I understand. That's very helpful, Mr Streeter. Thank you for taking the time to explain that.'

'Well, I think it's important to take the environment and the sensibilities of the local people into consideration, and I know Damian feels the same. And please call me *Robin*.'

'Thank you. *Amanda*.'

'*Amanda* it is. Anything you want to know just ask. I hear you're the local carpenter, or, rather, furniture restorer.'

'I am,' answered Amanda, with a smile.

'Well, we're not going to have anything antique or fancy, this is a working building, but it is good to know that there's local expertise available,' he said pleasantly.

Amanda warmed to him. 'Are you from around here, Robin?'

'Not now, my house is in Essex. But I grew up here as a boy. Both of us did.'

'Really. Where?'

'Upper Muttring.'

'No!' Amanda exclaimed in surprise.

'Yes, local boys made good, you might say.'

Miss de Havillande spoke up, 'Yes, they've done well for themselves as investment consultants, Amanda.'

'Oh well,' Robin replied, deprecatingly, 'Damian's the star of the show. But he's always had my loyal support.'

'That's a valuable commodity. I am sure you're too modest,' said Amanda.

Robin glanced over at Damian. 'Ok, if you'll excuse me, ladies, I'll see if he needs anything.'

'Of course,' said Miss de Havillande, inclining her head.

'I must be getting back too,' added Amanda.

She was walking to the car when her phone rang.

Thomas had paced up and down the small space of empty floor in his office, rehearsing what he would say.

The question was, was this personal or not? Would his memories make him some kind of witness in this case? If so, it was a combination of personal and professional. The *next* question was, to which approach would Miss Cadabra respond the more warmly?

Asking for help was always a good move.

'Hello, Miss Cadabra?'

'Detective Inspector Trelawney?'

His name must have shown up on her phone. Good.

'Yes, that's right.'

'Hello, Inspector. I wasn't expecting to hear from you for a few weeks. Did you want to book your tour of the village and surrounding beauty spots that I happily agreed to give you?' she asked lightly.

'Oh, definitely, but not quite yet. Actually, I was wondering if you could spare some time at the weekend for a chat about something else.'

'Of course. Do you have more evidence? Found the lady who reported the —?'

'No. Although it may be connected to the case, yes. But in a sense, it's also a personal matter. Former Chief Inspector Hogarth suggested that you may be able and willing to assist me,' he finished hopefully.

'Well, yes.' She sounded doubtful to his ears.

'Thank you. That's extremely kind of you.'

'Erm, well … how about Sunday?'

'Sunday would be fine.'

'Somewhere quiet … Sinner's Rue, … after the kitchen closes, say, … 3.30?'

'That's great. I appreciate you taking the time, Miss Cadabra. I'll see you at 3.30 on Sunday at The Sinner's Rue.'

'OK, see you then.' She still sounded friendly but nonplussed.

'Till then. Goodbye.' He hung up. He hoped to heaven she wasn't feeling railroaded.

'Well!' said Amanda to Tempest who was looking up at her demandingly. 'I expect you know who that was. It's no use looking at me like that. I have no idea what that was all about. I wonder how he thinks I can help him. It's an odd request. He always seems so self-contained, self-sufficient. I can't imagine that he'd ever need "personal" help from anyone. I suppose we'll just have to wait and see.'

Chapter 13

჻

RECALL

Trelawney was at the same table as when Amanda had met him here before. The only difference was that Tempest was already there, tucked under the table, chewing on a cold sausage the kitchen staff had been wise enough to supply him with before leaving.

The sun was shining into the front of the building, but the inevitable fire was still a-crackle for effect. Trelawney rose politely at her entrance, and they shook hands and sat down. He'd already ordered hot chocolate for her and tea for himself.

Amanda smiled. 'You remembered my favourite drink. How thoughtful. Thank you, Inspector.'

'The least I could do.'

It struck her that he was uncomfortable. Amanda had never seen him like that before, not even when Granny had been playing cat-and-mouse with him. To make him feel more at ease, she asked after the Chief Inspector and the weather in Cornwall.

'Have you always lived there?' she asked.

'Yes, I was born there. Although, … well …' Trelawney was

unused to talking about himself.

'Oh, did you go away to school?'

'No ... you see, my mother is English, and my parents divorced when I was 11 or 12. My mother came to live in London, in Crouch End, and I spent the school holidays with her and term time with my father.'

'That must have been difficult for you to adjust to,' said Amanda, sympathetically.

'Yes ... it was ... but ....'

She waited patiently.

'Just recently, I've started to wonder if it wasn't more difficult than I remember .... The fact is, that I didn't remember .... I didn't remember much of anything that happened before they broke up.'

'I hear isn't unusual for people to forget the time before the age of ten.'

'Perhaps not but ... I've started to have dreams in which I was back at the family home.'

Amanda was trying to imagine what this had to do with the case of the mysterious deaths of her relations. Trelawney read that much in her face, and added, 'I think that it's related to the case of the incident, related to your family in some way ... that it's important.'

'You think that your subconscious is allowing a memory to surface?' Amanda suggested, helpfully.

'Yes,' he answered, but uncertainly.

'OK, well ... why don't you tell me, and I'll see if any of it rings any kind of bell? Only, Inspector, I don't remember Cornwall at all. I remember nothing before Sunken Madley and living with my grandparents. I don't remember any other family members at all. Oh, I have a brief mental snapshot of my grandparents smiling down at me or holding my hands, but that's all.' She stopped.. 'That is ....'

He looked at her questioningly.

'That is ...?' he prompted gently.

'Oh!' Abruptly and irrelevantly her mind had made a connection ... she blushed ... Tall, fair and handsome ... oh, surely not!

'Did you cross ...?' she began. But, of course, he had. He'd crossed the Tamar River. Honestly! No wonder Aunt Amelia was so amused .... Tall and handsome ... was he? .... She'd never looked at him as a man before. She thought of him more an irritant on legs, who could be good company on occasion, when he wasn't turning up when he wasn't wanted or asking a lot of probing questions.

Trelawney noticed the blush and was aware that her eyes were travelling around his face, and taking in his appearance ... what on earth?

He had, Amanda reflected, come to the funerals to pay his respects, and he'd brought flowers that time. And actually, he'd been kind, giving her his card and personal number in case she needed him. They'd got on pretty well, and he had come all this way to tell her ... something. But then she hadn't liked the way he'd asked her for an explanation that day; the day he came to tell her about the stuff on the road. It was as though he suspected the Cadabras of involvement. Well! Granny and Grandpa were beyond his reach, and how could she, a three-year-old at the time, be implicated?

Nevertheless ... well. she supposed he was ... to do him justice ... yes ... but really! Tall, fair and handsome and it turns out to be only the inspector. Just my luck!

'Did I cross ...?'

'Never mind. It's nothing,' she said, recalling herself.

'You were saying,' Trelawney reminded Amanda, 'that all you could remember and then, "That is, dot dot dot".'

'Yes ... well ... I had a flashback and then a dream ... a few days ago. I think from before I was three ... at the family home ... I mean the ancestral home.'

'Yes, me too.'

'Really? OK,' Amanda said, warily. 'Maybe if you tell me

about yours first.'

'Of course. If you'd prefer.' He took a breath.

Amanda started him off. 'You were back in the family house.'

'It was a mansion, old, large rooms, a wooden floor. My feet make a sound on the flooring when I walk. I'm closer to the ground. As a child would be. I can smell something. My father's there. He's nervous. He's with an old, grand lady and some other men in black suits. They keep asking my father about me. I hear bits of conversation. A name keeps cropping up … It sounds like a spring, bouncing or a coil.'

She nodded encouragingly, and Trelawney continued.

'Last night I had another dream, the same scene, and then I was in the Arctic, I think …. ice and snow everywhere …. then a fire was raging all around me and then … and then I saw an old-fashioned penny with Queen Victoria's head on it, then it changed to the Georges, then Elizabeth II, then it became a silver denarius, I think, with the head of Caesar on it.' He stopped. 'And then I woke up,' he ended.

'That's strange.'

'I know,' agreed Trelawney.

'I mean, that's strange because, in my dream, I was being held like a child, I think, by a woman who was showing me a portrait ….'

Suddenly Amanda was back there …. The pub disappeared, and she was in a long gallery. The woman, clad in black, directed Amanda's attention, with a long, sharp-nailed, gnarled finger, towards the painting in front of them.

'These are not the very oldest portraits, but *they* might frighten you,' said the woman, with a touch of scorn. 'This is Branked Cardiubarn. He fell from the East turret. Sadly missed,' she commented in a mimicry of regret.

Amanda was carried to the next picture. 'But succeeded by his wife who married Caswaran Flamgoyne … shortly after which she drowned in the moat. Much regretted.'

She didn't sound sorry, to the ears of Amanda. They had moved on.

'Casworan Flamgoyne-Cardiubarn was one of the few who insisted on adding his family name to his new surname ... until the portcullis came down unexpectedly. Unfortunate,' said the old woman with relish.

'We'll skip these. I wouldn't want to tire you. Your grandmother makes such a fuss,' said the woman bitterly. She put Amanda on the floor and led her past several more painted faces.

They halted. Amanda was picked up again.

'This is Massen Cardiubarn who was sucked into a bog on Dartmoor. He *would* go travelling,' she smirked. 'Being already a widower he was succeeded by his daughter Cryda.' They advanced a few paces. 'This is she. Cryda Cardiubarn had the good sense to keep to her mother's surname. But she went down in a boating accident on the Dozmary Pool. *Boats*. What can I say?' She shrugged her black shoulders idly.

The old woman walked on, continuing, 'Cryda was followed by her sister, Eselda, over here. She carelessly fell down the stairs one night, leaving only a grief-stricken grandson.'

With a side-step or two, they arrived at 'Treeve Cardiubarn. He accidentally consumed wolf's bane at a family party, leaving a hole in the life of his devoted daughter.'

She hitched up Amanda, 'My word you're heavy. What does Senara feed you! His daughter hangs here. She was the other member of the family to join her mother's name to ours: Gonetta Flamgoyne-Cardiubarn. She mistook a punnet of cuckoo pint for red currents – alas ....

'Her daughter Lamorna was more careful about what she ate, until a loose stone from the battlements fell on her and her husband. Deeply mourned by their sole surviving daughter, Jowanet. You can't be too careful,' she said with a chilling smile.

Amanda was put back on her feet.

'Now that's quite enough of a treat for you for one day. And your grandmother will be here soon to take you away.'

'Amanda ... Miss Cadabra.'

'Hm?' She had returned to The Sinner's Rue.

'Are you all right?' asked Trelawney, with concern. 'I lost you for a moment there.'

'What? Oh ... it happened again ... suddenly I was back there .... She was taking me from portrait to portrait. Actually, it was funny! Like something out of *Kind Hearts and Coronets*! You know? Dennis Price bumping off all of the relatives that stood between him and the succession to the — '

'And they're all played by Alec Guinness,' he added, with a grin. 'Oh yes, that's a classic.'

'You *know* that film?' Amanda asked, with distracted delight.

'Of course. I don't spend *all* of my time pursuing the Cause of Justice and righting wrongs.'

The atmosphere had lightened, and Amanda's head was clearing.

'So ...?' asked Trelawney.

'Well, there was a name ... oh no, it's gone! ... it's .... Wait.'

'Ice and snow?' he prompted with images from his dream that might connect. 'Arctic? Antarctic? Scott?'

She shook her head. 'The money ....'

'King? Queen? Monarch?'

'What do they have in common?' asked Amanda.

'They're all rulers?'

'I've got it! Coins,' said Amanda.

'Right. Coin something? Doesn't sound very Cornish to me,' responded Trelawney doubtfully.

'Fire,' continued Amanda.

'Hot,' replied Trelawney.

'Flame ....'

'Flame. That rings a bell. Yes, close,' he said.

'Coin flame ...,' Amanda suggested.

'Flame coin.'

'Flamcoin,' she said excitedly.

'Flamgoyne!' Trelawney exclaimed.

'Yes!' answered Amanda. 'Good. OK, Flamgoyne. Now. What about the ice and snow?'

'Poles,' he said.

'Polflamgoyne?' she tried.

'No,' he corrected. 'They *were* the Polgoynes.'

'Then they became the Flamgoynes?'

'Yes,' confirmed Trelawney, 'and they sometimes married the Car —'

'You're a Flamgoyne?' asked Amanda, aghast.

'You're a Cardiubarn!' retorted Thomas.

'No, I'm not!' they uttered simultaneously, with playground vehemence, leaning towards one another across the table.

'I'm a Cadabra!'

'I'm a Trelawney.'

They suddenly caught themselves, leaned back, embarrassed, Amanda half smiled, and Trelawney chuckled.

'So you are,' he agreed.

'So you are,' she echoed.

'Well, now,' said Thomas, 'since there seems to be a history of uneasy alliance between them … do you think it's possible one of my lot bumped off your lot? Sending them over a cliff would seem to be in keeping with the list of homicides your elderly relative recited to you with visual aids.'

'If they did, then tell me where to send the thank you note!' replied Amanda.

He laughed. 'Could it have been part of a feud? Does that sound familiar?'

'The first portraits were old, I think. The others she showed me were more recent, but she still had an edge to her voice whenever she said the name, Flamgoyne.'

'It's possible then,' said Trelawney.

'It's possible,' Amanda concurred.

'If you could remember more … the most recent portraits would have been after the last the woman in your dream told you about.'

'And I suppose they're still there,' she remarked.

'Well, ... surely you could access them?' Trelawney suggested tentatively.

'Me?' she asked, surprised. 'Why me?'

'Don't you know?'

'Know what?' Amanda asked uneasily.

'What you will inherit if we crack this case and establish cause of death.'

Amanda was relieved. 'Oh, some derelict or other.'

'No, Miss Cadabra.' Should he tell her? If not, all she had to do was look through Senara's papers. This way he could at least observe her reaction to the news.

'You are the heiress to Cardiubarn Hall.'

'What?' Amanda's voice was faint.

All at once, she saw it. A black stone, brick and metal castle-like structure, its tall, thin turrets a set of spikes piercing the thick, dark, low-hanging cloud above it that stretched out over the leaden lake of the Dozmary Pool. She was seeing it over Granny's shoulder as she was carried to the car ... saw it for the last time ... and she was feeling ... feeling what ...? Something had just happened, ... something she couldn't remember ... she *needed* to remember .... she needed to *tell Granny* ... but ....

'*That* place?' Amanda said. All she knew was that it was the last place she wanted to go back to. 'That's mine?'

'You are the heiress. They never told you?' he asked. This was unexpected.

'Good grief, no. Ugh!'

Her revulsion seemed real enough. 'Well, it's boarded up, surrounded by an electrified fence anyway. You wouldn't have right of entry ... but ... if we could prove —'

'No. No. I wouldn't go back there if you paid me! Anyway, isn't it enough that we've remembered the name and the connection? Can't you just go and find some Flamgoynes now?'

'Well yes, I do have a trail to follow,' he agreed. 'Thank

you, Miss Cadabra. You've been of great assistance. I hope that it's helped you too in some way.'

'Yes ... yes, I think it has. I've remembered what it was my subconscious or whatever wanted me to recall. Hopefully, all the dreams and flashbacks will go away now.' Amanda looked at him and shook her head. 'I can't believe we're ... you know?'

'Connected. Yes, I do know.'

'In the worst possible way!' she added.

'Oh, I don't know,' Trelawney countered pacifically, 'We do have the common ground of having antecedents of whom we're not very proud, and of being unwilling members of those ....' He was going to say, 'clans', a word Hogarth had used ... 'witch clans'. 'Dynasties,' he finished.

'True.' Amanda smiled. 'Brother and sister in misery then.'

'Let's say *misfortune* rather than misery,' he offered.

'Yes, that's much better,' she said.

'And there's nothing inherently dreadful about being distant cousins, is there?'

Amanda shook her head.

'Was there anything else,' asked Trelawney, 'that you remember or want to ...?'

'No, thank you,' she replied emphatically. 'That's quite enough for one afternoon.'

'Another drink? And how about out in the sunshine?'

'Yes, blow the cobwebs away.'

They sipped and chatted about the village, until Trelawney took his leave. He held out his hand.

'Thank you again, Miss Cadabra.'

'You're welcome, Inspector. Thank you too.'

'I hope it hasn't been upsetting.'

'No, I'm fine.'

'I'd still like the tour,' he said on a lighter note.

'Just let me know when. I'll be here,' Amanda promised.

'Thank you, I will. And if there's anything else ... you want to talk about or need help with ... you know ... just call.'

'I will,' she agreed. 'Safe journey.'

'Thank you.'

As he drove away, Tempest nuzzled against her legs reassuringly.

That night, Amanda and Trelawney slept soundly. Whatever had been rattling around in the cage of memory had now been released. Released and free to unleash, slowly and quietly, more of its kind.

Chapter 14

╰┈➤

THE TRUTH ABOUT MISS ARMSTRONG-WITWORTH

Amanda looked at the blast radius of damage to the room. The noise must have been colossal.

How come no one had heard it? she wondered
Or had they heard it but didn't come?
Didn't come because they knew what it was?
Knew what it was because they had planned it.
Had they planned that I should find the body?
 Are they watching me now?

* * * * *

Former Chief Inspector Michael Hogarth sensed the man long before he saw him, or his neighbour, Alf, mentioned the matter. It was a small seaside village. Strangers in Mornan Bay were noticeable.

Hogarth thoughtfully went to the kitchen and took out the big bag of Epsom salts that he kept under the sink. He went out of the back door that led to the garden, and slowly began pouring it out in a continuous line, from the right of the door around the back and side of the house to the front. There he left a break for the entrance, and carried on letting the white stream fall from the packet until he heard Alf calling out to him.

'Arter noon, me'ansum.'

'Good afternoon, Alf, how are you doing today?'

'Fine, fine. 'Ere. You see 'im?'

'The stranger?'

'No emmet, I censure.'

'I agree, I don't think he *is* a tourist.'

Alf looked at the trail of salt.

'They pestic slugs a-bretherin a, again?'

'It's the time of year,' commented Hogarth. 'This should discourage them from eating the young vegetables.'

'Strange as ow nerry don't brether me.'

'You're lucky they leave you alone. Perhaps it's my compost.'

'Yas, that might be it.'

'Well, best get it done,' Hogarth said philosophically.

'Leave a to it then. I let a know if I see 'im agen.'

'Yes, if you would. Thanks, Alf.'

Hogarth finished the job. Then went inside to pack and send a one-word text to his sister:

Ready

* * * * *

Amanda arrived at The Grange expecting to see Miss de Havillande, considering it was Cynthia with whom she'd made the appointment.

Surprisingly, however, the door was answered by Miss de Havillande's diminutive bosom friend, Miss Armstrong-Witworth.

She wore a sun hat decorated in pale lilac wisps of delicate fabric and white artificial tea roses. It matched her ballet-length, light, muslin dress with three-quarter sleeves. She was stripping off her gardening gloves.

'Hello, dear, do come in. Cynthia will be sorry to have missed you but Churchill was feeling the call of nature rather, and I expect dear Cynthia had something urgent she wished to say to Jane. She usually does, as I am sure you know, dear. Shall I call Moffat to help you bring your things from your car?'

'No, that's all right, Miss Armstrong-Witworth, I can manage.' Amanda went to the boot of the Astra and came back carrying a light box of cloths.

'Oh, do call me Gwendolen. Come into the dining room. Cynthia told me she had seen you at the site.'

'Yes.'

'And what do you make of it all, dear.'

Amanda was taken aback by the question.

'Well, … it's a very worthy project.'

'But?' asked Gwendolen, turning a mildly inquisitive little face up towards Amanda.

'Oh, it's just maybe not the best possible choice of location.'

'Ah. Lost Madley,' agreed Gwendolen, nodding.

Amanda had an idea. 'Miss Armstrong-Witwor—'

'Gwendolen. I insist. It makes me feel old you calling me Miss Armstrong-Witworth all the time. And I have a feeling about you and me. I think we're going to be good friends.'

Amanda smiled. 'Gwendolen. Do you remember it, Lost Madley, as it was before it was ….'

'Oh yes. I do. I had a friend there: Violet. It was all rather sad.'

'Was she killed?'

'No. But her young man was. They had just got engaged.'

'Was he killed at the front?'

'No, no, he wasn't a soldier. He was doing important work though. That I do happen to know.'

'Where?'

'There, in Little Madley, as it was called then. At home in his workshop at the back of his house. Like yours, dear.'

'How come your friend survived and he didn't? If I may ask?'

'They were supposed to meet in The Apple Cart, the inn there. When the air-raid warning sounded, she went into the shelter. He didn't follow. They found him the next day when it was light, in the inn. It had collapsed. I don't think she ever got over it entirely. After the war, she married, had children, and has outlived them all.'

'Your friend is still alive?'

'Yes, Violet is in Pipkin Acres Residential Home, between here and Upper Muttring. That reminds me, I must go and see her. I don't think she has much longer, to be honest. Her mind wanders rather. I'm not entirely sure if she knows who I am. I think she goes into the past sometimes …. So many women lost their menfolk you know … hmm …'

'You too, Miss — Gwendolen?' Amanda asked, tentatively.

'Oh yes, I was married.'

'And he …?'

'Yes, he was killed in the war.'

'I'm sorry.'

'Oh don't be, dear,' replied Gwendolen cheerily, 'I wasn't. He wasn't really quite the thing.' She rubbed her cheek and arm absent-mindedly, which gave Amanda a pretty good clue as to the way in which he had not been 'quite the thing'. 'And I got a chance at another life,' she continued, 'and very interesting it was too.'

Amanda's curiosity was aroused.

'May I ask, in what way?'

'Well, dear, I got the chance to travel.'

'In import-export? Tourism?'

'In a way, dear, yes.'

'Ah, as a rep or a buyer?'

'As a matter of fact, it was for the British Government.'

'You were a diplomat?' hazarded Amanda.

'Not exactly. I was an agent.'

'An agent?'

'A field agent.'

Amanda had seen enough action films to recognise the term.

'Miss Armstrong-Witworth, you don't mean that you were a ... a spy?'

'Oh dear, you make it sound so dramatic. It really was not like you see in the films, you know. Really not at all glamorous.'

'But ... but how were you ... erm ... recruited?' Amanda's attention was caught, the dining room table utterly forgotten.

'Not off the street or out of a Cambridge university, no. You see, I went to work for dear Sir Ambrose, a friend of Papa's, at the Home Office. A very minor department and just filing and typing. But it came to light that I had a certain flair for languages.'

'Such as?'

'I spoke fluent Russian.'

'Russian?'

'Yes. Dear Papa taught us. He was very fond of Russian culture. He always said that it was the language of the soul. We used to have readings from the great Russian authors every evening. We went to the Russian opera, the ballet, we sang songs, his friends from Russia visited. We had émigrés staying with us. Hmm.' She smiled gently, reminiscing. 'What jolly times.'

Amanda made a connection.

'Of course. Your cats: Pushkin, after the writer, and Natasha, the heroine from *War and Peace*.'

'That's right, dear. Let me make you some tea. I can see you've had rather a shock.'

'Well, it *is* a surprise. Here I was thinking all these years that you were just … that you …'

'That I was a sweet little old lady.'

'Erm, yes,' confessed Amanda, apologetically.

'You should know,' said Miss Armstrong-Witworth mildly, 'that there is no such thing as a sweet little old lady. The person might be sweet, she might be small in stature, she may be senior in years and, indeed, a lady, but not what all of those words strung together have come to mean.'

'Clearly not,' agreed Amanda with sincerity.

'No, that is just a construct that has served many of us exceedingly well.'

'How so?'

'It acts like an invisibility cloak, rendering the wearer able to come and go and ask questions and overhear information whenever and wherever she pleases. They see me in the street and will say, "Oh, it's just Miss Armstrong-Witworth."

'But when they see *you* in the village, they say, "There goes our furniture restorer. Perran and Senara adopted her, you know. Her family perished in strange circumstances, you know, and she's at least 30 and not yet married. What do you think of all of that?" You may not realise it, but you have glamour, my dear, you are an oddity. Doing a man's job, living alone with just your cat for company.'

Amanda looked concerned.

'And yet,' continued Miss Armstrong-Witworth comfortingly, 'you are loved, and you are *our* oddity. The Japanese vase that is valued all the more for the crack in the glaze.'

Amanda relaxed. She didn't mind if people thought she was cracked. 'That's kind of you, Gwendolen.'

'You see, you're not invisible like I am, in spite of your quiet ways. Now let me get the tea.'

Amanda sat down at the dining room table and shook her head, wondering if anyone in this village was what she thought they were. Here was Miss Armstrong-Witworth, whom she thought she'd known her whole life, and all the while ….

The former spy came in from the small adjoining dining-room with the tea tray.

'Miss, erm, Gwendolen.'

'Yes, dear?'

'May I ask you a question?'

'Of course.'

'Did you have a gun?'

'A pistol? Naturally,' Miss Armstrong-Witworth replied calmly, as she poured out the tea into two bone china, hibiscus patterned, Wedgwood teacups.

'And ... did you ... ever kill anyone?'

'Yes, but they were all bad, I do assure you.'

Amanda opened her mouth to speak but no sound issued forth.

'Drink your tea, dear.'

Amanda sipped at the delicate lapsang souchong, feeling the urge to lie down in a darkened room for half an hour with a cold compress to her temples, while the world resolved itself back into its familiar shape.

'You're quite right, Amanda, dear,' said the 007 in the muslin dress. 'People are not always what they appear to be. That is why you have to be so careful whom you trust. Especially on dating sites.'

'You know about dating sites?'

'This is a grange, not a convent, dear, we do have contact with the outside world. Our wifi is really quite excellent since I installed the new router.'

'You ...?'

'Oh well, in the Service we were trained in the use of radio equipment. If you keep up with technology, it isn't really that difficult.'

'Perhaps you'd like to have a look at my connection sometime,' Amanda uttered, mesmerized, 'It's been running slow.'

'Of course, dear. Let me know when. Well, I must let you get on.'

Amanda was overwhelmed by a sense of unreality. Dear Miss Armstrong-Witworth who had just brought in the tea, in her pretty hat and floating gown, had had a licence to kill?

Miss Bond patted Amanda's cheek. 'It's come as a shock. Then again. You with your sweet face and your child's eyes, yes, I expect it's something that you experience yourself quite often. Especially from gentlemen who imagine you are a helpless ingénue. I imagine they get quite a shock when it turns out that you are really quite self-sufficient. For you are not at *all* helpless, are you, dear?'

Amanda looked back at the gentle blue gaze. What did she mean?

Then Miss Armstrong-Witworth continued, 'No granddaughter of Senara's would be brought up to be helpless.'

Amanda breathed an internal sigh of relief. 'Well. I hope that I'm reasonably independent.'

'I'm sure you are, dear. No.' Miss Armstrong-Witworth looked at Amanda reflectively. 'You don't need a rescuer.' She paused then added, 'Or a limelight grabber either. Someone with quiet intellect and humour, and the something extra, just like you. No,' she said again as she wandered out of the room, 'I don't think Mr Ford will do for you.'

Mr Ford? Of course, the whole village had been speculating about her and Ryan Ford. Perhaps Miss Armstrong-Witworth was right. It crossed Amanda's mind that much of Gwendolen's description could apply to Trelawney, but he would not do at all either. He was too decidedly Normal, in spite of his family connexions. No, the right man would have to be someone of her magical world, and Trelawney could not be further from that.

Whoever it was ... had yet to show himself.

Chapter 15

ॐ

THE GERMANS ARE COMING

No sooner was The Pouring finished than the villagers began talking about the next big event. The concrete was drying nicely flat, and was, at least partially, cured. Everything had gone according to plan and on schedule. It was now far more than rumour: the Germans were coming.

Inevitably, Amanda heard it from Joan.

'That'll be nice for Irma Uberhausfest, to have someone to talk to in her own language.'

Perran who was standing nearby, unseen, of course, by the postlady but perfectly solid to Amanda, commented, 'Irma's been here more years than in Germany. I'd say *English* is her own language.'

'And Irma speaks it better than half the village who was born here!' added Granny, caustically. Senara had Views on the state of the British education system.

'I wonder how much they'll socialise, though, Joan,' Amanda mused, ignoring her grandparents.

'Oh, Irma's having one to stay. She's got the extra rooms

and sometimes does take in paying guests. Makes a nice addition to the income from her business.'

Irma Uberhausfest had the distinction of being, at 91, the oldest party planner in England. Long retired from a career in accountancy, Irma had discovered a talent for organising personalised entertainment for the over-70s. After experimenting with parties for friends, word of mouth spread sufficiently for Irma to decide on a radical life change.

She gave herself a makeover, had her hair restyled, gave her sensible wardrobe to a local charity shop, and created a new elegant, fashionable, artistic look for herself. Next Irma sold her Mercedes hatchback and obtained for herself a remarkable reconditioned VW Beetle former police vehicle, with a Porsche engine, in metallic purple. (Dazzled, Dennis Hanley-Page proposed on the spot. Irma laughed and told him that she wasn't currently in the market for a toyboy.) Irma set up a website and got some business cards printed: Finely Aged Festivities was born.

'Older people are not children, you know, my dear, they want more than balloons and sing-songs,' Irma told her when Amanda went to assess the cost of post-birthday-bash repairs for the insurance. The event Irma organised for Mr Fortescue's 80th, with a burlesque theme, featuring a dancer of the exotic variety, caused a scandal in minor parts of the village and a flood of bookings from over four counties.

It was Irma who was the second to give her the news, when Amanda popped into the post-office to dispatch a completed repair that had been sent to her. Amanda usually had insurance-funded work of some description after Irma's parties, so they were on especially friendly terms.

'Amanda, they are coming. So many nice young men. One who is staying with me, oh, his family is so nice.'

'I'm sure they're all lovely, Mrs Uberhausfest, but they all one have one drawback: they live in Germany. I live here.'

'People move. I did.'

'Yes, but you moved here with your husband.'

'No, no, we do not want to lose you, Amanda. *He* will move *here!*'

'Er, well, I think that this is all premature. They haven't even arrived yet. Anyway what exactly does this company do?' she asked, equally interested to know and eager to change the subject.

Irma was predictably knowledgeable. She explained that the business, Huf Haus, began with dream houses. To minimise time on site, every preparation possible was crafted in the warehouse. Each home was designed according to the customer's needs and desires, then entire panels, walls, roof structures and beams transported to the location, and within days, stylish mini-palaces of wood and glass grew up, fixtured and fitted, ready to be inhabited, decorated and loved.

From there the company had expanded to include larger commercial buildings. The asthma research centre would be the first of its kind to grace the United Kingdom. Damian had enticed the sponsors with the idea of having a stake in architectural innovation, as well as a cause that would also be good for their own public relations.

Actually, a small team of Germans had already come and gone, working with the British builders on the concrete. A mere cameo before the main event.

'On Monday they will be here,' announced Mrs Uberhausfest. An inspired thought was kindled in her fun-loving soul. 'Maybe I should throw a party for them.'

'I'm not sure they will want one. Of course, you can ask them.'

'Amanda,' said Mrs Uberhausfest, looking seriously into her young friend's eyes, 'I see you only working. When do you have fun? Come to my next party!'

'You can hardly take a guest to a client's party, Mrs Uberhausfest.'

'Oh, I can plus one if I want. You need to get out, have fun.'

'I think your parties might be a bit much for me.'

'Oh yes, these young people are wild, wild!' To Irma, anyone in their 70s was designated as 'young people'. 'But it is good to enjoy yourself. You will think about it?' Irma took Amanda's hands and patted them. 'I know your grandmother would wish me to encourage you to "hang loose" sometimes. You know, she and I, we are friends for over *fifty* years.'

Amanda smiled affectionately, and kissed Irma's cheek. 'I know, Mrs Uberhausfest. Thank you for your invitation. I promise to think about.'

'Good. Anyway, they arrive on Monday, Monday. Many nice young men. You will see.'

Only the earliest risers saw the first arrivals: Joan the postlady and Joe the milkman from Madley Cows Dairy, naturally. Sylvia the lollipop lady (she of the circular 'stop' sign on a pole, used to halt traffic so that school children could safely traverse the roads twice a day) and her husband were also up, as were insomniacs, and those roused betimes by hungry infants or door-flapless cats returning late from all-nighters.

These alone witnessed, just after dawn, the headlamps of the first giant truck sweep gently through the village, and then turn off to the right to light the track to Lost Madley. The sun rose as further trucks and vans arrived. The villagers, Damian and Robin assembled. There was the inevitable wait for the British crane, and then the German team swung into action with seamless ease. By the time Amanda and Tempest arrived, late in the afternoon, whole wall panels were in place. It was a wonder, like watching a time-lapse video.

As Amanda stood transfixed, Tempest grumbled in his throat and pushed at her legs. She looked down, then followed his stare. There he was, the strange man, near the builders. But this time he was not looking at *her* but at one of the crew; a tall man of about Amanda's age, she judged. He was brown-haired with golden roots. She could not tell his eye colour from a distance but thought they might be blue. Looking up from a task he had just completed, the builder caught her gazing at him and smiled. She blushed and grinned back self-consciously. Thereafter, her eyes strayed to the two men, until the construction team finished for the day.

Amanda felt she owed the smiling man an apology for staring and waved at him. He came over to say hello.

'I'm Hugo.'

'Hello, I'm Amanda, I'm sorry for staring at you like that. It's just that the man in the suit was looking at you and I just wondered why.'

Hugo flicked a look around. He said quietly, 'Do you have time for a cup of coffee perhaps? My accommodations are in Sunken Madley at the pub, The Snout and Trough, I think?'

Amanda was surprised by his manner and invitation. Both intrigued and willing, she replied, 'Yes, we can have coffee there.'

He went to have a word with his foreman, and soon they were sitting with hot drinks in Amanda's favourite corner of The Other Pub.

'The man in the suit,' began Hugo in fluent English, with a slight Bavarian accent.

'Yes?'

'You see him?'

'Yes, of course,' answered Amanda, surprised by the question.

'Well, no one else does. Except me. My colleagues don't.'

'Really? They can't miss him. He's right on the concrete slab.'

'We have not reached there with the panels yet, but you will see. They will be walking straight through him.'

'Oh,' said Amanda. She saw Granny and Grandpa standing behind Hugo. She wondered, if he turned, whether he would be able to see them. She was sufficiently well-trained to be cautious of a trap. Was Hugo friend or foe?

However, Grandpa was giving the thumbs up sign. Hugo glanced over his shoulder to see what she was looking at. But Perran and Senara were too quick for him and, with a wink from

Grandpa, had vanished.

Amanda said, 'He's a ghost, then.'

'Or a recording. You know about these things?'

'Yes, I'm a furniture restorer. My grandfather told me about them. I remember the first one I came across. A chair with a sort of roof over it? Do you know what I mean?'

'Yes.'

'When I came near, and stood in front of it in a certain place, I would see a man in a Victorian black suit, sitting with a maid in a long dress on his knee. When she saw me, she would look shocked and get up very quickly, and then they would disappear.'

That made Hugo laugh. 'Exactly what I mean,' he confirmed. 'Yes, the man could be like that. Tell me, does he do the same thing every time he appears? And are you always in the same place when you see him?'

'No,' she said slowly. 'In fact, the first two times I saw him, he looked at *me*, but today I saw him looking at *you*.'

'And I was not in the same place as you either, Amanda, so …'

'All right, then. He's not a recording. Then why is he here?' she wondered. 'And why does he appear only to us?'

'I think you know the answer to that,' replied Hugo. He lowered his voice. 'You are one of the magic people, yes? You see other dimensions. Your cat too. I saw him looking at the man.'

Her heart quickened. He was the first man she had met, apart from Grandpa and Dr Bergstrom, who was a witch. It was as though the shutters of a darkened room were opening, letting in the light, banishing the everlasting need for secrecy that dominated nearly every single interaction with the people in her life.

'Yes,' she answered quietly, her eyes sparkling.

Hugo nodded. 'I come from such a family also. In my village, we too live quietly, like you. We work with wood for many generations; carpentry, joinery, carving.'

'Yes,' said Amanda eagerly, 'mine too! My grandfather's family. In that case … could it be that the man is a carpenter? He looked pleased to see me.'

'And me.'

'Have you tried to speak to him?' Amanda asked.

Hugo shook his head. 'There is always someone else around. And he is not there all of the time.'

They paused for thought.

Hugo asked, 'What is underneath where we are building?'

'An old abandoned village. It was bombed during the war — oh! No offence.'

'It was a long time ago. I apologise anyway,' he said ruefully.

Amanda laughed 'I was about to say that it's nothing to do with us … but somehow it looks like it is.'

'I will try to find out about what is underneath.'

'Me too,' said Amanda, readily.

'Be careful, be casual,' Hugo warned her.

'I will,' she reassured him. 'I have a friend, Claire, who works in media, who started out as a reporter. She has research resources. I could ask her.'

'Are you sure she won't leave a trace or ask the wrong person?'

Amanda thought. Claire might know how to dig things up, but covert ops was hardly what she associated with her best friend.

'No. No, I can't. OK, I'll ask at the library. They won't be surprised. They know I'm interested in history, including local history. I'll let you know what I find out.' They exchanged phone numbers.

'Oh, and I can look at the photographs. One of the librarians took pictures of the site. I'll bet that man doesn't appear in any of them. Now,' said Amanda, 'I must let you get cleaned up and rested.'

'Thank you and ….' There was no time for more. 'Here are my friends coming who are staying here also.' He stood up and waved. His two younger crewmates came over, and said 'hello' politely.

Hugo introduced them. 'This is Niko and Yannik.'

They shook hands. Amanda greeted them, then excused herself. 'I was just going. We are all very impressed with your work, by the way. Enjoy your evening.'

She turned and bumped into Joan.

'That was quick work, dearie,' she said in Amanda's ear, with a jerk of her head in Hugo's direction. Joan looked at the men, saying aloud, 'All right, my loves? Introduce me then, Amanda. Don't keep them all to yourself!'

'This is Joan, our postlady. Joan, this is Hugo, Niko and Yannik.' They stood up to greet the newcomer.

'All lovely boys I see. You staying 'ere?'

'Yes,' they assented. '

'Well, you'll all be up at the crack o' dawn I expect, and they don't serve breakfast 'ere until long after you're all up and doing. So you drop by my place five o'clock sharp in the mornings, and you can eat with me and my Jim, all right?'

Their faces were alive with a mixture of hesitation, relief and delight.

'Are you sure, er, Mrs Joan?' asked Hugo.

'Just *Joan* will do, and yes, I am sure. Number 2 Rectory Close, behind the church. You can't miss it.'

'This is most kind,' said Hugo.

'We will pay, of course,' added Niko.

'Well, we'll see about that. I like a full English of a morning, but I expect you'll like your sausages and cheese, and I've got muesli, if that's your fancy. I must be off. See you bright 'n' early, boys.'

They sent her on her way with thanks, and Joan linked her arm through Amanda's as they went out into the late afternoon sunshine.

'Well, well, what a nice bunch. I like your young man, I must say.'

'He's not my young man, Joan,' Amanda replied, with practiced patience. 'We only met about fifteen minutes ago.'

'Ah, love at first sight. I know all about that.'

'No, it's really not —'

'Sometimes, one look is all it takes,' said Joan knowingly.

'But ... I —'

'See you out and about, dearie,' called Joan, leaving Amanda beside her car, and striding off along the high road.

Chapter 16

✍

LITTLE MADLEY

The next morning, as Amanda set about tightening the stretchers on an Edwardian oak, barley twist chair, and filling a gouge in a console table, she found herself somewhat distracted. Her clamping spells were not all that they could have been, and she set the glue brush to stir by itself without remembering to turn the electric hob on under the pot. She caught herself in a pier glass, smiling for no reason.

By lunchtime, Amanda had done enough, and could leave glue and polish to dry. She shuffled out of her overalls and boots, changed into jeans and comfortable shoes, and drove quickly to the library. There was an event on at the school, so the road was parked up, and she had to leave the car so far away she might as well have walked from home.

Amanda was intercepted by Sylvia, the lollipop lady,

'Ello, lovie, 'ow's your young man?'

'My young man?'

'That 'andsome 'unk. You know. Hugo!'

'He's not my young man,' Amanda recited.

'Well, he should be! Oh, they're lovely boys, every one of

them. Tell you what, if I didn't have my George and I was 40 years younger I'd be there like a shot. Not just 'andsome but such nice manners.'

At that moment they approached a narrow space on the pavement between a lamppost and an over-exuberant fall of lobelias on a garden wall. Olivia Mazurek, coming from the opposite direction, charged the gap, bumping Sylvia's arm as she hurried past.

'Oh! Maybe they could give evening classes to our teenagers in how to behave!' Sylvia said markedly after Miss Mazurek.

'Sorry, Sylvia!' Olivia called back apologetically, 'I'm late for the dentist!'

'Hm, well, that one's usually better than the rest,' commented Sylvia. 'At least, she's being brung up proper. Like your Ruth.'

'My Ruth?'

'Ruth Reiser, that nice one you 'elp with her 'omework.'

'Only now and then. She's very capable.'

'Yes, I like her, with her quiet ways. Puts me in mind of you at her age. Not that you seem any older to us.'

'Don't I?' asked Amanda, in surprise.

'No dear, with your big child's eyes and your little face.' Sylvia patted Amanda's cheek. Funny, thought Amanda, Miss Armstrong-Witworth said something similar.

'Thank you, Joan. Not that I can hold a candle to our local model, Jessica James, or Claire.'

'Oh yes, you can't but notice our village belles. But I've noticed there are those who prefer you.'

'One or two perhaps,' Amanda conceded.

'Well, what with all the scientists coming, I'm sure you'll 'ave your pick, dearie.'

'They're coming here to *work*, Sylvia, not provide husbands for Sunken Madley spinsters!' teased Amanda.

'I don't see why they can't do both,' Sylvia replied practically. 'Well, mind 'ow you go. Give my best to Mrs Pagely.'

Amanda was about to ask how Sylvia knew that she was going to the library but gave up. This was Sylvia. She knew where everyone was going and why.

Amanda pushed open the library double doors.

'Hello, Amanda,' said the comforting and matronly Mrs Pagely, sitting at the counter looking across at one of her favourite readers. 'What can I do for you today?'

Amanda looked around with admiration. 'I see you've got everything back to normal.'

'Oh yes, no storm can keep a good library down. Now, did you still want that pamphlet?'

'No, thank you, Mrs Pagely, it's something else now. The building work has sparked my interest in Lost Madley.'

'Oh yes? Now, that's understandable, dear.'

'Well, I wondered if there were any plans, maps or photos of it, from before it was destroyed.'

'Hm ... let me see ... it's such a tiny little place ... I shouldn't think there's anything especially about that. You'd be more likely to find it on an old map of Sunken Madley, one big enough to cover Little Madley, as it was called.'

Suddenly Mrs Pagely stopped, stood still and looked up meditatively.

'Do you know, Amanda, in all the years I've been a librarian here, never *once* has anyone asked about that place.'

'Really?'

'No ... hmm. So if we have anything, it'll most likely be down in the stacks. I'd better look for it myself. Jonathan!'

Her assistant appeared from the children's section, carrying the books he was in the middle of shelving.

Jonathan Sheppard was possibly the most beautiful example of manhood ever to grace Sunken Madley, with raven black hair, liquid brown eyes, perfect white teeth, high cheekbones and flawlessly cut lips. His shy air and hesitant manner made him all the more alluring to the teenage female population, in particular, and reader numbers and book loans had tripled in the short time since his arrival.

However, rather than enjoying his popularity Jonathan found it more overwhelming than anything, and was happy to busy himself with his duties in a corner of the library, the more hidden the better. However, Mrs Pagely had, after a fashion, adopted him, and Amanda held no terrors for him, for they had already established a rapport, and he came over willingly at his boss's call.

'Hello, Amanda. Yes, Mrs Pagely?'

'Can you man the fort while I go down to the basement?'

'Of course,' Jonathan answered readily.

'You stay here, Amanda,' Mrs Pagely bade her.

Jonathan apologised for the second time for taking Amanda down there on a previous occasion when she had been spooked into a mild asthma attack.

'It's really all right, Jonathan,' Amanda replied reassuringly, 'you weren't to know.'

'But I do know what an unsettling place it can be. Not surprising, considering its history.'

'Yes,' she responded, 'you mentioned that there was .,.?'

'Yes, you see, back in …'

But Amanda was not destined to be apprised of the basement's murky past because teenager Becky Whittle had arrived with a book, and was leaning her ample curves over the counter, while gazing saucily at Jonathan.

Amanda was more relieved than anything else. If something untoward of a paranormal nature were pending in the stacks, it would inevitably wash up on her beach at some point. But right now, she had Lost Madley to deal with, and that was more than enough.

Mrs Pagely reappeared through the green metal door behind the counter, and switched off the light that illuminated the stone stairs to the basement.

'Here you are, Amanda. Come over here to the table.' She spread out a map and used a pencil as a pointer. 'Right. Here you can see Little Madley's location. So here's the High Road going up into Muttring Lane and here the lane branches off into the trees. Now here, the buildings start, and you can see the biggest one in the centre of the line of houses.'

'Ah yes,' said Amanda leaning over the large sheet of cartography.

'Now,' continued Mrs Pagely patting a thin, faded red book in her hand, 'this is a rare copy of *Madley Wood Life* by Teresa Goode.' The librarian opened it at a place where she'd marked the page with a scrap of paper. 'Here in the middle, are a few photographs, and these pages here show the hamlet. See? This is the pub, The Apple Cart, which was in the middle of the row of cottages, the biggest building that I showed you on the map. It had rooms for rent above the bar.'

The photos were in black and white and slightly fuzzy.

'Yes, there's someone waving out of one of the windows,' observed Amanda. 'And that man with the apron must be the proprietor, standing outside with, maybe, one of his staff.'

'Yes, very likely,' agreed Mrs Pagely. 'Now this photo here is taken from the end of the hamlet showing more of the line of structures.'

'Which end?' queried Amanda. 'Must be the north-west, the one furthest from Sunken Madley?'.

'Yes, I'd say so.'

'So this … wait ….' Amanda had just spotted something. There was a man, who looked like he'd just leaned out of his front door. He looked vaguely familiar. Could he be …? He had on a brown lab coat like the one Grandpa used to wear and she put on herself sometimes. She pointed. 'Who is this? Does it say?'

Mrs Pagely looked at the captions and the neighbouring text. 'No.'

'What's that in his hand?' Amanda asked pointing with the nail of her little finger. 'The photos so grainy. Is it …?'

'Wait.' Mrs Pagely bustled off and was soon back carrying a magnifying glass. 'Here. You look, dear. Your eyes are better than mine.'

Amanda peered through the lens. 'I think it could be a chisel or a big screwdriver. What do you think, Mrs Pagely?' She handed over the glass.

'Hmm, I think you're right,' the librarian concurred. She smiled. 'Of course, that would interest *you*.'

Amanda nodded. 'I wonder who it was.'

'I'm afraid the caption only gives the name of the pub and Little Madley Lane,' said Mrs Pagely, regretfully.

'Could I photocopy the photos and this section of the map?' asked Amanda.

'Of course, you go ahead.'

Amanda had a quick look through the book to see if there were any references to any of the inhabitants, but it was principally a botanical and zoological work, concerned with humans only in regard to their place in the ecosystem. It said that the proprietor of The Apple Cart had caught a deer on camera, and it was one of the photographs included. He had, no doubt, been rewarded for his contribution with an image of his establishment as the centrefold.

Back home, Amanda found Tempest asleep on her computer keyboard. She lifted him off gently, put him on her lap, and went online to the local planning department. There she found a copy of the plans for the research centre and downloaded them. With a little rescaling, she was able to make out where, in relation to Little Madley, the new build was being erected.

Tempest woke up, and poked his head above the level of the table to study the screen. Amanda relinquished her seat to her familiar.

'Here, you look at it while I get some tracing paper.'

She printed out the plans and placed them over the map. Tempest jumped onto the table and sat on the papers. Amanda slid him to one side.

'You can stop it from rolling up. Now ... look. This half of the research centre is being built on top of the south half of

Lost Madley from our end to ... sort of half over the pub. The carpenter's house was on the north end, so his house isn't being built over.'

Amanda straightened up and mused. She looked back at the plans. 'All three times I've seen that man he's been here, over the pub. Now, why? And he's not in his work coat; he's in a suit ... a 1940s suit! That's what's wrong with the trousers! They're high-waisted! Like they were back then.' She stroked Tempest, pleased to have solved at least one puzzle. But there was another. 'What's the connection to the pub?'

No inspiration came.

'I need to talk to Hugo,' Amanda announced. She sent him a text. It was a while before he responded. It said:

Let's meet on Friday evening at 7.30 in The Sinner's Rue, Hugo

'Good idea,' Amanda said to Tempest. 'It'll look like a date. No one will think anything of it, except what they're *already* all thinking anyway, thanks to Joan!'

Chapter 17

ॐ

RECONNAISSANCE

It was a test for Amanda to wait out the days. She told herself that it was purely to do with their investigation. Finally, Friday evening came. Amanda dressed in a skirt and medium heels, as if for a romantic rendezvous, and arrived promptly. Hugo came out of The Sinner's Rue as she approached.

'Hello, Amanda. It's quite full and noisy in there. Is there somewhere else we can talk?'

'Yes,' she said, at once, 'there's a cafe in Romping-in-the-Heye that stays open until 8.30. The food's good too.'

Amanda drove them to the neighbouring village, regaling her passenger with tales of the epic battles between the cricket teams of Romping and Sunken Madley.

Seated at a red-and-white-check-clothed table, Amanda recommended the shepherd's pie, and they ordered. While they waited, she took a quick instinctive look around, and then pulled the plans, map and photos from her black velvet holdall.

'Regarding the carpenter we both saw,' said Hugo, 'I was thinking, could he have been in the pub when he was killed in the bombing?'

'Yes, but why wouldn't he have been in the air raid shelter?' asked Amanda.

'Good question,' said Hugo. 'Do we know where the air raid shelter was?'

'Was? Is? I could go and have a look,' she offered, enthusiastically.

'Ah. Amanda. About that ….' He looked serious.

'What?' she responded, anxiously.

'I have been asking one or two questions. I tried to ask the clients, Mr Gibbs and er …'

'Robin Streeter?'

'Yes. They said they didn't know much about the history to the place. They were OK, but later, my foreman, Jan, he was … what is the exact word? … stern … strict. He is not usually like that. He told me it is better for me to concentrate on the job and not to ask so many questions. He said it nicely, you know, but he has never spoken like that before. I think they had complained maybe. I tried to ask around the crew, but they don't want to talk or think about it. I think you should not go poking around the place, Amanda. I think there is something not right here. I do not want anything bad to happen to you.'

Amanda took him at his word. 'Thank you. Hugo. I understand. OK. I can't go myself … but I know someone who can. Someone no one would notice.'

'Who?' he asked, curiously.

Amanda looked down at her feet. Hugo slid his chair a little back from the table, so that he could casually see underneath it. A warm, furry, grey bundle was sitting on Amanda's shoes, and was weighing him up with an acid yellow stare.

'Your familiar?' he asked. She nodded. 'Can you meet me again on Sunday, Amanda?'

'Sure, we can confer again then,' she replied without hesitation. 'Would you like to see our famous orchard?'

'I did not know it was famous,' he said with humour, 'but

yes, please!'

After the café closed, Amanda dropped Hugo off outside the Snout and Trough, and drove back to Orchard Row. She opened the front door and let Tempest in first, wondering how to approach him. Had he heard and understood what she'd said to Hugo about the 'someone who can'?

First she fed him a sachet of Monarch's Minced Chicken, and waited nonchalantly for him to settle himself for a post-dinner nap on the sofa. She knelt on the floor and stroked him, uttering blandishments.

'Who's my handsome man, den? Who's da most bootiful kittykins?' He purred and closed his eyes.

'Temmmpessst, … would you like to do something for Ammy?'

He had not been deceived. He stopped purring and opened his lemon lamps on full beam. Amanda's familiar directed them unwaveringly into her eyes. She knew in that instant that he knew. And now he knew she knew he knew.

'Ok,' she said, abandoning her coaxing. She whipped a shallow glass jar of caviar from her pocket. It was only lumpfish; she hoped it wouldn't take the far more expensive sturgeon variety. 'I'd like you to take a little walk. I need you to do some reconnaissance and I can't go myself. Don't pretend that you don't know all about it.'

He gave her a bored look that said it all.

'So. You can have half of this while I run the bath, and then we can take a little stroll up the road to Lost Madley. We just need to find the air raid shelter and then you can come back home and have the rest of this delicious treat. Pleeeeease, Tempest? You know that I can't do this without you. You know that without you your Ammy is just one helpless ickle witch.'

Tempest sighed with the air of one much tried. Finally he uncoiled himself and led the way to the kitchen. Amanda picked him up, cuddled and kissed him.

'Thank oo, Tempest!'

She put him down on his favourite chair and served him half of the tin, at the table, then left the room. Tempest looked up from his caviar at her retreating form. A single word summed up his emotions:

Humans!

Amanda made her way upstairs into the bathroom. She ran the taps, and lit some candles. After a few minutes she was soaking under a quilt of bubbles, lavender scented, and slipping into her meditative state. Waiting for it to come.

The vision.

There it was. The kitchen back door, towering above, but blurred. The décor, a wash of greens and blues.

Cat's eyes.

This was the unique nature of Amanda's bond with her familiar, his ability to share what he saw with her. Most of her life with him, she had enjoyed it for recreational purposes to go to places, see things, that her physical limitations would not allow her. The freedom and experience that the gift had given Amanda had transformed her life. That was how she'd seen Lost Madley. Just exploring. But that had changed to something even more important a matter of weeks ago. And now, once again, together they were on the trail of something sinister.

Into the dusk they went. It was strange, the pavement being so close, the garden walls so high. Tempest crossed the road onto the north side of Orchard Row, so that he could keep to the trees at the edge of the playing fields as he travelled east. At the top of the road, he moved from garden to garden, then crossed Hog Lane to the back of the green.

The headlamps of a passing car illuminated Muttring Lane while Tempest crept behind the shrubs near the last house. All clear. He ducked from bush to bush in the garden of The Elms, home of Irene James and her famous model daughter, Jessica. Soon he was into the trees of Madley Wood.

The cat picked up speed then abruptly stopped stock-still. Amanda could see that he was nearer to the ground. He must be crouching, she thought. He remained motionless for what seemed an age. The bath water was beginning to lose its superheated edge, but Amanda knew better than to urge him on.

There was a flicker of darker in the darkness, a jerk forward, a thin pale flailing tail, then … ugh … some sort of rodent was in Tempest's jaws, then falling and trapped under paws. He watched it wriggle, unharmed but alarmed.

The paws lifted and the rat-shaped shadow scuttled away to live another day. Tempest stood up, and continued along Lost Madley Lane. The building site came into view. The security lights were on. There was at least one person on duty. The cat skirted the trees on the other side of the track until he was opposite where the concrete platform ended, and the ruins began.

He crossed over to them, and began a systematic tour, up the lane of Lost Madley, picking his way around rubble, splintered and broken wood, glass, abandoned textiles, dust and cobwebs. It was impossible to make out where one house ended and the next began, until the last untidy mound was passed.

And here it was, a hump in the ground, half covered by the fallen debris from the last dwelling, a depression shadowing darkly into its mouth.

'Yes, Tempest, yes. Good boy,' breathed Amanda. He scraped away with his paws, digging out a bigger hole. He leaned in and down into the depths of the old bomb shelter, hard to see even with cat vision, but surely large enough for the whole hamlet.

'That's it. Good. Clever kitty. Come home, now, Tempest. Have the rest of your luxury snack.' He withdrew his head and she had a view of Lost Madley, down the length of the lane, stretching to the concrete of the research-centre-to-be.

But Tempest was not finished. He was out on the tiles. It was still playtime. Caviar would be there when he got back. He padded and crouched, swiped at a moth, and pursued a spider along the ruins.

He was nearly at the building site, when a favourite quarry

whistled and whirled past him. He gave chase until the bat disappeared into a narrow horizontal crack in the ground, just beside the slab. Tempest got a paw into the crevice and clawed away, until he could get enough of his face in to get a look at what lay inside. Big enough for a bat to take refuge in, it might have other interesting occupants.

Needles of faint light were finding their way in through other cracks in the rubble. Enough to see a room-sized cavity crisscrossed with fallen beams, and piled with chunks of plaster and stone. Impossible to see more, or to enter. Tempest swept some small loose rocks back over the entrance and lost interest. He crossed back to the trees and padded homeward.

Amanda reflected that she'd need Tempest if she wanted to find the hole again. She opened her eyes, leaned forward and ran the hot tap, thinking. She'd have news on Sunday for Hugo.

Hugo ... he was certainly a new and wonderful experience. They made a good team. Someone like him could be a real partner in life. Like Senara and Perran, like the Bergstroms. Something she'd wondered if she could ever have. But, Amanda had no illusions. In a matter of days, Hugo would be leaving. Still, there was no harm in day-dreaming about ....

There was a rattle at the kitchen door. His Highness had returned. With a sigh, Amanda got out of the water, dressed and went downstairs to give Tempest the other half of the bargain.

As she watched him devour the caviar, then follow her to the sofa for a snuggle, it struck her that she *did* have a partner, one who shared her magical world.

'I can always be myself wiv oo, can't I, pwecious?'

Tempest purred in answer.

'Yes, oo is my handsome boy, isn't oo?' Not tall, not dark or fair, but ...'Oo is sooo handsome, my kitty.'

Tempest thought that, for all her human failings, his witch had, at least, got that right.

Chapter 18

༄

LOOKING FOR FLAMGOYNE

Here's something new, thought Hogarth, observing Thomas standing before one of the bookcases that flanked the fireplace. Normally he was collapsed into one of the Chesterfield armchairs, head back, eyes closed, relaxing after the day, the week, the half-week, while Hogarth made the tea or got trays for them to eat their takeaways off.

Now, what is he looking for? Hogarth wondered.

Thomas was a reader. Had been as long as Hogarth had known him. But he only ever occasionally borrowed books from Hogarth's library; an obscure volume on police work or an out-of-print novel.

Thomas had once spent a weekend staying over while a sprained ankle had healed. Not, alas, damaged in the line of duty or even sport, but by a newly formed pothole in the station car park, much to the mirth of colleagues and juniors. Thomas had taken the inevitable ragging in good part. That was one of his most endearing qualities, reflected Hogarth, for all the gravity of the job he did, Thomas didn't take himself too seriously.

That weekend, Thomas had spent a good many hours reading on the sofa with his foot elevated. But today, he had two sound ankles, and the intensity of his expression, Hogarth judged, was not in keeping with a search for an airport novel.

Hogarth manoeuvred to follow the direction of Thomas's gaze to near the end of the second shelf from the top, to two books, one fat, one slim, wedged in tightly. They were the two books Hogarth had shown him that day, at least a year ago. It was the Sunday that Thomas had made an impromptu visit to Amanda Cadabra and had come back disturbed by what his senses had detected in her workshop.

'Here's your tea, lad,' said Hogarth, interrupting Trelawney's reverie.

Thomas turned with a slight start.

'Oh. Thanks, Mike.'

'Seen something that interests you?'

'Just browsing. Sort of.'

'You're welcome to.'

Thomas sat down and stirred his tea.

'Actually, I was thinking about those books you showed me ages ago, wondering if you had anything else, sort of, on the subject.'

'The history of Cornwall? I'm sure I could find something if I knew better what you were after.'

Thomas hesitated.

Hogarth took a shrewd guess and offered him a way in. 'Been doing some research, following what you and Miss Cadabra put together during your conference?'

'Yes. Yes, that's right. There's nothing online about any Polgoyne or Flamgoyne family members. Nothing about the history and none of them is making any appearance on social networking sites, or any other sites.'

'And you didn't want to ask me because you want information that's, er ... purely secular, shall we say?'

'Exactly. I don't want it all clouded by the hocus pocus

Cornish witch clans business.'

'You could ask your father. It's his family, after all.'

'I did. He became tense, said they were distant relations. I asked what exactly the relationship was. He eventually told me then clammed up. I tried my mother. She just said, "ask your father", and changed the subject faster than a speeding bullet.'

'All right. What do you deduce from your conference with Amanda that you're comfortable with?' asked Hogarth, with a touch of humour.

'I'm not being chicken, Mike. I just want to keep things clear,' insisted Thomas

'Okay.'

'Well, judging from my memories of the Flamgoyne mansion, and their uneasy alliance with the Cardiubarns, and Miss Cadabra's recollections of her family's grand establishment, I'd say they were, or are, both powerful families. Who's to say if it's still the case, but they had the trappings of wealth and the air of influence, in the past, at least.'

'And their relationship to you is ...?'

'My grandfather Jeremy Trelawney married Emblyn Flamgoyne. Obviously, my mother didn't approve of her in-laws.'

'Your mother wasn't present at all, in the dream you had of being back at the Flamgoyne house?'

'No.'

'And the in-laws are a sore subject even now?'

'Yes.'

'Do you think it was a factor in your parents' decision to divorce?' Hogarth asked gently. He was aware of how close he was to the bone now.

Thomas put down his tea. 'Mind if I have a drink, Mike?'

'Course not. Go ahead.'

Thomas got up and went to the cabinet where the spirits were kept. 'Join me?'

'Why not?'

Thomas knew the way that Mike liked his whiskey and

handed him the glass. Unusually, on this occasion, Trelawney took his neat. 'I've never told this to a soul. Not even to myself, when I could help it.'

Hogarth waited.

Thomas had yet to take a sip, but the sight of the golden liquid in the tumbler seemed to give him courage.

'It's not like my parents ever got on. Not since I can remember. But there was this one night. It was my 10th birthday. I'd had the cake, the presents, and, I suppose. I'd overdone the treats and couldn't sleep. You know?'

Hogarth nodded.

'I heard their voices in the kitchen downstairs. Nothing unusual about that. I went to the landing. I remember squatting and holding on to the bannisters. They are quite quietly spoken people, my parents. Their voices were more like a murmur. And then it came. Like a shriek. My mother. Just one word. Full of hate and accusation and desperation.'

Thomas stopped as though the word stuck in his throat.

'What was it, lad?'

Thomas looked up, white-faced. 'Sorcery.' He sat, hunched over in the armchair. 'The next thing I knew, they were telling me they were getting divorced, and if it were OK with me, I'd spend term-time with dad and hols with mum.'

Suddenly his demeanour changed. He sat up, frowning.

'Wait. There's something more. I remember this now. It was before ….Yes, she said it more than once, to my father: "We had a deal!"'

Abruptly Thomas stood up and looked around for his jacket.

'I'm sorry, Mike, I have to go.'

'Let me guess,' Hogarth smiled.

'Yes. To London. And this time my mother is going to answer my questions!'

'Good luck, lad.'

Thomas was out the door and starting his car as Hogarth

stood listening and looking up at the bookcase. He said aloud to himself,

'But will you like what she tells you, Thomas?'

Chapter 19

୧ର

RESOLUTION

On Sunday, Amanda gave Hugo the latest report. Hugo had nothing new to tell. As they walked between the Hormead Pearmain apple trees, she saw the sun shining on his hair.

'May I ask you a personal question?' she requested.

Hugo smiled. 'Of course.'

'Your hair .... erm ... brown with golden roots. Unusual.'

'Ah, yes ... I had no time before I left. I colour my hair brown. You know? Blonde hair and blue eyes and Bavarian? People tease me and say, have I just walked out of an Oktoberfest theme party!'

Amanda laughed. 'I understand.'

'May I ask you a personal question too?'

'Yes,' she answered readily.

'What is your gift? Your, er ... talent?'

'Levitation.'

He stopped and stared at her.

'No. Really?'

'Yes. Why? Is it yours too?'

'No. No, I have nothing like that. Can you show me? Please? I have never seen this.'

'But you know other witches. You must have seen it used before?'

'You really don't know, do you?' Hugo marvelled. 'This gift is very rare. You are very special, even among witches.'

'Noooo. I find that hard to believe,' Amanda answered sceptically.

'How many other witches do you know?'

Amanda paused and counted: Granny and Grandpa, Aunt Amelia and the Bergstroms.

'Not many,' she admitted.

'And your grandparents, never told you how extraordinary it is?'

'Well, it runs in Grandpa's family, you see, so I suppose it didn't come across as anything out of the ordinary. I thought all witches had a special skill. Now, you should meet my aunt. Her *divination* skills are amazing. I'm just hopeless at that. But sure, I can show you levitation. What shall I do?'

Hugo looked up at an infant green apple just out of their reach. He pointed.

'Can you get that?'

'Hmm, what about the one next to it? It looks like it's been got at by a bird or something. The farmer won't mind if I pick that.'

'Ok, that one is fine.'

Amanda looked at the stalk and said simply, '*Beterrac.*'

A crack appeared in the stem, and the little fruit came loose. '*Fleotneiyn,*' Amanda added quickly, and it hung in midair.

'Hold out your hand,' she said, and Hugo spread his palm.

'*Sedaasig ynentel,*' she said. And it sank gently, and landed in his hand.

He applauded. 'Now that is something to tell the family!'

'I had no idea it was considered so spectacular,' Amanda responded, taken aback.

'Oh yes.'

'But you must have a gift too.'

'No, just to see other dimensions,' he said casually, 'like you do.'

'Like seeing the ghost?'

'Yes, and other things. There is more than one other dimension, as you know.'

'Really? My grandparents only told me about one other.'

'And you don't see more?' asked Hugo, surprised.

'I don't think so,' said Amanda.

'Ah, well there is more than one, and that is my family gift then, I suppose.'

Amanda looked around. 'So, do you see others now?'

'Yes, of course,' Hugo replied, perfectly at his ease.

Her head flicked from side to side, nervously. 'You mean there are other ... people ... things here now?'

'Of course. But they are not interested in us, or they do not see us. Please relax, Amanda, it is not so strange. Let me see.' He looked down at the base of a tree ahead of them. He pointed.

'There are two or three beings there. But this is not so unusual. People have been seeing them all over the place, all over the world for thousands of years.'

'What are they?' she asked curiously, looking in the direction of his finger, but seeing nothing beyond the trunk and grass.

'They have many names ... er ... you say in English .... Let's see .... Fee ... er, fay? Ferry?'

'Fairy! *Fairies?*'

'Yes, yes, this the word, I think.'

Amanda laughed. 'I thought they were just fantasy.'

Hugo smiled, and said, 'People think *witches* are just fantasy.'

Amanda had a great deal to think about as she lay that night waiting for sleep. She half sat up, leaning on her elbows.

'Tempest,' she asked him, as he lay curled up against her

hip in the darkness. 'Am I really special?' she asked.

He raised his head and gave her scornful look expressive of 'No, you're just an irritating human who's woken me up.'

She lay down again, somehow relieved. 'I didn't think so.' Amanda mused. So the Cadabra gift was levitation. What was the Cardiubarn gift? Or the Flamgoyne gift? Or that of the Polgoynes, even? She really must remember to ask Granny ….

Not just Hugo but all of the German crew endeared themselves to the village. The strawberry season was upon them, and the culinarily inclined made strawberry flans, strawberry tarts, strawberry jam, strawberry jelly, strawberry fools, trifles and Victorian sponge, filled and topped with the luscious red fruit. A fair number of these found their way to the guests working on the site, for snacks and treats, and were delivered to the places where they were staying.

Over the days, the first floor of the building was in place, then the second, and the roof added. The tiles went on, fixtures and fittings were completed. The appointed time for the supervisor to make her inspection was set.

Amanda and Hugo walked in the orchard, for what she suspected would be the last time.

They had known one another for just weeks that had flown by. It was too soon to be having The Conversation. And yet … Amanda's mind went back to Lost Madley, Little Madley. Back then, hadn't it been like this for thousands of couples who were soon to be separated, by war, by distance, maybe even by …

'Amanda.'

She was brought back to the orchard and the 21st century by his voice.

'Yes, Hugo?'

'I have enjoyed so much our time together, working on the puzzle of Lost Madley, meeting someone else like me.'

'Me too.'

'If it were possible, I would like there to have been more, much more.'

Amanda smiled

'But I cannot come and be here. My family ... they need me. With this work, I have some flexibility. I can go home when I need to. My father, his health is not so good. I have a younger brother and sister. They depend on me. I don't mind that. I love them. I love my village.'

She nodded understandingly.

'And I know that they would love you, Amanda. They would welcome you, welcome you into the family. Your levitation, it is so rare a mystical gift. They would prize it, they would prize you. You could visit. We could see. If you want.'

Amanda stopped walking and turned to him. She knew, in that moment, that what Hugo was asking was something she could not do.

Amanda shook her head regretfully.

'Thank you for that Hugo. It would mean a great deal to me to be accepted by your family for the witch that I am. There. I have said it. But ... it isn't just that my business is here and the only family I have ever known or that, for all my oddities, I am somehow cared for here. But ... you know, even when I used to travel with my grandparents, something always drew me back here, even before the trips were over. Like an elastic between this place and my soul. I don't know why. But I can't accept your invitation, Hugo, and I won't lead you or your family up the garden path by trying. I hope that you understand.'

'Yes, I do,' he said at once. 'And I thought that this is what you would say.' They were quiet for a moment.

'I will leave tomorrow, I think, but, please, know that if you should ever have need of me, I will try to come here.'

'Thank you.'

He held out his hand.

'Friends?'

She laughed with relief and pleasure. She couldn't remember any man ever offering her that before. She put her hand in his.

'Friends.'

They shook on it.

'We will keep in touch, yes?' Hugo asked.

'Yes. I'll let you know how the Centre gets on.'

'And how Joan is?' he said humorously.

'Oh, Joan! Yes of course. Although it wouldn't surprise me if *she* gave me news of *you*!'

* * * * *

The supervisor arrived. One or two tweaks were made, and the inspection passed. The crew did the last of the packing, gave their thanks, made their farewells, and piled into the vehicles ready for the trip home. They drove south through Sunken Madley at high noon for the last time, to the cheers and good wishes from the villagers.

Amanda waited at the far southern end, by the last building, the Snout and Trough. Hugo and Amanda smiled at one another as he went by. She waved until he passed the bend, and disappeared behind the trees.

She found Tempest at her feet.

'Well. Who'd have thought? I found a friend. A friend like me. Oh, of course, I mean a mere *human* like me! And if I can do it once, I can do it again. And if I can find a magical friend, who is to say I can't find even more than that?' said Amanda looking down at her familiar.

Tempest's citron stare was unwavering. And then, slowly, he blinked. Once for 'yes'.

Chapter 20

༅

INAUGURATION

Amanda, phone in hand, took a step. She froze. The forensic team would be able to track her footprints. If her story was going to be that she was rooted to the spot with horror, she couldn't go traipsing around the crime scene as though she was viewing an exhibition.

She took a careful step back, set the camera app to record, pressed the button, flattened her palm so that the phone was resting on it, and whispered. It rose.

Then with the words, '*Winstre, rihthdhou, aereval, sedaasig, kileiniga, forthwg, kileiniga adhelnde,*' left, right, up, down, tilt forwards, tilt backwards, Amanda sent it flying. The experience she'd had with the model planes she sent on missions around her bedroom was coming in handy. Aerial photography.

It was taking time, however.

Precious time.

The CCTV cameras that had recorded her progress into the lab would be counting the seconds.

* * * * *

Everyone was there; every notable in the village, all in their Sunday finery. The Patels, the Mazureks, Joan and Jim, Sylvia and her husband, the Sharmas, Mrs Uberhausfest, Mrs Pagely the librarian, and her assistant Jonathan Sheppard, the Poveys who were the new owners of Sunken Madley Manor, Gordan French, the retired village headmaster, Irene James of The Elms, the ladies from the Grange attended by Moffat, Mr Hanley-Page, the Reisers, the Fleetfoots, the Demirs, the Reids, Pawel the Royal Mail driver, Penny, the Patel's receptionist with her fiancé, the Whittles and the Kemps. Local press had turned up. Amanda arrived in good time and parked the Astra. She followed the signs heralding a red carpet laid around the south end of the building.

'Amanda!' She turned to see ... Ryan with his sunny locks aglow, looking smart in a linen suit and white shirt.

'Cricketing colours, I notice,' she said, as he caught up with her. 'How's the season going?'

'Over soon. I still mean for us to have that dinner. It's so frustrating. I keep *seeing* you, but somehow we never have the chance to *talk*.'

'Not to worry, Ryan. Anyway, I'm not sure Miss Gibbs would appreciate you taking another woman out on a date.'

'Oh, Samantha ... she's just ... young.'

'Well, I wouldn't want to meet her in a fit of jealousy down a dark alley,' said Amanda.

'Really, Amanda., please —'

'Ry-Ry!' came the familiar husky voice.

'Oh no,' said Ryan. 'I'll call you,' he promised Amanda.

'And I'll make a swift exit,' she countered, quickening her pace away.

Amanda looked at the architecture, and its view of the

countryside. The bright chartreuse green of spring had deepened over the weeks to the deep emerald of summer. The blackberries were ripening in the hedgerows and plums were ready for picking. Soon the conkers would be falling from the horse chestnut trees, and the damsons and greengages would be gathered in.

It had rained in the night but blue sky was making headway, and the audience had dressed optimistically for a pleasant August day. Nevertheless, with characteristic British caution, most were wearing jackets and cardigans for insurance. Even one or two furled umbrellas were in evidence, among those who had walked from Sunken Madley, because 'you never know.'

An announcement invited the guests to take their places. The chairs had been set out in ranks on the grass in front of the central section of the Centre that gave on to the open field beyond the Wood. There was Jessica James in supermodel Ice Queen guise. Amanda was surprised to observe Sir Michael whom she recognised from the pavilion at Lords cricket ground. The lady next to him was presumably his wife. Samantha had secured Ryan in the seat next to her. She kept leaning close to whisper in his ear.

Claire had sent Amanda a text asking her to save a seat. Now a series of excuse-me's and sorry's and thank-you's as people moved their knees aside, proclaimed Claire's careful progress along the row to Amanda's side.

'Hello, my lovely,' said Claire as they hugged, 'sorry I'm late, can't stay long. It's murder. We're on site in Richmond for only a few days before we go to Thailand.'

'How's the shooting going?'

'The usual. Pretty good, actually. The movie's utter tripe, but I just grit my teeth and think of the money, darling,' she said merrily.

Claire had climbed the grueling producer's ladder. The low budget, hugely popular but absurd film *Block-buster!*, about a karate expert who becomes a movie mogul, had supplied the deposit on her cottage in Orchard Row. A string of TV jobs had got up the mortgage payments until the successful movie about an airhead who becomes a soccer star, entitled *Mindless Dribble*. Now Claire was producing *Block-buster! II*, which, she hoped, would get her closer to her goal of paying off her house, so she could work on the kind of films to which she aspired.

'I'm so glad you could make it,' said Amanda delightedly.

'Couldn't miss this. I wouldn't be considered Village if I didn't show my face today, Ammy,' answered Claire, arranging her pale blue, silk, shirt-dress over her knees and patting her chocolate brown bob into place.

Robin gave the opening address, then handed over to Sir Michael Loughty, as one of the sponsors. He passed the microphone to Ryan, as a village celebrity, who finally introduced Damian. He spoke entertainingly, and then movingly, of his beloved mother, Marion Gibbs, suffering through asthma, and how much he missed her since her passing.

'That's awful!' Amanda whispered to Claire. 'I had no idea his mother died of asthma.'

'She didn't,' replied Claire, succinctly. 'She'd have lasted longer if she hadn't smoked forty fags a day, but it was the brandy that saw her off.'

'What?'

'Liver. No one could sustain that level of alcohol. She must have had shares in a distillery. She drank it like lemonade.'

Amanda suppressed a giggle. 'But he makes it sound like ...!'

'Spin, darling. It's called *spin*,' said Claire, with a saucy smile.

Finally, Jessica James glided across the platform to cut the ribbon. Applause and champagne followed, and the guests trooped in through the doors of the glass front of the building. They moved caterpillar-like along the carpet, across the tatami mats donated by one of the sponsors, through the therapy rooms, the group rooms, admiring the big lab, pharmacy and accommodation upstairs, that would hopefully help to maintain the running of the Centre.

Around the café they wandered and through more rooms. As yet unoccupied, they were rather samey, but it was all fresh and new, curved wood, soft lighting, soothing colours, cream, mushroom, and palest russet. Finally, they went out to the reception, milled around, and back to the refreshment stands outside.

Claire had slunk off to chat to Joan and catch up on 'the goss.'

Amanda speculated where she would be seen at the Centre when she came officially on medical business, and by whom. Robin and Damian came to say hello. They brought an imposing, biblical figure, a tall, broad-shouldered and generously girthed man with a dark brown beard and bald crown.

'Amanda,' said Damian, 'this is Robert Crossley who is going to be in charge of the lab upstairs, so you probably won't see much of him, but I thought you might like to meet another member of the team.'

'Aha, Miss Cadabra, I understand,' said Crossley peering at her over his half-glasses with benevolent curiosity. 'Interesting name. A future patient. Splendid, splendid. Bum ta-ta bum-pom-pom,' he ended.

She grinned in spite of herself. 'You are fond of music, doctor?'

'Was I singing? Sorry. Habit of mine. My wife is always telling me about it. She's here somewhere.' He looked around. 'Pom pom pa-pom. A lot of curly red hair. Can't miss her. Do say hello if you see her.'

'OK, I will. Thank you, Dr Crossley.'

'Excuse me if I go and raid the buffet before it all goes. The sausage rolls are awfully, awfully good. Didi bom bom bom deee bom.' And off he went.

'Please, excuse Crossley. He's a trifle eccentric but an excellent chap,' said Robin. 'We three go way back.'

'No doubt,' said Amanda. 'Robin, do you know when I'll get my appointment?'

'It's in the post, I do believe. It will be with Dr Vina Schofield, a highly qualified physician, I've known her for years. I'm sure she'll look after you. You should get the appointment tomorrow. The first wave is timed for when all of the equipment is in place, and the therapists have prepared their rooms. A matter of days. That will be convenient, I hope?'

'Oh yes. I'll turn up.'

'Well, enjoy yourself, Miss Cadabra.'

'I will. Please do go off and mingle, I know you're both on duty today.'

'I'm sure we'll all bump into one another,' said Damian.

They said goodbye, and Amanda looked around for Ryan. He was nowhere to be seen.

She greeted some of the villagers, fed some delicacies to Tempest and then got bored. Amanda remembered that Mr Hanley-Page had offered to take her for a ride in his Rolls, but he was nowhere in evidence and, truth to tell, she wanted to go home. Suddenly Claire dashed up to say goodbye.

'Must be off. Wish me luck in Thailand.' She hugged Amanda. 'Wish you all the luck in the world with your appointments here. Soooo hope they can help.'

'Thank you, Claire. Take care.'

'You too, darling.' And she was gone in a whirl of flying dark hair.

Watching her hurry to her car, Amanda caught sight of a crop of auburn curls, twirling this way and that. She looked about the right age, 40-to 50-ish, she judged.

'Mrs Crossley?' said Amanda tentatively.

'Hello,' came the friendly reply.

'I'm Amanda. I'm going to be a patient here. Your husband described you and said to say hello.'

'Of course. Oh, you've met him, then.'

'Er, yes.'

'He's an odd stick but not so bad when you get to know him,' said his wife tolerantly

'Yes, he, er … does he play an instrument?'

'No,' Mrs Crossley emphatically, 'can't even carry a tune. But I know what you mean. The singing. He comes across a bit vague and out of it, but he's actually rather a genius, even if I do say so myself.'

'I'm sure,' said Amanda, politely.

'You don't have any idea where he might be, do you?'

'He went to get some sausage rolls.'

'Oh yes, of course, he did. He's supposed to be on a diet. Let me catch up with him before he sees off every pastry at the buffet. Nice to meet you, Amanda.'

'You too, Mrs Crossley.'

She was turning away when Damian came up.

'Amanda, you haven't seen Sam, by any chance? My daughter.'

What am I? thought Amanda, Missing Persons?

'I haven't been watching Samantha's movements.' She glanced about. 'No, no, sorry, Damian, I haven't.'

'Don't know where she's got to. I wanted her to be in some of the photos, and Sir Michael too, if I can round him up from wherever he's got to. Oh well, never mind. Glad you could make it. Best wishes for your improved good health and hopefully, as close to a cure as we can get.'

'Thank you, Damian.'

'Sure we'll all bump into each other. Bye for now.'

She walked off slowly towards the Astra. Ryan missing and Samantha missing. Hmm, thought Amanda.

Chapter 21

~

APPOINTMENTS

Amanda looked at the body on the phone screen as she zoomed in.

How different it was when you had known the person ...

* * * * *

Amanda reported to reception at 8.45 am on the day of her first appointment at the Marion Gibbs Asthma Research Centre. Letter in hand, she approached the counter. A tall, fit, broad-shouldered man, with a white beard and grey, slightly receded hair, sat behind the desk.

'Hello there, lassie,' he greeted her in a broad Scottish accent. 'Yooor bright 'n' airly!'

'Yes, it's my first day, and I wanted to make sure I was on time,' explained Amanda.

'Vairy gude. What's yer name?'

'Amanda Cadabra.'

'Really? I bet ya geht a reaction ev'ry time ye say that!'

She laughed. What a relief it was to hear someone come and out and say that. 'Yes, I do.'

'All right, wehll, I've got ye down here. You going ta be a regular, are ye?'

'Yes, I hope so.'

'In that case, I'm Bill, Bill MacNair. I'm security. So if you need me, you know who I am. I'm usually on nights, so this is the end o' my shift. But I live on site. Gloria's just gettin' herrr coffee, then she'll tek over.'

'Thank you. Nice to meet you, Bill.'

'You too, lassie. The waitin' room is through those double doors, down the corrida, through the doors at the end. Opal waiting room. They're all named after precious gems.'

'Ok. Thank you, Bill,' Amanda replied appreciatively.

She found her way and sat down on a mushroom-coloured sofa opposite the window. There was a pale young man on one end of it and, in a chair, a mother with a small daughter sitting listlessly on her lap. Amanda looked around for something to do, and investigated the children's toy box with some success.

A dark cloud of curls, framing a square-jawed face and sharp grey eyes, appeared around the door that bore the name 'Dr Schofield'.

'Amanda Cadabra?'

The other patients looked up, wondering if they had heard correctly.

Amanda immediately put down the Sticklebrick boat she had been attempting to construct, and stood up. 'Yes?'

'Please come in.'

The doctor sat behind her desk, and gestured to a chair on the opposite side.

'Please sit down. Welcome to the Marion Gibbs Research Centre for Asthma. We hope that we can help you.'

Amanda thought the woman sounded like someone reading off a screen at a call centre. The doctor was indeed looking at her monitor.

'Let me just confirm some details.' She checked Amanda's name, contact information and date of birth.

'So ... Amanda. Is it OK if I call you, Amanda?'

Actually, Amanda would have preferred it if this woman called her Miss Cadabra, but she didn't want to appear standoffish. 'Yes, sure,' she replied politely.

'Your asthma began at the age of three?'

'I think shortly before, maybe,' replied Amanda.

'Do you know for certain?'

'No,' she admitted.

'Let's leave it at three then,' said the doctor, with slightly laboured patience. 'And you've been using inhalers.'

'Yes.'

'Have you tried any ... complementary therapies before?' The expression seemed to bother her. That was strange because the appointment letter said that Dr Schofield was a homoeopath as well as a conventional doctor.

'Yes, herbal. My grandparents treated me,' added Amanda, then wished she hadn't.

'I see. And did it lead to any improvement?'

'I am much better than I was when I was a child,' was all Amanda could say.

'But you are still restricted in what you can do?'

'Yes.'

'You have completely explored what mainstream medicine has to offer?' The woman's voice had an edge that was grating on Amanda.

'Dr Schofield,' Amanda replied firmly. 'Hospital staff saved my life several times, and I am extremely appreciative of everything they have done. But if mainstream medicine had been able to effect a full recovery then I would not be here at the suggestion and referral of my GP,' she ended crisply.

The doctor tapped away on her keyboard. Then asked, as though changing the subject, 'What brings on your asthma?'

'Exertion, stress, pollen, dust, dander, the usual things,' answered Amanda.

'I see that you are a furniture restorer.' It sounded like an accusation.

'Yes.'

'Hardly ideal,' commented the doctor.

'I wear a mask, I vacuum, take precautions.'

'Have you thought of changing your profession? It seems to me that if you were really serious about improving your health, then it would be something that you would be willing to think about.'

'My work is not a problem,' Amanda responded calmly.

Tap tap tap.

'How about climate?' asked the doctor.

'Excuse me?'

'Are you better in certain types of weather?'

'Well, dry and warm are better, yes,' Amanda responded.

'Have you considered emigrating to a more suitable location? Spain, Italy, south of France?'

'No,' replied Amanda in surprise. This woman was certainly into drastic measures. What would she suggest next?

'It's something to think about,' said the doctor, then opened a desk drawer, and took out an A4 sheet that she handed to Amanda. 'Here is a list of complementary therapies. Is there anything there that you want to try?'

Amanda had expected the doctor to recommend one, and said so.

'Very well,' replied the woman. 'Have you had acupuncture?'

'No.'

'OK, let's try you on acupuncture. If you want to look in on a meditation group or yoga, you can do that too. There's a map of Centre on the other side of the page. I'll see you in six weeks.'

The appointment seemed to be over.

'Thank you, Dr Schofield,' Amanda said, civilly.

'Goodbye, Amanda.'

She left the Centre in a state of shock and disappointment. It hadn't been anything like she'd expected. What was *with* that woman? Change your job? *Emigrate?*

'Well!' commented Granny, as she and Perran appeared either side of their granddaughter. 'I don't think much of her!'

Amanda took a quick look round to check that no one was near, then agreed, 'It's like she didn't care. In fact, like she had contempt for the Centre, and didn't much like *me* either.'

'What's she doing there, then?' asked Granny.

'My question exactly,' said Amanda.

'What do you think about acupuncture, Ammy?' asked Grandpa.

'I don't mind trying. It might help. As long as the therapist is nicer than *she* is!'

* * * * *

Within days, Amanda was back in a different waiting room to see the acupuncturist.

A medium-height, 20-something, white-overall-clad, attractive young woman with long brown wavy hair issued forth from a door to her left. She smiled with a white, perfect set of teeth.

'Hiya. Amanda?'

'Yes.'

'Come in, I'm Charlotte Streeter. I'm going to be your acupuncturist today.' Amanda felt like she was with a tour guide. Hold on. Streeter?

'Are you related to Robin Streeter?'

'Yeah, he's my uncle,' she answered. 'Have you met him? Lovely man, isn't he? He just paid for my dental work.'

'Oh, that was kind. Yes, yes he is,' said Amanda, glad that they had some common ground.

Charlotte checked details.

'Soooo … you were referred by Dr Schofield.'

'That's right,' said Amanda, coolly.

'Yeah,' said Charlotte, sympathetically, 'I know she can come across as edgy, but it's probably the effect of having to commute from Dover every day. Long drive. I think, it contributes. And this set up is a tad out of her comfort zone, but I'm sure you'll get used to her if you give her a chance.'

Amanda nodded. 'Sure,' she conceded.

Charlotte read Dr Schofield's notes. 'You OK with needles? Or did Dr S ask you that already … I can't see it here.'

'Yes, thank you, I'm fine with needles.'

'Good. Mind you, these aren't like the ones when you have a blood test. They're very fine, and you shouldn't feel a thing.'

And Amanda didn't. Charlotte was careful and gentle. At the end of the session, she asked her patient, 'All right?'

'I certainly feel relaxed. Thank you, Charlotte.'

'Good. Well, I'll see you next week then. And you can tell me how you've felt in the meantime,' said Charlotte brightly.

'Yes,' agreed Amanda, rather dreamily.

'Bye.'

'Hm,' said Granny to Amanda on the way through the car park. 'Knows her job but has got all the intuition of a lamppost.'

'At least she was nice. But I must admit, this isn't quite the place I imagined, Granny.'

'Why don't you have a wander around, and talk to some of the other therapists?' suggested Grandpa.

Amanda agreed, went back in and was given a pass by Gloria on reception. She met Jack, the healer, He was 80 years old, gentle and insightful. Nat, the Chinese medicine specialist, was 30 years younger but merry and wise. Joy who led the yoga and meditation sessions lived up to her name. Kathleen, who did reiki, and Melanie, who did aromatherapy with massage, had a depth and kindness about them that accorded with their professions. But they were all part-time staff. They had no permanent plaques on their doors.

The weeks passed. Amanda felt relaxed after each session, but there was no improvement in her asthma.

After the third visit to Charlotte, Amanda was walking from the café, where she'd stopped for hot chocolate, when she heard the doors behind her open and the sound of voices and laughter.

'Teedle tiddle dum pom dum pom diddle.' That could only be Dr Crossley.

'Robert, why don't you join us?' Amanda recognised Damian Gibbs' tones.

'Sorry, I have plans.'

'You *always* have plans on Tuesdays. And on Fridays. What is it that you *do*?'

'I do have a wife, you know, Damian. You should try it some time.'

'I think we all know what happened last time I did that,' he replied sardonically.

'Samantha's not a total disaster.'

'It's kind of you to say that, Robert. She obviously hasn't been making advances to you.'

'No! Well, not *exactly*… she's very young still.'

'That's what bothers me,' said Damian, gloomily. 'It means she has years to continue embarrassing me by systematically working her way through my friends.'

'She'll grow out of it,' encouraged Robin, 'and, in the meantime, not every man falls for her charms.'

'Thank you,' said Damian slightly cheered. 'I guess she's just bored. Maybe she'll find her niche in life and … oh well.'

Amanda wasn't in the mood for a chat. She quickened her pace and exited to the car park.

Following Dr Schofield's advice, Amanda joined a kundalini yoga group at the Centre, and that helped with her breathing. However, during the meditation, her mind would often flash back to the memory of being in front of the portraits with the old woman. Then next she would be in retreat from Cardiubarn Hall, desperately trying to remember … something that had just happened … if only she could remember and tell Granny ….

Sometimes she'd be walking down stairs, her hand held by the old woman …walking down some stairs. Not the grand staircase … stone steps … a door …. It was agitating. She half-wanted to avoid the yoga sessions, half-wanted somehow to get closer to that one essential memory ….

Amanda noticed that two of the therapists, Melanie and Kathleen, were replaced by others. She asked where they'd gone. No one knew. They'd just left.

Amanda dreaded the six weeks being up and having to sit across the desk from the cold Dr Schofield again.

As it happened, she was to be spared.

Chapter 22

༄

TOBY

Amanda sat, once again, in the Opal waiting room, which seemed to have shrunk a good deal since her last visit. She was staring at the plaque on the doctor's door in some trepidation when it moved, and a different face to the one she had been expecting showed itself: large, round, brown eyes, alive with curiosity and gentleness, and widely smiling soft lips. His hair was dark and wavy, topping a tall, fit figure in a white coat.

His gaze followed the direction of where she had been looking, and saw the sign with Dr Schofield's name on.

'Better change that!' he said. 'Amanda Cadabra?'

'Yes.'

'Bewitching name. And I'm sure that you are,' he said with an inclination of the head. 'Won't you come in? Please, make yourself comfortable. I am Dr Toby Sidiqi.'

'Hello, doctor, ... erm, what happened to Dr Schofield?'

'Left. Maternity leave. Bed rest been prescribed. I'm sure we all wish her well.'

'Hm,' said Amanda.

'On the other hand, it does mean that this amazing

opportunity has come my way.'

'Right.'

Amanda, truth to tell, was dazzled. She had always had a thing about attractive men in white coats. Amanda knew perfectly well why. It went back to when she was five years old.

* * * * *

Amanda was in Barnet Hill Hospital after an asthma attack that she had survived by only a hair's breadth.

She had passed out and, as she regained consciousness, a dark, wavy-haired man with a smiling face had swum into view. He wore a white coat. Amanda knew who he was: the new medic, Dr Tahami. He spoke.

'Hello, there. Nice to have you back with us.'

Amanda heard the wind of her breath whistling through her lungs. She recognised that she was in the intensive care unit.

'Am I going to die?' she asked, with a mixture of concern and curiosity.

He sat down on the bed beside her. 'Not on my watch.'

Amanda considered. 'I'm too big to ... fit on your watch.'

'It's an expression. From the days of the old sailing ships. The hands, the members of the crew, used to take turns to work or stand lookout.'

'For pirates?'

'Any kind of danger. A man overboard, maybe.'

Amanda visualised this image. Then she said between shallow breaths, 'That's me when I have a bad attack .... I'm sinking under the sea, but it's ... a warm sea and cosy and quiet and ... I'm going to sleep.'

'Well, when that happens, Amanda, I want you to listen for my voice. And when you hear me calling, I want you to look up, and swim to the surface as fast as you can, and with all your might. Will you do that for me?'

Amanda thought. It seemed very important to him. 'All right,' she agreed.

'Promise?' His eyes were alight with kindness and concern.

'I promise,' she agreed, her little face solemn.

Three weeks later, Granny was in the kitchen making jam tarts. Amanda was barred because the flour was filling the air. She loitered outside in the hall being driven to distraction by the smell. Then … the garden door could be heard opening …. Granny must have gone to see Grandpa.

Amanda reasoned that, if the outside door was ajar it should clear the air. She opened the kitchen portal a crack. Granny had told her to stay in the hall but hadn't said she couldn't look into the kitchen. Amanda could see the tarts cooling on the table. She opened the door further. The breeze from the garden sent a current wafting the aroma of strawberry jam and warm pastry towards her, laden with fatal flour particles. Amanda inhaled.

The water was warm, rocking her from side to side as she sank deeper and deeper.

'Amanda.' The voice was distorted and far away but familiar … it was Dr Tahami's voice … she remembered hazily making a promise … comforting as it was, she couldn't stay down here … she had to swim, swim for the surface… swim with all her might ….

Amanda opened her eyes. There was the doctor, in his white coat, sitting beside her on the bed. But his legs were stripey.

'Why are you wearing pyjamas,' she asked breathily.

'My ship's watch started unexpectedly.'

'I'm not going to die,' said Amanda with conviction.

'That's right. You're going to live for a long, long time.'

'Happily ever after?' she asked.

'Yes, Amanda.'

A notion came to her. Spending a good deal of time in hospital, she had opportunity to observe the interactions of her carers. Amanda had noticed the susceptibility of both the doctor and the nurses, as well as his flirtatious disposition.

'Are you married?' she asked.

'No,' replied Dr Tahami, with smiling, carefree directness. 'Why not?'

'Because I'm waiting for you,' he replied simply.

Amanda searched for the right phrase with which to reply. She recalled something she'd heard one of the nurses say to him. It seemed apt now:

'I bet you say that to all the girls,' she said.

He laughed. 'No, only you.'

* * * * *

Amanda had got better, especially once she started learning and practicing magic, and attended the hospital less and less. Dr Tahami moved on to another clinic, and faded in her memory. Yet she liked to imagine that somewhere, in some other form, he was waiting for her and one day would appear. He now seemed to have manifested himself in Toby Sidiqi guise.

Of course, he would have to be part of her magical world. That factor was a given, and Amanda was sensing only a little of that nature about the man sitting around the corner of the desk.

Toby had seated her to one side of it, and made sure that she could see the computer screen. It was an open and companionable arrangement.

'OK to call you, Amanda?'

In his case, she really didn't mind. 'Yes, of course.'

'Have to ask. Rules of priority. How's the chair? Best I could obtain from the biggest group-therapy room.'

'I'm sure you were very persuasive,' she said, lightly.

'You're too kind,' he returned graciously

'And it's certainly comfortable, thank you, Dr Sadiqi.'

'Please call me *Toby*. I find all of this titles business a bit antiquated, don't you? We're both a bit young for that, wouldn't you say?'

Amanda wasn't sure how old he was. He looked 25 but was probably nearer 30, given the length of time it took to become a fully-fledged physician.

She nodded good-naturedly. 'You're right. Toby, it is.' He turned the screen towards her. 'All details present and correct?'

Amanda confirmed that they were, and he continued, 'My approach is a little different from Dr Schofield's.'

Amanda relief was visible.

He went on, 'I'm a digger.'

'A digger?' she said, with amused scepticism. 'You look like a doctor to me.'

He laughed

'It's the white coat,' she jested.

'Misleading, isn't it?' he said merrily. 'What I mean is. I like to get to the bottom of things, find the root cause, what's underneath.'

'You're a frustrated archaeologist?' she smiled.

'Yes! I am at heart a Howard Carter, an Indiana Jones, if you will.'

'Without the hat,' Amanda observed, getting into the spirit of the thing.

'Indeed,' he agreed. 'So I hope you won't mind a lot of questions and going over old ground, so I can get a picture of the lie of the land, and perhaps a peek at the bedrock.'

'Of course,' she agreed, readily.

Senara and Perran had appeared seated in chairs, to the left and a little back from Amanda and Toby, but where they could still see the screen. They each gave a little wave, which Amanda stoically ignored.

'So when did the asthma start?' asked Toby.

'Just before I was three years old, according to my grandparents,' replied Amanda.

'That's right, love,' said Perran.

'Any other members of either family have a history of asthma, eczema, anything like that?' Toby checked.

Senara and Perran both shook their heads.

'None whatever,' said Senara.

'They say — said not, ' replied Amanda, hastily correcting her tense.

'Any respiratory infections at that age?'

'No,' said Senara definitely.

'No,' repeated Amanda.

'Do you remember being exposed to any chemicals that could have set it off?' Toby queried.

Senara and Perran looked at one another then shook their heads.

'No,' said Amanda.

'You sound sure,' observed Toby.

'My grandparents were very informative on the matter,' responded Amanda, truthfully. 'I too wondered, years ago, what might have started it.'

'Well, it's all helpful. It means we can eliminate those factors. Had any scans?'

'Not for years.'

'OK, I'm going to send you for one. How about blood tests?' He looked at the screen, scrolling down. 'I can't see that Dr Schofield ...'

'No, no, she didn't, and I haven't had any for years.'

'Let's do some now. OK with needles?'

Amanda smiled. 'Fine.'

'We'll leave you to it,' said Grandpa.

'This one's much better,' noted Granny, nodding with satisfaction. They waved and melted into the ether. Amanda was relieved. She felt that having her grandparents present was somewhat cramping her style.

'Just going to pop into the lab here,' said Toby, gesturing behind him as he got up.

'I wondered about that,' said Amanda. 'It wasn't here last

time.'

'No,' he called through the open door. 'They created it especially for me, would you believe? Isn't that nice of them?'

Amanda wasn't sure how to respond. The word 'why' presented itself to her, but she was searching for a polite way to say it.

'Ever wondered about the running costs of this centre?' he asked.

'Erm ... sponsors?' tried Amanda. 'And they said something at the inauguration about the facilities upstairs?'.

'Sponsors, yes, for the setup costs,' he said coming back into the room with a small trolley carrying a kidney-shaped disk, a long, slender, flexible tube and some phials. 'Have you seen the big lab upstairs?' he asked.

'Yes, on Inauguration Day.'

'Well, that has been handling mainly lab work for other health organisations. That's one source of income. Another is the accommodation on the same floor for patients visiting from afar. There's also the café, and the therapists' rooms.'

'The therapists' rooms?'

'Yes, they rent them. They were only on full-time contracts for the first month. Now the therapists come in, as and when, as freelancers. But for the first two months of a treatment course, this place foots the bill and, after that , ... well, low-income patients are subsidised, but anyone else who can afford to pay has the option of continuing privately.'

'I noticed that some therapists had left and others had replaced them,' commented Amanda.

'Yes, I noticed that too. Curious. Because the low room rents are still attractive.'

'And no one seemed to know why they left.'

'Did you ask around?' enquired Toby.

'Yes.'

He smiled and looked up at her appreciatively. 'Good for you. I can see that we're going to get on famously.'

Amanda twinkled but said, recalling him to the original subject 'So *why* have they built this lab for you?'

'Ah, well, I am a trained lab technician, so I was happy to double up with the bloodwork when I don't have patients. For the most part, I'm just a portal to the other practitioners, so I do have the time, and it saves the Centre money.'

'You're not a homoeopath then like Dr Schofield?'

'No, that's now one of the freelance therapists since she left. Now please could I have your arm, and don't worry about a thing. I am a trained phlebotomist,' said Toby.

'Why doesn't that surprise me? asked Amanda rhetorically.

He grinned. 'Just a keen student of whatever comes my way.' Toby continued to chat as he took the blood tests. 'Even though I work all hours, I do take breaks. Lunch breaks even. How would you like to continue our consideration of the Mystery of the Disappearing Therapists over lunch at er ... The Snout and Trough, is it?'

'Hold on,' said Amanda. 'Are you allowed to do that? Aren't you supposed to keep professional and social relationships separate, or something?'

'Once I refer you, you won't be my patient anymore. I told you, I'm just a portal.'

'Well, you haven't referred me *yet*,' pointed out Amanda firmly.

'Coffee in the café here then. We can sit at separate tables if you like,' he offered.

Amanda laughed. 'That I can agree to.'

'Just a moment,' he said, and picked up the phone on his desk. 'Hi, Robert? .... Good, thanks. ... Got any scan time today? ... When is she in? ... Uhuh .... OK, I've got a patient here I'd like .... Sure I'll hold.' He looked at Amanda saying. 'He's going to see if he can get the radiologist to come in tomorrow.'

They waited in silence until Amanda said, quietly. 'I appreciate your expediting matters.'

'You're welcome. I am eager to find out what there is to be

discover —. Yes, Robert, still here … that's great.' He put a hand over the phone. 'Tomorrow afternoon?'

'Sure!'

'Thanks, Robert, and thanks to Jen.' He put the phone down. 'Right. Tomorrow.'

'Thank you!'

'It'll take a few days to process the results. Then we'll take it from there. Should be all ready by this time next week. Good for you?'

'Yes,' she agreed willingly.

'Coffee?'

Amanda grinned. 'OK.'

Seated at the same table, with large steaming cups before them, they conferred.

'You know, I did apply for this job in the very beginning,' Toby told Amanda. 'Thought I was neck and neck but the best man, er, person won.'

'I expect Dr Schofield may have been relieved about the post winding up for her,' Amanda responded. 'After all, she was travelling every day all the way from Dover.'

'Phew, that's a hike.'

Echoing what Charlotte had said, Amanda continued, 'And I'm not sure she really felt she fitted in here, anyway.'

'But she's a homoeopath, I thought.'

'So did I.'

'Interesting,' said Toby, his eyes gleaming with interest. 'So you've been on board from the beginning of the whole project, being a local villager? Notice anything else odd?'

'Yes, I became friends with a member of the construction crew. We were curious about what was underneath the north wing. When he asked around, he got a slap on the wrist, and the other team members didn't want to talk about it.'

'Do you know what's underneath?' Toby asked, curiously.

'Just a bombed-out pub and some cottages. It's not like it's King Tutankhamen's tomb.'

'Hm. Wonder if there's any way to get down there, though?' pondered Toby thoughtfully.

'The area is cordoned off. Haven't you noticed?'

'Yes, but it's only tape; it's not like it's an electrified fence.'

'But wouldn't that be trespassing?' asked Amanda. 'I wouldn't want you to get into trouble.'

'It's nice of you to care,' he said, hopefully.

'Well, you're the best doctor I've seen here,' she countered pragmatically.

'Er … thank you.'

'Promise me you won't do anything until you've made some very discreet enquiries,' urged Amanda.

'I can have a chat with one or two of the therapists,' suggested Toby,' or maybe Bill. Yes, Bill!'

'Be careful. I must get to work now, Toby. Thank you for the consultation and the fast track scan. See you next week.'

He stood up. 'Back to work for me too. I'll get another cup to take back to the office. Till next week.'

As Amanda turned out of the door, she smiled knowingly, observing Toby chatting up the attractive café counter staff.

Chapter 23

༦

THOMAS VERSUS PENELOPE

Hogarth calculated, as he observed Thomas standing in front of the bookcase again. It had been almost two months since the evening that Thomas had dashed out of Hogarth's cottage, and raced off to London to question his mother.

Thomas had not been forthcoming about that visit, and Hogarth had known better than to probe. However, he noticed that his younger friend was often distracted, and every visit saw him scanning Hogarth's bookcase.

Mike set the tea tray on the coffee table. Then he went over to the other bookcase and leaned on it, openly watching Thomas. Suddenly Trelawney noticed his mentor viewing him with some amusement, and smiled.

'I'm not going to find my answers in these spines, am I?'

'That depends on the questions, lad.'

'I suppose that I was hoping that if I ignored them, they'd just go away. That works for some things but not this.'

'Are you ready to tell me what happened, Thomas?'

'Yes.'

'Want to tell me before we eat? Can always heat it up.'

'Yes, I'll feel more like food once I've ....'

'Ok. Go ahead then, lad.'

They sat down, and Thomas took a sip of tea and a long slow breath.

'Well. After I left here and grabbed an overnight bag ...'

Trelawney had had a quick journey over the Tamar, up the M3 motorway towards London, around the M25 orbital to the North of the metropolis, and down a few miles to his mother's house.

Thomas let himself in and startled her. Penelope Trelawney, for she had kept her married name, concerned that the suggestion that her son had been born out of wedlock might impede his progress, was still trim of figure and youthful of countenance. She was sitting on the sofa, in pyjamas, typing away on her laptop. Her short, well-cut blonde hair was wet, and her face free of makeup. There was a glass of wine on the sustainable wood coffee table in front of her.

'Good heavens, Thomas!' she exclaimed.

'Hello, Mum,' he greeted her, with a smile, going over to kiss her cheek.

'What are you *doing* here?'

'I need to talk to you.'

'Well, you *might* have called,' she said, with mild exasperation. 'You're usually so good about that.'

'It was a spur of the moment thing.'

'So I gather.'

'Why? You don't mind, do you?' asked Thomas in surprise, hanging his jacket up in the hall.

'Well, darling ... I might have had a man here!'

'A man? What man?' asked her bewildered son, coming back into the room, and looking around.

'You know? A date?' prompted his mother.

'A date?' The thought was new to him.

'Yes,' said his mother, testily. 'Exhibit A: my birth certificate indicating I am not yet in my dotage. Exhibit B: Degree Absolute proving I am divorced from your father. Please see absence of death certificate.'

'Oh, I see what you mean,' said Thomas grinning. 'Yes … er, I'm sorry, Mum … only I thought you broke up with Judas last year.'

'His name was Jude, and that was five years ago. Do *try* to keep up, darling.'

'Oh, sorry. Look —'

'Sit down,' she instructed her son. 'I'm about to order pizza. Do you want some?'

'Bit late, isn't it?' commented Thomas, perching on the edge of an armchair next to the sofa.

'I wasn't hungry before. I'm hungry now, and I'm going to order. I'm having the Vegan Four Seasons. Would you like something?'

'I'll have the same,' he said, distractedly.

'Darling, you don't like Vegan Four Seasons. Have Ham and Mushroom Miracolo.'

'Er, yes, thanks, Mum. Ham and Mushroom Miracolo,' Thomas echoed automatically.

As his mother ordered online, Thomas considered that he was good at his job, thought to be one of the most skilful interviewers in Cornwall, in fact. After all, he had been able, over three weeks of careful conversation, to persuade Fangs Mcnarl to grass up Jimmy The Leg. The court had secured a conviction and Thomas had even got a commendation for it.

And yet, somehow, within minutes, he would utterly lose the thread of a conversation to his mother. Of course, the fact that she was his mother, and had been the one to tell him to eat his breakfast and to make him do his homework at the beginning of the holidays, might have had something to do with it.

Penelope pressed the final submit button on the order screen and looked up.

'There. Now, what was it that has put you in such a fever to converse with your maternal parent that you have come hotfoot from the south-east at this time of night?'

Witnesses and offenders didn't say that either. He had forgotten his opening speech that he had been rehearsing on the journey up.

'Um. There was ... is ... something that I need to know, Mum.'

'Something you can't google, I gather,' said his mother, kindly.

'About our family,' he explained.

'Ah,' she uttered, cryptically.

Thomas knew that tone.

'Please, please, don't put me off,' he entreated. Somehow he had to get her on his side. 'I haven't been sleeping well. I've been having dreams. Dreams about the old house and Dad's family.'

'Oh, I'm sorry, love,' said his mother contritely, reaching out her hand to him. 'Yes, I see now that you do look a shade worn down. All right. What is it that you want to know?'

He paused preparing to gather momentum with his next sentence. It was interrupted.

'Please, darling, don't use any of your police warm-up techniques on me. Just say it.'

'What was the deal?' he asked.

'What deal?'

'I've remembered. I used to hear you say to Dad, "We had a deal."'

His mother stared at him. In spite of her insistence that Thomas should come out with whatever it was, she was unprepared for this bald question.

'Mum ... what was the deal?'

'Ahhh,' she said. Penelope put her laptop aside and leaned forward to pick up her glass and take a sip. It was her turn to choose her words.

'Your father's family was very ... dominating ... I don't want to speak ill of them because they are related to you.'

'No, please, go ahead,' he encouraged her.

She continued. 'I didn't like them. Actually, neither did your father. But they had some kind of a hold over him. For me, it was a deal-breaker. I suppose we should never have set up home there, in Cornwall. Things might have been different but … I don't think so. They kept pulling him back into the fold. I put up with it … because I loved him, I suppose … and then *you* came along, and we made a deal. He had to break with them, or I would take you and leave.'

'Oh,' said Thomas. It sounded drastic.

'He agreed,' Penelope went on. 'He stopped taking their calls, answering their letters … and then … when you were nine, they pressed his buttons and pulled his levers. Maybe they threatened us, who knows? But I found out that he'd been taking you there.'

'Where?'

'You know where, Thomas,' she said, quietly.

'Flamgoyne,' he supplied.

'Yes. I kept hoping it was a one-off. Your father would say sorry and promise that he'd never do it again. Then there was some shady business. They called on him to come late one night The next day, someone associated with the family died in inexplicable circumstances.'

'The day of my tenth birthday,' murmured Thomas.

'How do you know that?' asked his mother sharply.

'Because I remember what you said, what you cried out to Dad that night.'

She looked at him uneasily.

'Sorcery,' said Thomas. 'That was your word: sorcery.'

'Oh … I was being dramatic,' she insisted uncomfortably, looking down at her wine.

'What did you really mean, Mum?' said Thomas, employing just a shade of his policeman's voice.

Penelope thought, tracing the rim of her glass. 'All right. Your father's family practised some hocus pocus. It's probably just all psychological claptrap, NLP or whatever, but they manipulated people and circumstances.'

'Did you ever see Dad do that?'

'No,' she said decidedly. 'No, I would never have fallen in love with him, married him, if I had, Thomas. Your father was a good man. I still believe that. He's just .... They were too strong for him.'

He took a deep breath, stepped way beyond the boundaries of his comfort zone and asked a painful question.

'Did you ever see Dad do anything that couldn't be explained in terms of the laws of physics or the experience of the five senses?'

She looked up at him, rattled. 'No,' she said shortly. 'No.'

And here it came, the most agonising and daring question of all: 'Or me?'

'Don't be ridiculous,' she responded at once, impatiently, dismissing the very idea with a quick jerk of her hand. She got up and went over to the curtains, closing them more tightly. 'Look. It's all nonsense. The fact is, that we did have a deal and he broke it, over and over. In the end, I had to protect you, and myself.' She ran her hands down the folds of the drapes, then went on,

'It was a condition of the divorce, and your residence with him, that he would not bring you into contact of any kind with any member of his family at any time. On that condition, you stayed with him during term time.' Penelope looked back at her son, 'I assume that he kept to that.'

'Yes, Mum, I promise you that he did.'

'Is that all?' asked Penelope hopefully, fluffing up her damp hair and returning to the sofa.

Thomas felt that he had tried his mother enough, and had been lucky to have got her to part with this much information, for the first time. She was clearly intensely discomforted.

'Yes, Mum. Thank you. Maybe I'll sleep better now.' He gave her a hug. She returned it affectionately.

'Oh, I hope so, my love,' she said, her tension melting into concern for her son. 'I never thought all that dreadful stuff would come back to haunt you. Let's talk about something else. How is that nice Constable Nancarrow?'

'How do you know Nancarrow?' Thomas asked suspiciously.

'I had to call you that time about arrangements for your aunt's birthday party, and your phone battery had died, so I called the station and she picked up.'

'I see. I expect that in the space of five minutes you had learned her age, marital status, vital statistics and her hobbies,' said Thomas wryly.

'I took an interest, naturally. So ...?' prompted Penelope.

'She's erm ... in good health. Performing well,' Thomas responded, a little at sea.

'That's *not* what I meant,' said his mother, pointedly.

'Oh!' The penny dropped. 'I see what you mean. No, no, mum, she's not my type; far too young and anyway I'm her superior. It wouldn't be appropriate.'

'Well, what about that girl you keep interviewing?'

'What girl?' asked Thomas.

'The one up here. The one you drive north about eight miles north to visit.'

'Mum,' replied Thomas, with strained calm, 'she's someone I see in connection with a case. And how do you know ...? Oh, never mind.'

'Well, who do you think you inherited your detecting talents from? It was a simple matter of observing your milometer. But anyway, if she's part of a case then that won't do. I know that much. Such a shame you and Michelle didn't get together.'

'Michelle I was at college with?'

'Yes, darling,' his mother replied happily.

'Mum,' he said with a sense of outrage, 'you said you never liked her!'

'Well, at least she was normal. Not a witness or a member of the criminal classes,' Penelope pointed out.

Thomas sat deprived of speech. Fortunately, at that

juncture, the doorbell rang.

'Get that will you, darling.'

A minute later, Thomas brought in the pizza.

'Now, why don't you pour us both a nice glass of wine,' his mother suggested, soothingly.

'My idea entirely,' said Thomas, with feeling, and reached for the bottle.

Hogarth had remained silent throughout Trelawney's discourse. Thomas concluded with, '… I stayed overnight and came home the next day. We never said another word about it, either of us.'

Chapter 24

❧

CURTAINS AND CARPET

Having got to the end of his narrative, Thomas relaxed back into the Chesterfield chair opposite Hogarth's, put his hands behind his head and breathed a sigh of relief. Yet his gaze, fixed on the ceiling, showed that his ease was less than complete.

Hogarth waited. Finally, Thomas leaned forward and reached for his tea. It had cooled to unpalatable, and he put it down at once. To give him some time, Hogarth got up and, without a word, took it out to the kitchen to make a fresh cup. A few minutes later he returned, threw a few twigs onto the small fire, put the tea in front of Thomas, and sat back down.

'Thanks, Mike. I'd like to be able to say, "and that was that". Only for me, it wasn't.'

'What is it that troubles you, Thomas?'

'I didn't believe her,' he said frankly. 'As her son, I wanted to, *want* to, but as …'

'Detective Inspector Thomas Trelawney …'

'I know that she was … I hesitate to use the word "lying" because I think it's more a case of the fiction that she's told herself all these years.'

'About your father?'

'No, actually, I don't think she did ever see him do anything out of the ordinary. I think that he loved her so much that any … strange side of himself, that Flamgoyne side of himself, any unusual abilities that he possessed I think he did suppress that entire aspect of himself. I think that whatever he did or involved himself in, he did away from our home.'

'Then … about you?'

'Yes. It was the most difficult question of all for me to ask. And when I did ask her if she ever saw me do anything out of the ordinary, it wasn't just that she was so vehement —'

'"The lady doth protest too much"?' suggested Hogarth.

'Exactly, but … it was the curtains that gave her away. It was after dark, and she'd closed them before I arrived. There was only a small gap in them, yet she got up so abruptly and jerked them tightly together. What do curtains mean? Shutting out the dark, shutting out prying eyes, creating a cosy, safe haven from the night. It was an act of denial about me, shutting out an unacceptable memory.'

'I see why you needed time to come to terms with this,' said Mike, sympathetically.

'Yes, I did need time. But I have come to terms with it. I've been dismissing it all as preposterous, but I keep dreaming of being back in that house. After all these weeks, finally, yes I can accept now that my mother did see … something … I did, could do, something. But what? I have no … magical powers! I can't do anything out of the ordinary. And if I could, I don't remember it. And if I don't remember it, *why* don't I remember? Was something done to me so that I wouldn't? If so, what? When? Where? By whom? And was it just all in their imagination? Oh, I keep feeling like I want to wash my hands.'

'You feel tainted?'

'Yes, I suppose I do. Ridiculous as that seems, considering that it's something that I don't even give credence to!'

'Thomas, throughout the history of myth, legend, tales, reports, not all magic has been evil, nor all who have gifts of that nature. In those stories, there are many kinds of magic, and many that are, and can be, used for good. Your mother said that your father is a good man. Would you agree with that?'

'Of course.'

'If he was left to himself, no Flamgoynes in his life, and let's suppose, hypothetically, that he had a mystical gift, do you think that he would use it for good, or for ill?'

'For good, certainly.'

'Well, that's my point. You have no reason to feel tainted.'

Thomas nodded.

'You will remember, in time. The answers to all of your questions are in your memory. Actually, the answers to all of your and Amanda Cadabra's questions are in the memories of you both. Look how you found the family names between you.'

'That's true. I do feel better now I've told you about it. It's been weighing on my mind like the Rock of Gibraltar. The main thing is, that whatever it is that I could do, that's in the past, I can't do it now. I feel perfectly normal. I have a normal job in a normal world, thank goodness. Oh ... and a reasonably normal mother!'

Hogarth grinned.

'Let's eat!' said Thomas, cheerfully.

'I'll heat it up.' Hogarth went out to the kitchen.

Well done, Thomas, he thought, that was one of the most spectacular sweeping-under-the-carpet jobs it's ever been my privilege to witness. Now, let's see how long it stays there.

Chapter 25

༄

FIRST DATE

Amanda was standing at the Centre reception desk, signing in. Suddenly the double doors to her left were flung open. A leggy brunette strutted out on six-inch stilettos swinging a Chanel bag.

Samantha Gibbs walked past Amanda without registering recognition. Amanda considered. Those doors led to only one place: Toby Sidiqi's office. First Ryan, now Toby. Oh well, why not?

A few minutes later, Amanda was in his office herself.

'No help, I'm afraid,' said Toby regretfully, reviewing the results of the scans and blood tests. 'Except we can rule out things like malformation or anything really nasty.'

'OK ... well, that's good,' said Amanda, reaching for the positive.

Toby exhaled, put his fingertips together and looked at her meditatively.

'I'm not sure how to broach this,' he said hesitantly. 'I don't know how open you are to ... esoteric ideas.'

Amanda was more open to them that she was going to

admit here. She'd have to feel her way through this one. '"There are more things in heaven and earth …'

'… than are dreamed of in your philosophy."' He paused. 'My family goes back to ancient Persia. We've been here for four generations, but … we have a legacy of understanding of … other possibilities of …. There are more ways than one to get sick and to get well, let's say.'

Amanda nodded warily. 'Yes, I agree with that.'

'Since we have no conventional evidence of a cause, I would like you to explore … other ideas.'

'OK,' agreed Amanda. Toby took a list from his desk drawer and handed it to her. 'Which of these therapists was here when you first arrived?'

Amanda looked at the sheet. 'Well, the healer —'

'All right. I'm going to hand you over to the healer. I'd like you to have the full set of treatments that are on the house. See what he finds. Will you do that?'

'Yes, of course.' What was he getting at? Amanda pondered, This was mostly an alternative medicine centre. Weren't *they* 'other possibilities'?

Toby tapped away at the computer keyboard, then started up the printer. 'Let me just access his diary. Jack is it?'

'I think so, yes.'

'Jack Benner … right. You're in luck, he's available tomorrow, but the only slot that's free is the early bird that no one wants: 9 o'clock? Good?'

'Sure. That leaves the rest of the day clear for work.'

'OK. You are now about to be his patient,' pronounced Toby, with a congratulatory air.

'Aren't the complementary therapies under the wing of the clinic?'

'We all coordinate our data but, as most complementary therapies are not approved by the mainstream body that allows us to practice as doctors in this country, we make a separation. The patient undertakes the therapy at his or her own risk. We can suggest but ….'

'I see,' said Amanda comfortably. 'That's all fine with me.'

Toby offered her a pen. 'Sign here, please … and here ….
Great. All done. Lunch?'

Amanda laughed. 'Is that what this handover is really about?'

'Of course,' he replied, merrily.

The Snout and Trough was the village's gastropub. It possessed neither the age nor status of the 400-year-old The Sinner's Rue. Consequently, as a comparative newcomer, it was dubbed 'The Other Pub' by the locals. The food was excellent, and Sandra the proprietor had her eye on a Michelin star one fine day.

'So, … how are you liking your playroom?' asked Amanda, roguishly.

'Aha, my lab?' responded Toby, enthusiastically. 'Yes, very nice. Has all the requisite mod cons including centrifuge, CBC analyzer — just old second-hand ones but they do the job.'

'What do they do?' she enquired.

'A centrifuge spins the blood around very fast to separate it out, and the — look, I tell you what, why don't you come early for your appointment with Jack, and I can show you my machines?'

'That sounds like a Victorian gentleman inviting a lady to see his etchings,' commented Amanda.

'But *so* much more interesting,' countered Toby.

'Yes, I'd like that. I must admit that I am curious. OK. Thank you.'

'Let's say 8.30? Not too early?'

'I'm sure it'll be worth it.'

'It's a date then,' he said playfully.

Amanda grinned. Even with his possibly mystical background, he was far too much a flirt for any serious relationship. But he was fun, and it would be refreshing to engage in a little light dalliance with someone who understood the rules, and wouldn't try to own or rescue her.

'It's a date,' she agreed.

'I'd have asked you to dinner tonight only I want to have a poke around beside the lab once it gets dark,' explained Toby, brightly.

'In the ruins?' Amanda asked, anxiously.

'Yes,' he said, happily.

'Toby do be careful.'

'What's the worst that can happen?' he asked, smiling, 'I scrape my knee? That's all right, I'm a doctor. Oh, you're thinking about Batman and Robin. Yes, I might get a rap over the knuckles from the CEO and the manager, but they're not going to fire me; I'm far too good value for money.'

'Well, if you must. There's an old bomb shelter at the end of the ruins. You might see if you can get a look in there. And right next to the slab on which the Centre is built, is a horizontal crevice. There's — probably there's a bit of a cavity through there. Maybe you can get a torch and an eye to that, and see what's in there.' She was about to offer to go with him, but remembered she'd given her word to Hugo that she would not.

'Good leads. Thanks, Amanda,' said Toby excitedly.

'Please, take care,' she urged him.

But Toby's eyes were shining with enthusiasm. 'I promise. No worrying; it's bad for your health. I'll tell you all about it tomorrow.'

They parted in the carpark with a wave and a wish from Toby,

'Sweet dreams, fair Amanda!'

Chapter 26

≈

THE RUINS

Amanda had had a disturbed night, dreaming of the man in the 1940s suit, the village as it had once been, and then the sound of the bombs crashing.

She awoke to the unmistakable rattle and boom of the milk float, as it crossed a prominent drain cover in Orchard Row. Tempest, curled up beside her, was rousing himself at the sound. He enjoyed the milk float. The opportunities for mischief were myriad. He hopped off the bed and hurried downstairs to the cat flap.

Amanda groaned. Joe from Madley Cows Dairy called only once a week, to deliver a couple of cartons of coconut milk and half a dozen eggs. When she was lucky, Tempest slept through his arrival. Today she was *not* lucky. She got out of bed, pattered down the stairs, fastening her dressing-gown, and got to the door as Joe was bending to place her order on the step.

''Allo 'Allo. All right, young Amanda?' he said, straightening up.

Amanda, viewing him through sleep-blurred eyes, managed only a burble in reply.

''Ow's your young man, then?' asked Joe, trying to peer inside the cottage and up the stairs.

'My wha'?' asked Amanda, bewildered.

'That nice young doctor,' Joe answered perkily.

'No,' said Amanda flatly. 'He's *not* my young man.'

'At least he lives round here and won't be going home to Germany. Shame that didn't work out. We all liked that Hugo.'

Amanda gave up the struggle. 'Just a minute, Joe, I'll get you the money. What do I owe you?'

'Next week's fine. You go back to bed and get some shut-eye. Want to look your best for 'im, after all, don't cha!'

Before she could protest, Joe had turned to head off down the path, spotting Tempest on top of a crate of milk bottles, one claw poised to puncture the foil cap of a pint of Jersey cream.

''Ere You! Moggy! 'Oppit.'

'Tempest,' called Amanda. Her familiar descended daintily. She knew he was less interest in the cream than in getting an irate reaction from Joe.

The cat followed her back upstairs, sat in the bathroom and sauna-ed in the steam from Amanda's shower. She called out from the waterfall, 'Give the poor man a break, Tempest.'

He smirked. That was what he had in mind. His favourite sound was of a milk bottle smashing onto the pavement. One day, Joe wouldn't be quick enough.

Amanda dressed in light tan linen trousers, pale orange top and cream blazer. Pretty enough for a date and practical enough for a therapy session.

'Morrrnin', Miss Cadabra,' said Bill, as he unlocked the reception doors. 'Bright and airly as expected. Dr Sidiqi told me last night you were comin'. Vairy keen, he was. Told me to send you right in. You know your way, don't ye? Double doors, corrida, double doors then into the doctor's room and through that to the lab.'

'Thank you, Bill,'

'And you look vairy nice, Miss.'

Amanda smiled, and said, with a faint blush, 'Thank you!'

She swung and sailed into the waiting room. It felt daring crossing the office and penetrating into the zone beyond. She called out politely.

'Toby.'

No answer.

She knocked.

No answer.

'Toby? ... I'm here ... Amanda ....'

Slowly, she pushed open the door.

The room was a chaos of furniture askew. The computer and keyboard had been hurled to the ground. The screen was smashed. The panels of a machine near the desk had flown off. The top of it had buckled. There were metal fragments everywhere, and the walls were a mass of dents and ragged pits, where the surface had been ripped out.

Amanda walked in a few paces and stood like Dido among the ruins of Carthage. She looked down. There was Toby, lying on the floor.

She checked for a pulse, but it had long ceased. It looked like the impact from a chunk of metal had collided with Toby's head. She hoped that death had been instantaneous.

Minutes.

She had minutes.

Amanda observed and photographed. It occurred to her irreverently, 'There goes my date.'

It was time to leave and raise the alarm. Amanda turned to take one careful step towards the door.

That was when she saw him. Right there. Three feet away and looking straight at her. The man in the 1940s suit.

Amanda was not afraid. As Granny had always said to her, 'Just because someone is dead, is no reason to hold it against them.'

'Have you seen her?' asked the man urgently.

'Who?'

'I have to tell her. I don't want her mixed up in this. I want her to be safe.'

'Sir,' she said. 'Did you see what happened?'

'It was the same person,' he said insistently.

'As what? As who?'

'The one who stole the plans!'

'What plans?'

'You're one of us,' he said, nodding. 'I know you are.'

'A carpenter?' Amanda asked.

'That's right. Have you been working on the wonder too?'

'I, er .... Where were the plans stolen from?'

'The hall,' he replied at once. 'I know where they're hidden. I can show you. Tonight. I'll meet you in here tonight.'

'Tell me what happened here today,' she urged him.

He seemed distracted, saying, 'Terrible mess, and the noise ....'

'Please,' Amanda entreated, 'what happened?'

But he had gone.

Amanda hurried out into the waiting room, and briefly sat on a chair so that she could say she was so shocked she'd had to sit down. Then quickly she went up the corridor, and staggered into the reception where Bill was still on duty.

'Bill!' she cried, in an appropriately distraught voice. 'Come quickly! There's been a terrible accident!'

He strode ahead of her back into the lab.

'Go and sit down in reception,' Bill instructed Amanda. 'I'll be right with you. I'm going to phone the police.' He was already on his phone, pressing 999.

The lab was sealed, and the Centre cordoned off as a crime scene. Amanda knew that she must at all costs get back into that lab. The ghost had the keys to it all. He was surely the only witness. But how to gain access?

Chapter 27

❧

POLICE CORDON

There was always one, mused Detective Sergeant Baker. Why in the name of heaven was there always one?

'I blame the telly,' he said aloud to his junior, who was busily writing up a report.

Detective Constable Nikolaides knew this speech well.

'You're probably right, Serg,' she responded.

'Agatha Christie has a lot to answer for, if you ask me.'

'Hmm,' intoned the constable, well aware that Baker didn't need a reply; just a call-and-response sound would do.

'You'd think finding the body would be enough for 'er. But no, she wants to feeeel her way to solving the whole mystery. Can I just 'ave five minutes in the lab, Sergeant. Something might come to me, Sergeant. I might remember something that's significant. It's reeely important, Sergeant.'

'She *is* a witness though, Serg. I expect she's anxious to see it all wrapped up. So she can move on. You know?' offered Nikolaides pacifically. 'It's not unusual for people to feel attached to a case when they're a witness. Want to help.'

'Well, I know that,' replied Baker. 'And didn't I offer to *give* 'er five minutes? You were there. Didn't I say to you, to take the young lady to the room?'

'Yes, Serg.'

'But, "oh, no, Sergeant," she says, "I 'ave to be alone there or it won't work, it'd be too distracting if someone else was present. All I need is five minutes." Now, where would we be if we left witnesses alone at the crime scene, wandering willy-nilly all over it, getting vibes or whatever? I mean, I *ask* you.'

Nikolaides stopped tapping and looked around at her boss. 'She did seem a bit worked up about it. Are you sure that wasn't suspicious, Sergeant?'

'Oh, of course, she didn't do it. She'd only met him five minutes ago. And she's as curious about it as any of us. More so. Besides, it was an accident, as far as we can tell. These things do happen, you know. You'll find out all the different ways a individual can meet their Maker afore their time, young Nikolaides.'

'Yes, Serg.' She continued expertly imputing ninety words per minute, while continuing to play her part in the dialogue. He gave an approving nod in her direction. He was well aware that she was a good deal smarter than he was. A first-class honours degree and sharp as a tack. She'd be promoted out of his office in no time at all, and outrank him, and that was all right with him.

Nikolaides, for her part, was equally well aware that Baker was, first and foremost, a fine, solid, experienced policeman, down to his well-polished boots. She'd asked for her present post and felt that she couldn't have done better.

'I dunno,' he continued, his mind returning disapprovingly to the works of Miss Christie. 'A individual watches an episode, and suddenly they're Miss Marple. Think they can run around, ask a coupla questions and suddenly they've solved the crime. I dunno what they think we're 'ere for.'

'I know what you mean, Serg.'

'*Procedure*, Nikolaides. That's what solves crimes. Relentless interviewing, evaluating, re-interviewing, gathering and considering evidence and more interviewing, and paperwork and just plain plodding through the job, until you get the picture. And then it's no use just working out who dunnit. You 'ave to build a case, a case that a prosecutor can take to the courts, and get a conviction with, or it's only so much thin air.'

'That's right, Serg.'

'It's the job. What do amachures think they teach us at Hendon Police College?

*****'

Amanda had tried.

She had been interviewed by Detective Constable Nikolaides who had been compassionate and considerate. Amanda had answered all of the questions to the best of her ability. No, she knew of no enemies the deceased might have had, or of anyone who held a grudge or might have wanted to harm him.

Yes, she had touched the body to check the pulse, but no, she had not moved it, no, or anything in the room.

How did she come to find the body?

'The doctor had offered to give me a brief tour of the lab, to explain what the various items of medical equipment were. I had expressed an interest the day before.'

'You were close friends?' asked the constable.

'No, we weren't close friends. We met in the office, just days ago, for a consultation. We had coffee in the café here. Then after Dr Sidiqi had signed me off and passed me onto one of the therapists, we met for lunch. That was when he invited me to see the lab this morning.

'I walked in, saw the disorder, then saw the body. I was … it was a shocking scene. I stood there for a while, I felt for a pulse, and then I went and sat in the waiting room to recover, and then I went to get Bill, erm, the warden, who was on security.'

'Thank you, Miss Cadabra. Is there anything else you can tell us?'

This is my chance, thought Amanda. 'Well. I'm a very intuitive person. I think there were things I missed. I think if I could just get back into the room, by myself, those things would come back to me.'

The constable kindly but firmly explained that that would not be possible. They could not allow the scene to be disturbed. They had a certain procedure that it was important to follow. She hoped Amanda could understand. Amanda said it was very important to her peace of mind, and could she possibly speak to the officer in charge.

Yes, Amanda had tried. Tried as hard as she could. But there was no getting past either Detective Constable Nikolaides or her superior, Detective Sergeant Baker. She would have to find another way.

Chapter 28

❧

RESOURCES

Once back inside the front door of the cottage, Amanda had the first opportunity to call on the cavalry.

'Granny! Grandpa!' Obligingly, they both appeared, and led the way into the living room.

'Let's all sit down,' said Granny practically.

'You've had a shock, pet,' observed Grandpa.

'Well yes, but that's not the point. I have to get back in there. That man. He *saw* it. He saw the murder, he *knows* who did it.'

'Now, Ammy. You have to take this one step at a time,' said Granny calmly, sitting, with characteristically straight back, beside her on the sofa. 'A witness from another dimension is not the same as one in your dimension. Tell us what he said.'

Amanda repeated the dialogue as best she could.

Grandpa considered and said, 'What he's seeing and experiencing could be crossing over between the two, between the now and the then.'

'Yes,' said Granny, 'your job is to disentangle one from the other.'

Amanda had an idea. 'Did you two see it?'

'Ammy dear, we can't be everywhere at once. And even if we did know, you can do this yourself. Just use your resources.'

'You'll be fine. We have every confidence in you, love,' said Grandpa. 'Like your Granny says, use your resources.'

They faded, leaving only Tempest looking at the spot where they'd been. He sat down and began to groom himself.

'Well! Once again, we're on our own,' Amanda announced, none too pleased. 'First thing I need is a cup of sweet hot tea.'

She sat in the kitchen, looking out at the fruit trees in the garden turning to silhouettes against the dusking October sky.

'Use your resources.'

* * * * *

Amanda was seven years old. She had a thing about aeroplanes even then. She used to make origami models and levitate them around her room. Amanda wasn't very expert at it, and, inevitably, they crashed and, sometimes, got stuck.

There was a particular place, on the top of the wardrobe, which was stacked with odds and ends she had yet to find a home for. This area seemed to attract aerial accidents. Sometimes Amanda could manoeuvre the plane out, but there was one occasion on which it was stuck fast. She tried standing on a chair, but she was too short to reach the aircraft.

She went down to Granny and Grandpa in the living room, having afternoon tea.

'I've got something stuck on the top of the wardrobe, and I can't reach it.'

'Use your resources, *bian*,' said Grandpa, with a wink and a quick movement of his head in the direction of the dining room. She knew what this signified.

Amanda hurried next door and opened Senara's hereditary tome *Wicc'huldol Galdorwrd Nha Koomwrtdreno Aon*. After leafing through the book, about two-thirds of the way, she found a shrinking spell.

'If I can make the box the plane's wedged against a little smaller then I can fly it out,' said Amanda, aloud to herself. She hurried back into the living room. 'Granny, please may I do the shrinking spell on a box on top of my wardrobe?'

'Yes, dear.'

It worked. However, changes in mass and shape where not Amanda's forté, and the box, which she had been rather attached to, came out of the process looking sadly crushed. Granny refused to fix it.

'This is an object lesson, Ammy dear,' she explained. 'Magic has consequences. I will give you this hint though: the counter-spell is in the latter quarter of the book.'

It had taken Amanda a week to get the box back into the semblance of its former shape.

* * * * *

Seated at the kitchen table, Amanda considered. 'What resources do I have? Well ... I'm a witch, aren't I? So I'll use spells. Yes, I know that that spell will have repercussions,' she said to Tempest, who had paused his consumption of Monarch's Luscious Liver to shoot her a warning look. 'But I *have* to get back in there. He never appears anywhere but in that space, and I know that he knows what happened. I have to try. After dark.'

Amanda dressed in jeans, shirt and jacket. There was as yet no autumn bite in the air. Rather, a storm had been threatening for the last week, without ever quite getting up the courage to let loose, and the atmosphere was humid. She came down the stairs from her room, patting her hip to make sure her Pocket-wand was in place.

'You coming?'

Tempest got up with an air of 'I've been ready for hours.'

'Let's go.'

They left the Astra just inside the Wood and went the short distance to the Centre on foot. Working magic on electronic items was easy. It was just another kind of energy. From the shadows, Amanda pointed her pocket wand up at the CCTV camera and softly pronounced, '*Kileiniga lytaz rihthdhou ynentel.*'

The camera swivelled to the right, away from the path to the reception.

'*Gestilfth.*' It stopped.

She could see through the glass doors that Bill MacNair, was on duty, sitting at the desk facing the door but reading a newspaper. Amanda sidled up to the entrance, wondering if the spell would work through a window. She flicked her wand towards the guard, whispering,

'*Cusslæpath.*' Bill's eyes closed and he slumped forward gently onto the desk. She felt a ripple in the ether. The same ripple she had felt, and ignored, the first and subsequent occasions that she had used a spell on a living creature. This time she had the good sense to heed it. Amanda wiped her forehead.

She pushed at the doors. Locked.

'*Agertyn,*' she commanded them, quietly. The bolt slid across, and she was soon in the foyer. If anyone was around, she couldn't hear them. Amanda moved with Tempest into the corridor and down to the next set of double doors. She peeped through the glass into the waiting room. Oh no! A police constable was standing right in front of it. If she used the spell, he'd fall over.

And he'd certainly have no explanation. A guard on night watch might fall asleep at his desk, but not one standing up. Plus he'd get hurt in the process and maybe into trouble. No. She must do no harm. Amanda knew how to hold an object still and lower it gently but not a human. It was too much magic on something organic, and far too risky

'Dammit. It's no good, Tempest,' she breathed. 'Come on.' They returned to the foyer, went out through the entrance, and locked the doors again, with a word, '*Luxera*.' Amanda tapped her wand towards the sleeping guard.

'*Awaekdenath*,' she breathed. She saw him begin to raise his head and dodged out of sight. Again, the ripple. Amanda wondered anxiously how far it was spreading out.

Witch and familiar made their way along the track. From a safe distance, she magically moved the camera back into position.

'I'll have to find another way,' said Amanda resignedly, but still with determination.

Chapter 29

❧

MORE RESOURCES

Amanda was seven and a half. And her plane was stuck again. This time she couldn't see the site of the crash and wedge. Even trying to change the shape of the surrounding objects was having no effect. She went downstairs to tell Granny.

'Ammy, dear,' came the patient reply, 'I'll say what I always say: use your resources.'

Amanda returned to the scene of the predicament and cogitated. An idea formed in her mind and she went back down to the ground floor, up the garden path and knocked at the workshop. This was a wise precaution when she didn't know how dust-free it was in there.

Grandpa came out and closed the door behind him.

'Hello, *bian*, come for a visit?'

'Yes. Grandpa,' she said coming straight to the point. 'You're someone I can ask to help me, aren't you?'

'I am, love.'

'Are you a resource, then?'

Grandpa laughed and put his arm around her.

'There's no arguing with that, *bian*. What do you want me to do?'

'You're tall. I want you to get my plane down for me, please, Grandpa.'

'Come on then.'

* * * * *

'Use your resources,' Amanda told herself, as she drove towards Orchard Row. 'Yes, sometimes a resource is a *person*, Tempest.'

She checked her watch.

'It's too late to call now. It'll have to wait until tomorrow.'

They reached home, and Amanda plonked herself down on the sofa. Tempest jumped onto her lap and began kneading her jeans. She addressed him with conviction,

'Granny and Grandpa are right. I need to calm down, curb my impatience and take this one step at a time, however challenging that might be!'

Tempest judged that Amanda's legs were sufficiently prepared. Putting his rear end in place, walked around it until he was a neat ball of body and tail, with paws tucked away.

'I do need to get in there. But besides that, if I'm going to separate what happened back during the war from what happened in the lab, then I need information about what went on around here before the bombs fell.'

Amanda stroked her familiar as she mused, 'There would have been rumours ... stories the next generations heard from their parents and grandparents. And I need someone who's good at intelligence gathering. Yes, *he's* the obvious choice.'

Tempest purred uncommunicatively.

'How to say it? How to ask? What kind of argument would

appeal to a policeman?' Amanda thought back to her interview with Detective Constable Nikolaides. 'What was it she kept talking about? ... Procedure ... yes ... procedure.'

* * * * *

'Mike?' Trelawney spoke into his phone.

'Hello, Thomas, all well?'

'I just had a call from Amanda Cadabra.'

'Ah yes?' said Hogarth, with interest.

'She, er, says that she needs to consult me.'

'About the death at the Centre?' queried Hogarth.

'Yes,' confirmed Trelawney. 'Miss Cadabra claims she needs me to explain the finer points of police procedure. She's confused and troubled, apparently.'

'Really? And you said ...?'

'Yes, yes, of course.'

Hogarth asked, 'When are you going up?'

'I've managed to arrange tomorrow.'

'You sound sceptical about her request, my lad,' Hogarth observed.

'I am. I think she told the truth, and nothing but the truth, but not the *whole* truth,' said Trelawney shrewdly. 'For one thing, I don't think Miss Cadabra is the, er, "confused and troubled" type. Those are more conditions she induces in others, I'd say,' he concluded drily.

'I trust your judgement, Thomas,' said Hogarth supportively. 'Meeting in the lovely old Sinner's Rue?'

'No ... the ...The Big Tease.' He knew Hogarth grinning.

'My lad, you might enjoy this more than you expect,' said his mentor, suggestively.

Trelawney had seen that coming and decided to ignore it.

'I only meant,' continued Hogarth innocently, 'that, if I'm not mistaken, she also wants a tutorial in professional intelligence gathering.'

'Perhaps. At any rate, I think this bears investigation,' said Thomas.

'And it may be a chance to reinforce the bridge between you,' Hogarth added.

Trelawney agreed. 'Yes, kill two birds with one stone.'

'One other thing. Could you ask her a question for me?' requested Hogarth.

'Of course.'

'Ask her if she ever feels like she's under surveillance. And find out if there have been any strangers or newcomers in the village.'

'May I ask why?'

'I have a feeling that our Amanda has attracted attention outside Sunken Madley. Just a feeling. Probably nothing. Ask her though, will you? Just in passing.'

'Certainly.'

'Keep me posted.'

'Will do.'

Chapter 30

ॐ

THE BIG TEASE

The Big Tease, the tea and coffee shop in Sunken Madley, was owned and run by Jules and Alexander, Sandy to his friends. They worked long hours, opening at 7 o'clock in the morning to serve breakfast to the commuters, and closing twelve hours later, when the takeaways and the two pubs took over to provide dinner for the hungry residents and their visitors.

They closed for a half day on Thursdays, and on Sundays for the cricket, at the insistence of the locals. Sandy was the team's ace-in-the-hole seam bowler. Many an overconfident opposing team batsman had fallen prey to the wicked curve of Sandy's bouncing bowl, as rivals from the neighbouring village of Romping-in-the-Heye knew all too well.

Of indeterminate ages of somewhere between 40 and 50, Sandy had done well as something in the City, or possibly in construction, and Jules had distinguished himself in the hair salons of London. Having been friends since Sunken Madley School-days, they had sequestered to their home village, to take over the decaying tea shop from Miss Hempling, when the demands of its upkeep were becoming too much for her. In her own words:

'I don't understand about all this going to the net market and social stages.'

They paid her a generous amount that had allowed her to move into the Pipkin Acres Residential Home, where her great friends were already being comfortably cared for, and 'the boys', as she affectionately referred to them, took over.

Every sausage roll, pasty, scone, angel cake, flan and pastry was made by the owners. With their West End and City contacts sampling and spreading the word, what had formerly been known as 'Ye Olde Tea Shoppe', was beginning to attract passers-by, as well as the denizens of the surrounding countryside. Some came from the towns to the south, Barnet and Southgate, and even Hatfield to the north in Hertfordshire. The village had a long way to go before it would become A Destination, but it was a start.

Amanda popped in there regularly for her favourite beverage: hot chocolate. Knowing about her asthma and her consequent avoidance of dairy, they always had cartons of almond and coconut milk for her, and coconut cream to whip her drink into a fondant of foamy deliciousness sprinkled with hazelnuts and drizzled with homemade chocolate sauce. No powder for Miss Ammy. It might start her coughing.

The Big Tease had a cat-and-dog-friendly corner. Alexander and Julian kept a store of tins of tuna and salmon, and referred to Tempest as 'his lordship', which he refused to regard as in any way teasing or ironic.

Amanda had never been the sociable type or had the desire to seek out others for information. She spent most of her time trying to avoid being a topic of it. Consequently, she would never have thought of this particular venue as a hotspot for intel, if it wasn't for something Erik her solicitor had said.

Erik had been the Cadabra's solicitor for many years, and,

even though he numbered several millionaires and billionaires amongst his clients, was never too busy to prepare to ride into battle on her behalf if necessary. He was a friendly, likeable, jovial man, who off-duty dressed in youthful casuals and was popular in the local hostelry. Suited and booted, he was justly feared by his legal opponents, and Amanda considered that there was no one better to entrust with the interests of her affairs.

'I just wanted to have these on file. In the event that anything untoward should befall me,' said Amanda, handing some documents across his desk.

Erik took off his glasses and polished them, while he regarded her with apparently mild, passing interest.

'While I was working at the Manor,' Amanda explained, 'I encountered some uninvited guests. I encouraged them to make restoration for the hospitality of which they had availed themselves. The documents there are … an incentive for them to keep their word and discourage them from lodging any … objections on my person,' she finished diplomatically.

Erik smiled knowingly, 'I understand perfectly.'

'Yes, I rather thought you might,' she replied, twinkling.

'Does your young man know about this?' asked EriK.

'What young man?'

'Your tame detective.'

'He's not my young man. How did you —?'

'My dear, you can't have dinner with a member of a territorial police force of England and Wales, in one of the only two pubs in Sunken Madley, and expect it not to spread like wildfire throughout the village by 9 o'clock the following morning.'

'It was *business*,' Amanda explained. 'About the family accident.'

'Yes, I expect so,' agreed Erik. 'But I gather he was under 60 years of age and of personable aspect.'

'Considerably under 60 years of age!' Amanda answered

hotly, for no reason that she cared to explore.

'The community,' commented her solicitor, 'is divided as to whether they prefer him or your other young man.'

'Other ...?'

'Oh come now, Amanda, you were seen in conversation with him at the playing fields on his first Sunday here, and from all accounts, he seemed rather taken with you.'

'Good grief!' exclaimed Amanda. 'Is your office Grapevine Central?'

'No, no, dear, that's The Big Tease. I happily yield second place to them. In fact ...,' he glanced at his watch, 'I don't have another client for half an hour. Have they made a fresh batch of Bakewell tarts this morning?'

'How should I know?' she asked, suspiciously.

Erik put on his glasses, looked at her over the top of them, and uttered in judiciary tones, 'You were seen entering their establishment on your way here, were you not, Miss Cadabra?'

She laughed. 'How could you possibly know that, Erik!?'

'My thoughtful receptionist had just brought me coffee from there before you arrived,' he replied, with amused aplomb.

Amanda giggled helplessly. 'All right. You win. It's a fair cop, guvn'r. I'll come clean. Guilty as charged. Yes, they *have* made a new batch of Bakewells. Well, I'll be off now. I have polish to apply, and you have to get your tarts before your next appointment. Thank you for seeing me, Erik.'

'Always a pleasure,' he replied, graciously. 'Take care now. And you know where to find me if you need me.'

'Yes,' Amanda answered, 'I'll just ask a villager!'

And so, that day, she knew exactly where to meet Detective Inspector Trelawney.

Chapter 31

ༀ

PREPARING

Amanda clocked off late-morning. She needed time to prepare, not just to shower and dress for the part, but to psyche herself up.

She and the inspector would be under observation, and she mustn't look like she was on a date, or that she was trying to employ her feminine wiles. On the other hand, she didn't want it to look too coldly business-like.

'Not a thigh-length skirt,' said Amanda to Tempest, as she looked through her wardrobe. 'Knee length ... but flippy ....
How about ... this?'

She presented him with a black skater skirt. He got up and turned his back.

'No? All right, I know you don't want to be involved, but this is important!' Amanda hung it back in the cupboard saying, 'Too sombre ... OK ... erm ... pale orange ... not too light ... with a dark orange top, tee-shirt .... And a jacket?'

'Rrrowlll.'

'You're right: too formal ... erm ... cardigan! Orange.'

'Grrlllll.'

'Well, I like orange.' She donned the ensemble and slipped her feet into burnt umber ballet pumps.

Tempest gave a cursory glance over his shoulder.

'Brrrrbrrrll.'

'I do *not* look like a pumpkin! I think it's fine. I feel confident, and that's what counts.'

Granny appeared, sitting up straight on the edge of the bed, with her hands folded in her lap.

'You're wearing that, are you, dear?'

'Please, Granny, not you too.'

'No, I think it will help break the ice.'

Amanda looked at her suspiciously.

'It's slightly formal with a hint of casual about it,' said Granny. 'Yes, dear, it will work very well.'

Amanda, on a new wave of sartorial enthusiasm, looked up at the top shelf of the wardrobe.

'*Cumdez*,' she said to her straw hat. However, as it floated down, Granny intervened.

'No, dear, too much.'

'Too much?'

Granny nodded.

'*Aereval*,' uttered her granddaughter resignedly, sending the chapeau back into its place.

Amanda went over to her discarded overalls, withdrew her IKEA pencil wand and put it in her skirt. The pocket was rather shallow. She pushed it in as deep as it would go.

'Thank you, Granny. Any other suggestions?'

'Yes, recommend the Earl Grey tea there. Tell him it's very good, and then order a pot.'

'Why a pot?'

'So you can share it. It will create a bond,' Granny explained.

'It's just a drink, not a contract,' replied Amanda flatly.

'And remember how he likes his tea.'

'Why?'

'If you expect to get round a man you should at least know

how he likes his tea, dear.'

'Get round …! Granny! What about female emancipation and all that?'

'Do you want to persuade him to help you or not?'

'I want to persuade him in the cause of justice, not seduce him with a hot beverage and a sugar lump!'

'Very good, dear, that's how he likes his tea. Milk, one sugar,' responded Granny with aplomb. Amanda fairly spluttered. Senara continued, 'Order something to eat. Have the same savoury as he has, and then something for pudding that's too much for one so you can share it.'

'Granny!'

'You need to make him comfortable with you, Amanda.'

'Well, how can I do that when I'm *un*comfortable myself?'

'You'll be fine, dear. You'll get your answers in the end, one way or another.'

'Well, thank you for the vote of confidence, Granny. Now. I want to get there before he does.'

'No,' said Granny decidedly.

'What? Why "no"?' asked Amanda in bewilderment.

'He likes getting himself settled and in position before you arrive. Haven't you noticed?'

'Erm.' Amanda gave it some thought. 'I suppose … yes.'

'He's a policeman, remember. And it will help if you let him feel that he has the advantage.'

'Well, he does, Granny,' said Amanda prosaically. 'He has the power to do something I need him to do. I can't see why he wouldn't so I don't see why I have to resort to … ploys and stratagems!'

'As you wish. Ready, dear?'

'Yes,' said Amanda, with a final look in the mirror, pulling her waist-length cardigan down a little.

'Off you go then,' said Granny. 'Is The Animal accompanying you?' Two pointed grey ears twitched.

'Tempest?' asked Amanda, 'You coming?'

Her familiar looked around wearily.

'The Big Teeeeease?'

That was different. It held out the promise of delicacies. Tempest stood up, stretching his legs mightily. Some things were worth getting out of bed for.

Grandpa appeared at her side as she neared the end of Orchard Row, not far from The Big Tease.

'The target is in position,' said Perran jauntily.

Amanda tutted, suppressing a smile. 'That's not funny, Grandpa.'

'You're on, *bian*.'

Chapter 32

৩

AT THE HUB

As Amanda approached, it was clear that the first wave of the traditional lunchtime queue had abated. Amanda made her entrance, and saw Trelawney seated in a corner at the left-hand end of the beech block counter, at one of the round pine tables. He rose as she approached. She had to give him that; he did have nice manners.

'Hello, Miss Cadabra. You're looking very … seasonal.'

'Hello, Inspector. Er … thank you,' she uncertainly.

'Although it isn't quite Halloween,' he acknowledged. 'Two more weeks to go.'

'Oh yes, … um … I like orange.'

'And it suits you, if I may say so.'

Amanda was relieved. 'Thank you.' She sat down. 'And thank you very much indeed for coming all this way.'

'Not at all, I'm hoping to make a long weekend of it at my mother's.'

'That's nice. I'm sure you've earned a break. Have you ordered?' she asked him.

'I thought I'd wait for you.'

'How kind. I can recommend the Earl Grey tea here. It's particularly good.'

'Excellent. I'm very fond of Earl Grey,' Trelawney replied.

'I'll get a pot then, shall I?' What's going on? Amanda asked herself. Has Granny set me to 'autopilot'?

'Certainly, thank you.'

Amanda went to the counter.

'Well, hello stranger!' exclaimed Jules. 'Haven't seen you for a coupla days. Where you bin hidin' yourself? I was just saying to Alexander — Alexander, *wasn't* I just saying? *Where's* our Miss Cadabra, I was sayin'.'

'He was,' confirmed Alexander, 'that's *just* what he was sayin', and here you are large as life and looking lovely! Lovely! Now, what can we get for you, lovie?'

'A pot of Earl Grey, please.'

'And two cups?' asked Alexander, looking over the counter to the left, at the inspector.

'Please.'

'Quite.' He caught sight of Amanda's cat. 'Oo, I can see what his lordship wants!'

Tempest had seated himself before one of the wooden pet tables, the surface raised a few inches off the ground, with two shining bowls set into circular holes.

'Tuna is it, Sir Tempest?'

Tempest blinked once for 'yes'.

'What about something for you two to eat, lovie? Got fresh pasties, pork pies and cheese and bacon flan. All with salad, natch.'

Trelawney looked at Amanda for guidance.

'All of their flans are delicious,' she said.

'I'll have that then,' he replied, amiably.

'Two flans and salad, please, Alexander.' I can't believe it, Amanda said to herself, I've just ordered the same savoury as him. I must be channelling Granny!

'Coming up, lovie. Want to order pud now for after? We've just made some trifle. Fancy some trifle? Coconut milk custard.'

Jules presented her with a large dish full.

'Oh, it looks rather a lot for one person,' said Amanda. What am I doing? she asked herself in alarm. Am I programmed or something?

'Two spoons and you can share ...?' suggested Alexander.

'Er, Inspector. Do you like trifle?' Amanda asked.

'I do,' he confirmed, with interest.

'Would you like to share one? They're rather large.'

'Of course,' he answered, thinking he'd rather like a whole one but could always order another. His mother tended to make more adventurous puddings like goji berry soufflé, and mango and pomegranate compote in a sugar-spun basket. Thomas hadn't the heart to keep reminding her that he preferred traditional desserts like bread and butter pudding and spotted dick.

'You go and sit down, lovie, and enjoy your chat with the inspector. We 'ad a nice chinwag before you came in, didn't we, Inspector?'

'We did,' Trelawney agreed, with a friendly smile.

Amanda sat down at the table in a chair near Trelawney. Like him, she preferred sitting in corners.

'Do you mind if I take my jacket off?' he asked courteously. 'It's rather close.'

'Please, go ahead. Yes, I noticed that. It's been so nice lately, but it's definitely getting a bit muggy.'

'So ... it's all been happening here, I gather,' he said for openers, removing his outer layer and hanging it on the back of his chair.

'Yes, indeed it has,' Amanda answered with feeling. 'What a thing to take place in our sleepy village! Although it wasn't exactly in Sunken Madley.'

'It must have been quite a shock for you, finding the body,' he commented sympathetically.

'Yes, it was rather. Actually, everything has happened very

quickly, and I'm trying to understand it all.'

'That's where I come in?'

'Yes,' said Amanda, glad he understood.

'Well ... how about if I explain what the various measures are that need to be taken in the case of an untimely death?' Trelawney offered.

'Untimely death? When it's unexpected or violent?'

'Precisely. Because this happened to a doctor in a laboratory, it comes under the heading of industrial. Would you say that it had the appearance of an industrial accident?'

'Yes. Yes, did *appear* that way.'

'You don't sound convinced,' he observed.

'It's just that .... It's too neat ... too coincidental.'

'Have you expressed your misgivings to the police who interviewed you?'

'Sort of, but it's all so ... it's not concrete ... it's hearsay, conjecture, feelings ... I could tell they didn't take it seriously.'

'Maybe you need to put it to them in terms that they can use to help them. Why don't you tell me from the beginning? When did you first start to feel ... uneasy?'

'It was actually when I heard they were going to build on Lost Madley. It's not a place with a ... happy reputation.'

Julian came to the table bearing a tea tray.

'Here you are, my lovelies.'

He arranged the teapot, the hot water pot, two cups, milk jug and sugar bowl in front of Amanda, saying, 'You can be mother,' and took away the tray.

They thanked Julian, and Amanda continued.

'Then it went ahead so quickly. I got curious about the part of the village that one wing of the Centre was going to be built over. I got friendly with one of the builders and asked him to find out, and he got warned off. But I know something's down there. There are places where you can peep through the rubble.

'I know that Toby — Dr Sidiqi — was just as curious as I was. The evening before ... it happened, he told me he was going to poke around in the ruins. I told him about the two places where he might be able to get a torch and see into. I told him to be careful. I told him what the builder had said, I warned him.'

'I see.'

'And there's more, Inspector,' she continued now in flow, picking up the teapot and pouring the dark bronze liquid into the white china cups, sitting in their saucers. 'When I first went to the Centre for my first appointment, the doctor I saw was rubbish.' Amanda added milk to the cups and a sugar lump to Trelawney's. 'She wasn't really interested, and she seemed to feel totally out of place in the ... holistic environment, and she travelled for miles every day to get there, from Dover! That day ...'

There was a rumble at the door as Mrs Patel junior wrestled her two-year-old son's pushchair over the threshold.

Chapter 33

᪐

TRELAWNEY ASSESSES THE EVIDENCE

'Hello, Priya,' Julian and Amanda greeted her.

'Hey, everyone,' she called back. Amir's eyes lit up at the sight of Amanda for whom he had a special fondness.

'Hello, Amir,' she greeted her little friend with delight.

'Ammeeee!'

He wriggled in the restraining straps of his buggy. 'All right, give me a moment, you'll soon be out,' said his mother, undoing the harness. Once liberated, he staggered over to Amanda and opted for a seat on her lap.

'You sit down, Priya, and I'll get your cappuccino,' called Alexander. 'Mini carrot cake for the little 'un, is it?'

'Please.'

'I'll just warm it up, how 'e likes it.'

Amanda performed the introductions. 'This is Amir Patel, Inspector. His mother, Priya.'

'Hi,' she said, with a smile, then took out her phone to use a rare moment's peace to check her emails.

'Amir is also grandson to my GP. Dr Patel was the one who

told me about the Centre and gave me a referral.'

Amir stared at Trelawney.

'Amir, this is Detective Inspector Trelawney.'

'Hello, Amir.'

The toddler, unimpressed, indicated that he wanted to be free to roam once more, and Amanda placed him again on his feet. As she bent, the angle of her skirt altered, and her IKEA pencil wand slipped from her shallow pocket. It rattled onto the floor under the table.

Amanda's face blanched and she gave a quick intake of breath. But the cavalry was at hand. Tempest who had settled beneath her chair, planted his body over the short wooden stalk, and Amir was already crawling in to retrieve it.

'Kitty!' he said with pleasure. Amir reached under the cat and passed the pencil up to Amanda. He put a finger to his lips with wide eyes. Amanda took it, nodding. Amir liked pretending they had secrets.

By the time Amada straightened up in her seat, she had recovered her complexion and her composure, and said,

'Thank you, Amir. That's very kind of you.'

'Amir!' called Priya. 'Be gentle with the kitty now!'

Amir toddled off.

'You're an IKEA fan, then, I see,' remarked Trelawney.

'Absolutely,' Amanda responded readily.

'Surprising, given that you're a furniture restorer.'

'Yes, you'd think the cottage would be stuffed full of Sheratons and Chippendales. It does have a lot of old stuff that my grandparents accumulated over the years, but my room is wall-to-wall IKEA, I assure you. And their little pencils are so handy for the workshop.'

'So handy that you carry one with you at all times,' he observed lightly, as though teasing her.

'You never know when you might need to write things down,' she countered.

'Many people make notes on their phone,' Trelawney

suggested.

'Yes, this being the 21st century and all! I suppose I'm just old school. You have your police notebook, don't you?' Amanda pointed out.

'True, I suppose I'm just old school too,' he agreed pleasantly. 'But we digress. You were telling me about your first day at the Centre.'

'Yes,' Amanda continued, from where she'd left off. 'I met most of the therapists. They were there on contract for one month only. Well, over time, I noticed more than one suddenly vanished and was replaced. Toby Sidiqi said it didn't make sense, because the Centre was charging really low rates for the therapists to rent the therapy rooms. And why would any of them just leave, and without telling any of their colleagues?'

'Well, maybe they were only interested in the one-month contract. Perhaps they moved on to other posts that were more reliable than freelancing,' theorised Trelawney.

'I guess so.'

'And some people do make long commutes, although it *is* strange that a doctor would take up such a job that she felt ill-suited to. Perhaps she hoped to adjust to it over time, especially if it was well-paid.'

'I suppose so.'

'I could dismantle all of these items one by one, Miss Cadabra, as a defence counsel would do, by the way. But taken all together, they may amount to something, especially as you are a local, with some familiarity with the site and its development.'

'Yes, I am, and I expect you won't be comfortable with this ....'

'Go ahead,' Trelawney encouraged her.

'That place, Lost Madley, dog walkers don't go there, the trees don't grow leaves, and the birds don't sing. Something happened there.'

'Well, I couldn't comment on that. I'm not sure it's admissible evidence.'

'The point is, that Dr Sidiqi said he was going to look at the ruins, and the next morning, he was ... deceased,' said Amanda.

'So you think that there is something in the ruins that someone didn't want him to find?'

'That's right.'

'Do you know whom he told that he was going to dig around?' Trelawney asked.

'Well ... he wasn't discreet. Honestly, he was like a little boy who'd discovered a new playground, and wanted to tell all his friends about it. And anyone could have overheard us at the Snout and Trough, but to answer your question ... only me as far as I know ...'

'Hmm. That could be rather incriminating. Where were you on Tuesday evening, Miss Cadabra?'

'I was at home.'

'Do you have any witnesses?'

'Just my cat ... I met Dr Sidiqi at the Snout and Trough for lunch, and that's when he said he was going to do some investigating that evening, and I went home. I went back to the workshop then just did the usual things in the evening. I don't have an alibi, do I?' she said with uneasy realisation. 'Then again ... I don't know how to make a centrifuge explode.'

'Has that been established as the cause of death?'

'I don't know. No one will tell me anything. But it certainly looked that way. It all flew apart, and a chunk of metal hit him on the head.'

'Have you ever visited the ruins, Miss Cadabra?' Trelawney enquired.

'No, not before the pegging out, when I went there with some of the other villagers. Anyway, how could I have got in and out without being seen by Bill?'

'Bill?'

'Bill MacNair, he's security, sits at the desk at night between making his rounds,' Amanda explained.

'Anyone entering the lab would have had to have come past

him?'

'Yes, the lab's at the end of the north wing of the Centre. There is a fire door but it's alarmed, and anyway, someone would have left tracks in the mud if they'd left that way.'

'And Mr MacNair says no one came in after Dr Sidiqi?'

Amanda shook her head. 'I don't know.'

Jules was passing with some used dishes from a table near the window.

'Excuse me for overhearin' but that I can answer. Bill was in here that day. Ever so upset he was, wasn't he, Sandy?'

'Oh, ever so,' agreed his partner. 'White as a sheet, he was. Said he'd lose his job for sure this time.'

'This time?' queried Amanda.

'Oo, yes,' said Jules, 'soon after he started there, someone said there'd been complaints about his conduct. What a cruel thing to say. He's such a gentleman, isn't he, Sandy?'

'Oh yes, he comes in 'ere, lovely manners.'

'Someone had said he didn't have no references, and he says "I've never needed references". Mr Gibbs give 'im 'is first job when he come out of the army and knows 'im for an honourable man and a good worker. Then, after what happened ... well, it was on his watch, he says, even though he swears he never saw a soul go by the lab after the doctor had gone in there.'

Steel heels clacked on the floor, attracting everyone's attention to The Big Tease door. Samantha, Prada shorts and top under a transparent Chanel mac, topped off with Dior shades and wafting the scent of RawChemistry, entered.

Chapter 34

༄

MISS GIBBS MEETS HER MATCH, AND AMANDA ASKS

With bored irritation, Samantha Gibbs glanced at the counter, and sat down at a table near the window.

She swept the shop with a disdainful glance, until it encountered Trelawney. Anyone watching could see her brain visibly clocking his pleasant features, fair hair and fit physique, under white shirt and tie. Amanda knew Samantha was recognising her as 'that girl who'd been at Lords', sizing Amanda up as no competition. I'll bet, thought Amanda, that she's the type with predatory instincts that likes a bit of a fight.

Samantha slowly took off her sunglasses, crossed her legs, swept her tongue over her glossed mouth and gently brushed her long dark hair away from her face. Trelawney's lips twitched. He'd had both the guilty perpetrator and the insecure witness pull this stunt.

'Oh no,' sighed Amanda quietly.

'You know this person?' he asked, in an undertone.

'It's Samantha Gibbs, daughter of the Centre CEO.

Actually, one day I saw her coming out of the doors leading to the lab. I had no idea Dr Sidiqi knew her. I didn't really think anything of it.'

'But you and he were beginning to see one another?'

'Nothing serious. He was the most incorrigible flirt.'

'Hmm, not sure Miss Gibbs looks the type to share her men.'

Miss Gibbs had plainly been planning to get the staff to come and wait on her, but she changed her mind, given that approaching the counter would give her the chance to sashay by Trelawney. It would also be an opportunity to get away from the cat with the toxic yellow eyes, threatening to adorn her designer boots with its grey hairs.

Trelawney returned his attention to the trifle. He sampled a spoonful. 'This is excellent,' he said to Amanda.

'Yes, it's pretty good here, isn't it?' said Samantha, in an unaccustomed attempt at chattiness.

'It is,' responded Amanda.

'The only decent place in this *dismal* hole,' Miss Gibbs drawled. 'The coffee at the Centre café is un*bear*able. Like totally.'

'Have you been visiting your father there?' Amanda asked in a friendly tone.

Samantha's gaze flickered to Trelawney then back to That Girl.

'Oh hi, we met at Lords, didn't we?' she said, unenthusiastically.

'That's right,' agreed Amanda.

The vamp looked at Trelawney. 'But I don't think *you* were there. I'm sure I would have remembered you,' she purred.

'I was not present on that occasion, no,' agreed Trelawney, in a formal voice.

She held out her pointed-nail-art-adorned hand to him. 'Samantha Gibbs.'

He stood up and took it. 'Thomas Trelawney.'

'Detective Inspector, he is,' called out Alexander, 'so just you watch yerself, Miss!' he added jovially.

'Okay, yeah, so … you're investigating what happened at the Centre,' deduced Samantha, pulling up a chair and sitting next to the inspector.

'Have you given a statement already, Miss Gibbs?' he asked, continuing his policeman's tone.

'Why would I give a statement?' Samantha challenged him.

'You did know the deceased,' he pointed out.

'Yah, but … I didn't kill him!' she objected, back-footed.

'Where were you on the evening of the 9th October, Miss Gibbs?'

'I dunno. I'd been shopping that afternoon, dropped in to see Tobes in his lab, and then left just before Daddy did. He was working late with Robin. I went home. I did some stuff and then … we had dinner.'

'We?'

'Daddy and I.'

'Was your father already home when you arrived?'

'We got home at around the same time, I think. What's this all about? Am I a suspect or something? How glam!' she added, in an attempt to recover her fashionable-young-seductress-about-town performance.

'This is a serious matter, Miss Gibbs,' said Trelawney, turning a steely gaze that Amanda had not previously witnessed upon the young woman.

Samantha got up impatiently. 'I don't have to answer any more of your questions.'

'That's quite right,' replied Trelawney coolly. 'You don't.'

Samantha shouldered her bag, pivoted on one heel and flounced out of the shop.

'Well!' exclaimed Amanda, '"Thou dissembler, thou!"'

He grinned.

'Was that strictly ethical?' she enquired.

'"I didn't lie. She *assumed* I was an investigating officer on the case.'

She leaned closer to him and said quietly, 'Is that one of your ... techniques?'

'You wish to gather information, do you not, Miss Cadabra?' asked Trelawney.

'Well ...'

He continued, 'You feel frustrated at being excluded from a possible crime, into which you may have some insight. I do understand.'

Amanda wondered if he did. She responded, 'I know you must have dealt with busybodies and people who may have just impeded your investigation by getting in the way. But what if I could come up with a theory that could explain the facts?'

'You'd have to support it with evidence,' Trelawney pointed out.

'Then the police would listen?'

'Of course,' he confirmed.

'Look ... when I was in the lab ... after I discovered ... the untimely death ... I ... sensed something. If I could get back in there, I'm sure it would come to me, ... something that could explain what had happened.'

'I see. And you asked if you could go back?'

'Yes, but ... well, they were very nice about it. The detective sergeant said I could have five minutes, but the constable would have to be with me, and I know it won't work unless I'm *alone* in there!'

'That's unfortunate. You asked the sergeant then if you could do that?'

'Yes, and he said no, and so .... As it's so vital to solving the case, or at least shedding some more light on it, could you ...?'

He looked at her questioningly.

'If you could maybe ask on my behalf?' Amanda entreated him.

'What?'

'If you could explain and ask the sergeant if I could —'

'I'm sorry, Miss Cadabra, I couldn't possibly interfere with the procedure of an investigation being conducted by another police force. This case has nothing to do with me. I have no jurisdiction here. You must understand that.'

'But he's a sergeant and you're an inspector. Doesn't that make a difference?'

'It would be unthinkable to pull rank. It would be highly inappropriate for me to even try, and there will be an inspector and possible a chief inspector in charge of this case.'

'But —'

'I really don't think you understand the protocols involved. I'm sorry. I will help you in any way I can, but I cannot do this,' he said with finality. 'I think it's best if we change the subject, Miss Cadabra. I don't want to fall out with you over this.'

Amanda was flushed with embarrassment.

'I'm sorry Inspector, I see now that it was highly improprietous of me to have asked you. Thank you for explaining. And I appreciate the information that you did get for me.'

'However underhanded the means?' he said with a smile.

'Quite!'

He looked around. 'So this, I gather, is the hub of the village?'

'Yes, even more so than The Sinner's Rue, according to my solicitor.'

'Everyone comes in here then?'

'Pretty much.'

'First port of call for visitors and new residents or is that the pub?' asked Trelawney.

'I'm not sure. I don't really notice things like that, to be honest. Alex and Jules would know. Jules?'

'Yes, lovely?'

'Would you say,' Amanda asked him, 'that this is the first place visitors, and people who have just moved in, would come to?'

'I like to think so. We open long before the pubs. We don't get much passing trade; Sunken Madley is off the beaten track.

Mr Ford come in 'ere when he first arrived, when he was moving into Madley Towers ... Jonathan Sheppard, that nice librarian ... yes, I remember he liked lemon tea, not many do .... Miss James, the model, she likes our fruit salad, doesn't she, Sandy? Oh, he does a *lovely* fruit salad, does Alexander. Then there's the lot up the Centre, but of course, they don't live in, except for Bill. Hmm, no, that's it, really. Right, must get on.'

Trelawney asked, 'And what does the village make of them all?'

'I think they're liked in various ways. I couldn't really say,' Amanda responded vaguely.

'How about you?'

'Yes, I like them all. Yes, why not?'

Trelawney was paving the way to execute Hogarth's commission.

'Do you ever feel ... watched?'

'Yes,' Amanda replied at once, 'all the time. I live in a village!'

Trelawney smiled. 'I mean do you ever feel like you're under surveillance of a sinister nature?'

Amanda remembered asking Aunt Amelia that. How strange, she thought. I wonder if I should mention it? Yes, no ... she and Amelia had always thought in terms of further afield. But what if the watcher or watchers were *here?* Right here in Sunken Madley? No, surely not.

'No,' she said aloud. 'Only if I've just watched a thriller and am feeling fanciful!'

'All right. Hm ... getting back to our mystery at the lab,' Trelawney said smoothly. 'Even though I can't help you in the way that you want me to, maybe I can assist in another way. Maybe together we can work out who dunnit. Or, at least, put together some theories. Who had means, motive and opportunity?'

Chapter 35

❧

THE SUSPECTS

'Well. Bill MacNair was the only one on site when it happened. He had control of the CCTV and he had the opportunity. He was in the army. What if he was a sapper? An engineer. He could have the know-how to rig the centrifuge so it would blow up. But motive? Oh.' She stopped in embarrassment as Bill appeared at the door.

'Hello, lassie.'

'Hello, Bill.'

Alexander hailed him, 'Come in Bill! I've just done a batch of pies. I know how you like your pies.'

'That I do, laddie, that I do.'

'Sit down and I'll make you a nice cuppa tea, just 'ow you like it. Cheer you up. Come on, it can't be that bad.'

'Oh, I don't know.' He looked at Trelawney. 'I don't really want to talk aboot it, in front of strangers. No offence, sir.'

'I'm Thomas Trelawney.'

Bill eyed him cautiously. 'You's a policeman.'

Amanda put a hand on Trelawney's arm to stay his reply.

'Yes, and he wants to help. Don't you?' she said, looking at the inspector meaningfully.

'I most certainly wish to serve the cause of justice at all times, Mr …?'

'Bill,' MacNair supplied.

'Bill.'

'Well, it's bad. I can't talk to them, those coppers up at the Centre. They think I did it, I know they do. Why would I do sech a thing? I barely knew the young fella. I can't think why anyone would want to harm him. Sech a nice laddie, he was. I remember the day he came for his interview, bless him. Oh, but that was a bad day. Mr Gibbs called me ina his office, and told me there'd been a complaint made about me. I could'na believe it.'

'Here you are, Bill. Nice cup o' tea.'

'Thanks Jules. I've never had a complaint before. I went to the café to recover, and then I saw Mr Gibbs and Mr Streeter come in. And I could tell they'd had a fallin' oot. Those two, been friends since they were tots. They're like a married couple, and here they were having had a row about me. I felt that bad.'

'Did you hear anything they said?' Amanda asked, gently.

'Only Mr Streeter saying, "I thought you trusted ma judgement." That was all.'

'Here's your pasty, Bill.'

'Cornish?' asked Trelawney curiously.

'Nay, these are Forfar Bridies!'

'He give us the recipe, didn't you, Bill?' said Jules.

'Oh yes, it's more of a pie than a pasty so your special Cornish dish is safe,' grinned Bill. 'Ye are Cornish, yes? Wi' a name like Trelawney.'

'Spot on,' Thomas agreed with a grin.

'Now don't you worry about all that business,' encouraged Jules soothingly. 'Most likely it was just an accident with the machine.'

'But why?' asked Bill, anxious again once more. 'I remember the day the equipment was delivered. It was at half eight in the mornin' so I was still on duty. They said sorry they were airly. Supposed to be coming at 9.30 Someone was supposed to be tekkin' delivery but they didn't have a name. Anyways, I let them in. I checked it. It didn't come from the manufacturer. It was second hand, and I know enough about machines to know that they need to be tested and certified. So I asked the delivery guys and they showed me the paperwork. It was kosha when it arrived. Nothin' wrong wi' it. So why did it go wrong that night?'

'Bill,' asked Amanda, 'do you know whose idea it was to create that new lab for Dr Sidiqi?'

'Nay, lassie, but I'd guess Dr Crossley. They want to get a big contract and be able to say that the lab upstairs would be dedicated to that client. He outfitted the big lab up there, and is the one with the know-how and the contacts, so I'd say it was him.'

Bill began wrapping his pasty in a napkin.

'Look, if ye don't mind, I'll tek this with me and be away to The Grange. Looks like it might come on to rain.'

'The Grange?' queried Amanda, surprised.

'Yes, those nice ladies are putting me up until they tek the crime scene tape down off of the Centre, and I can get back to my flat there. If I ever do.'

'Let me put that in a proper box for you, Bill,' said Julian, bringing one from behind the counter.

'Bill,' said Amanda, 'do you mind if I ask you one more thing before you go, please?'

'All right, lassie. Jest the one noo.'

'Thank you. It's about the day of the inauguration.'

'Aye?'

'After the speeches and everything, Samantha Gibbs and Ryan Ford both disappeared and —

'I know what you're thinkin', Miss, but you'd be wrong. Mr Ford had to be away to his cricket practice or a team meetin'. Nay, it wasn't Mr Ford Miss Gibbs was after.' Bill wasn't ready to say any more. But Amanda remembered something.

'Wait … there was someone else Damian was looking for … yes … for the photographs … it was …'

Bill knew she'd got there by herself and confirmed, 'Aye. Sir Michael.'

'Really?'

'Yes, I'm sorry to say.'

'But he's married,' objected Amanda naively.

'He is that, but you've seen what Samantha's like when she's playin' off her tricks. She likes men with power, and she was trainin' the full force of her charm on the man, and, bein' a good deal older, he was flattered out of his senses.'

'Good grief. Well, thank you, Bill.'

'See you all.'

The assembled group bade him farewell and meant it.

'Hm,' said Amanda, cryptically. 'Yes, well, I don't think Bill did it.'

'I'm inclined to agree,' said Trelawney.

'Then … let's see.' She began ticking them off on her fingers. 'Yes, Robert Crossley. If he was the one that knew about, and ordered, the equipment, then, surely, he'd know how to gemmy the centrifuge. His wife said he behaves oddly, but he's a genius.

'Damian Gibbs, the CEO. He's smart. What if he chose to build on this site because he knew something was down there and it would give him the opportunity to get it out?

'Robin Streeter. He's smart too, but building the Centre wasn't his idea, and he doesn't seem the type. And no motive.

'Samantha Gibbs. She's bored, predatory. Bored enough to commit murder as a diversion? Possibly. I'd wondered if Ryan Ford could have been an accomplice.'

'Ryan Ford?' queried Trelawney.

'Cricketer. Plays for Middlesex. Village VIP and golden boy. Samantha was all over him like a hot rash at Lords, and again at the inauguration of the Centre. Plus later they were both nowhere to be seen. I guess he was just a decoy. But also, one day I saw her coming from the direction of Sidiqi's office.

'So I wondered if she and Ryan could have colluded to kill the doctor. Or if she had acted alone out of a fit of jealousy? And just because she's an obnoxious fashion-victim doesn't mean she's not intelligent enough to figure out how to interfere with the medical equipment.'

'That's generous of you,' interpolated Trelawney blandly. Amanda suspected him of teasing her and ignored it.

'Plus,' she went on, 'with "Daddy" frequently visiting the Centre, she has the ideal excuse to wander in and out at will. However, given what Bill has just told us ... that put's paid to my Samantha-Ryan conspiracy theory. And it turns out she wasn't interested in Dr Sidiqi. I guess he was small fry by comparison with a sponsor of her father's company and the Middlesex cricket team. So much for my jealous rage shot-in-the-dark.'

'Yes,' commented Trelawney, with the hint of a twinkle in his eye, 'I thought you looked disappointed.'

She directed a quelling look in his direction, and said repressively, 'No comment.'

'Do go on,' he invited her, airily.

'The therapists? The old ones .... No ... wait. The acupuncturist, Robin's niece ... no. That's all of the people that were there that day. None of them seems like ... you know ... killers. Then there's me. I wasn't there that day, but I don't have an alibi. I suppose I could find out how to damage a machine if I looked online.'

Trelawney observed Amanda as she sat and thought. She looked up.

'There's a big old house in the village called The Grange. I've been doing some work there. It's owned by Miss de Havillande, and she lives there with her friend Miss Armstrong-Witworth. Miss de Havillande is a grand, fiery, old lady, but Miss Armstrong-Witworth, you'd think wouldn't say boo to a goose. *But* ... you know what?'

'What?'

'She was a spy!'

'Well, well.'

'After the war. She eliminated actual people. Said it was all ages ago, and she doesn't have a pistol or anything now. And I like her, I almost feel like a traitor including her in the list, but just want to be fair to everyone else on it and be thorough. Anyway, I know she has the ... psychological capacity to make someone pop their clogs.'

'Motive?' asked Trelawney.

'I don't know .... What if there was something down there, in the pub under the Centre site, something incriminating that she didn't want to be found. Any of the old people ... Miss de Havillande or Miss Armstrong-Witworth. Miss Armstrong-Witworth is electronically minded. She told me, how she, after the war — what time is it in Thailand?' Amanda asked abruptly.

'Erm. Let's see,' replied Trelawney, looking at his watch. 'About seven hours ahead of us.'

'Late but not dead of night?' Amanda checked.

'Exactly.'

'Do you mind if I make a call?'

'Not at all.'

'I'm going to go into the ladies. I don't want to be overheard. Just in case. I'll be right back.'

'Take your time.' Trelawney watched Amanda disappear into the back of the café. Interesting, he thought. She has a creative and objective mind. The way that she's applying it to the Centre case .... And yet, when he had asked her for a possible explanation of how an anomaly had appeared on a Cornish road, on the day her family was on its way to its collective fate, she had been almost off-hand, and pretty much told him to his face that she wasn't there to do his job for him.

Meanwhile, Amanda checked the cubicles. All clear. The chances of Claire picking up were slim, but it was worth a try. She was in luck.

'Hi, Ammy. Everything OK?' came the voice of her best friend.

'Yes, hope I haven't disturbed you?'

'No, just out of the shower, ready for bed. We start at an indecently early hour. What's up?'

'You have a location manager, don't you?' asked Amanda.

'Dan? Yes.'

'He knows the UK?'

'Like the back of his hand,' replied Claire.

'Hertfordshire? Around here?'

'Yes, I'd say so.'

'Can you ask him what was going on around here during the war? The second one. There's very little online about the villages here then.'

'OK, hold on, I'll call you back,' said Claire, never one to let the grass grow under her feet.

Amanda was so excited that she had to use the facilities. She washed her hands, used the drier, keeping an eye on her phone, and then leaned against the sinks, waiting and watching the little screen.

Finally, it rang.

'Darling? Dan says aircraft. Yes, Herts; it was the hub of the aircraft industry. Yes, long gone but he says if you're digging for info about your area, then that's where you should look. OK? Why, what am I missing?'

'I'll tell you all about it when you get home!' said Amanda.

'OK, darling.'

'Sweet dreams.'

'Thanks. Night, night.'

Amanda came back to the table. 'Aircraft,' she stated.

'Well, I can see that you're hot on the trail now, Miss Cadabra,' Trelawney said, reaching for his jacket. He took out his wallet.

'No, no, my treat,' Amanda insisted. 'I asked you to come up here.'

'All right. Thank you. Well, I'm glad I could be of some assistance.'

'Yes, you have, oddly enough,' said Amanda. 'I mean, in a roundabout way and others too,' she added awkwardly. They both got up and Amanda went to the counter and paid. Jules and Alexander bade them farewell and they left the café.

'If there's anything else, do let me know,' said Trelawney, kindly. 'I'm just down the road until Sunday.'

'Thank you.'

She waved him off, and then headed for the library, taking off her cardigan as she went. The humidity in the atmosphere was rising.

Chapter 36

❧

Thomas is Disturbed, and Into The Past

Trelawney sat on his bed as he pressed Hogarth's number on his phone.

'Hi, Mike?'

'What news, Sherlock?'

'It was a bit awkward. More than a bit.'

'Oh?'

'She wanted me to use whatever clout she thought I have, to get her back into the crime scene, the actual lab, by herself!'

'Really?' said Hogarth with interest.

'Wanted me to pull rank. It was all rather uncomfortable.'

'Why did she want that, Thomas?'

'Oh, some nonsense about sensing things, and if she could get back in there something would come to her. So much esoteric mumbo jumbo,' he said dismissively.

'I see,' commented Hogarth.

'I did what I could to help. Talking it all through. I think I redeemed myself to some extent, but I could see that she thought I was pretty useless.'

'You will indeed have to redeem yourself, Thomas,' Hogarth said firmly.

'How?'

'Next time she asks for your help you say, "Yes, Miss Cadabra."'

'What if it's unethical?' asked Trelawney, alarmed.

'Find a way to *make* it ethical.'

'Good grief …. All right,' Thomas agreed reluctantly.

'How's your mother after your little chat about your father and co?'

'Fine. Behaving as though the conversation never took place. That's all right with me. Probably for the best. Oh there was one odd thing about that lunch in the Big Tease.'

'Oh?'

'Well, … she knew how I like my tea. Why on earth would she know that? What woman in this day and age notices how a man likes his tea?'

Hogarth was suppressing his laughter valiantly at the other end of the phone. He got control of his mirth long enough to say, 'Yes, rather old-fashioned. More the sort of thing her grandmother would do.'

'Well, quite,' Thomas agreed, then, unaccountably, found himself not all at home with the thought. His mind deftly switched to a new anomaly. 'Oh, there was one other thing. Miss Cadabra dropped a pencil.'

'In the spirit of dropping a handkerchief?' asked Hogarth, with amusement. 'Is she after your hand, Thomas?'

'No, of course not. Nothing like that,' returned Trelawney, a trifle testily.

'Was there something remarkable about this writing implement?' Hogarth enquired.

'No, it was just an ordinary IKEA pencil. It wasn't that; it was her reaction. She turned white and gave a little gasp. That monstercat of hers sat on it, and then a baby she knows picked it up for her. And there she was, completely back to normal in the blink of an eye. It was all over in seconds. Why would a woman in a skirt and cardigan be carrying a pencil, anyway? No woman I've ever known carried pencils when she was dressed up.'

'It's not unheard of,' equivocated Hogarth.

'No, but why get so flustered when she dropped it?'

'Thomas,' Hogarth said carefully, 'have you seen a pencil like that before, that someone took special care of?'

Trelawney replied at once, 'No.' Then, 'Yes … no … I — I don't know.'

'Never mind. It's an interesting footnote. OK, well, thanks for keeping me in the loop. Enjoy your weekend now,' said Hogarth calmingly.

'You too, Mike.'

So … said Hogarth to himself, you have a pocket wand, do you, Amanda? And our young Thomas has seen one too, and that's what disturbs him. Now, where would he have seen one? Bertil Bergstrom doesn't hand them out like sweets, and I'll swear he'd never give one to any of the Flamgoynes. Still, there are underground retailers of such things.

He mused. Not like Senara and Perran's granddaughter to let something like that happen. Things are hotting up, Miss Cadabra, you're going to have to be a lot more careful than that …. On the other hand, it was only with Thomas …. Interesting, that it should accidentally fall into *his* view … Hmmm, magic wands can, every now and then, have a will of their own ….

So now young Thomas, you have two things that are deeply disturbing you. Disturbing you so much that you can barely think about them, I would guess, let alone talk to me about them. The smell of Amanda Cadabra's workshop and the pencil. What disturbs you is that you recognise them but don't want to contemplate how or why. Ah well. You'll come to it. In your own time.

I just wish I knew how much time we have.

***

'Tempest. I haven't been able to see the wood for the trees,' Amanda announced to her cat, 'I've been thinking too locally.'

She pushed open the glass doors of Sunken Madley library, and Mrs Pagely looked up from the computer screen on the counter.

'Hello, Amanda,' she said with pleasure.

'Hello, Mrs Pagely. I need to know,' responded Amanda, coming straight to the point, 'about the aircraft industry around here during the war.'

'Let's see. This would have been south Hertfordshire then …. De Havilland —'

'As in Miss de Havillande?' asked Amanda eagerly.

'Different family,' responded the librarian. 'I did ask when I first arrived. De Havilland would have been the closest manufacturer to here. You could visit the museum at Salisbury Hall.'

'Salisbury Hall?'

Hall … the ghost had said 'The Hall' not 'the hall'!

'Were they doing something special there during the war?' asked Amanda intently.

'It's where the design team worked on the Mosquito prototype.'

Amanda had made a model of a Mosquito when she was a teenager. It was the fastest, lightest fighter-bomber of its time.

'It was top secret even from the British government,' continued Mrs Pagely.

'Why?' asked Amanda.

'The government wanted a lot of bureaucrats interfering in the design. In the end, de Havilland was proved right and Whitehall rubber-stamped it, but while it was in the making it was kept highly confidential.'

The ghost had said … the plans, recalled Amanda. He had

seen 'the same person who stole the plans'. … Could they have been the Mosquito design schematics? Why would a carpenter like the ghost have known about that? Was he on the design team?

Aloud, Amanda asked, 'Do you know anything about the design team? Would they have had any cabinet makers, carpenters on it?'

'Oh, yes, it was made of wood. The Wooden Wonder they called it.'

The wonder …. He'd said, 'Have you been working on the wonder too?' The Wonder!

So that's what the ghost was telling her. But what did it have to do with Toby's death? The ghost had said 'it was the same person.' But Granny always said the dead cannot harm the living.

Mrs Pagely was speaking. 'Once it went into production, and they made about 7000 of them, it was made all over the place, here and in Canada, in big and small workshops, even groups of ladies made parts for it. They were glad to do it.' She smiled. 'It helped us to win the war.'

'Strange, I've never visited Salisbury Hall; only the RAF Museum at Hendon,' Amanda said thoughtfully.

'That's the famous one, of course,' conceded Mrs Pagely. 'But for the Mosquito, it's the Hall, you want, my dear, the de Havilland Aircraft Museum. They have the actual prototype there, the DH98, in its glorious Trainer Yellow. They've even got one of the practice bouncing bombs. You would love it.'

Some plans for the Wooden Wonder were stolen. The same person, said the ghost, … did what? The ghost hadn't said. Amanda had half the puzzle now. But what was the *other* half and how did the two fit together? She needed to talk to the ghost again. But how?

Mrs Pagely was presenting her with three books. 'Here dear, this is everything we have on it. They don't say who was on the design team except for the chief designer Eric Bishop, I'm afraid, but here's a photograph of them, if that's any help. Do you want these?'

'Yes, please, Mrs Pagely.'

After withdrawing the books, Amanda came out of the library with Tempest around her feet. She looked up at the clouds stacking on the horizon. As quickly as possible, they went home and found her grandparents watching television and drinking their dimensional version of tea.

'Granny, Grandpa,' said Amanda urgently, 'the man I saw, what do you know about him?'

'Now, dear, what fun would it be, if we told you all of the answers?' said Senara over her shoulder.

'Fun! Fun?' said Amanda outraged, coming into the middle of the room. 'How is this fun? I found a body!'

'Your second one,' said Grandpa, with a congratulatory air. 'Well done. And this one's —'

'Grandpa! Granny! This isn't a *game*. Come on, please. I've used my resources. I tried using magic. I could only use a spell on poor Bill then found a policeman guarding the lab, and he was *standing* so I couldn't use it on him, and then I had to go and undo the first one, and it means I made ripples *twice*! For nothing! I tried Trelawney, and I'm not saying he was worse than useless or anything, but he wouldn't get me in. *Now* ....'

Grandpa looked at his wife, then said:

'Roses are red, Violet's blue.

Go for a visit then you'll know why too.'

'Violets?' queried Amanda. 'Violet! Miss Armstrong-Witworth's friend who lived in Lost Madley ... whose boyfriend was George. Thank you, Grandpa!'

Chapter 37

~

VIOLET, AND THE RESOURCE

Amanda phoned the Grange, and asked Miss Armstrong-Witworth if she was free.

'Could you, please, come with me to the residential home and introduce me to Violet?'

'Yes, dear, give me half an hour.'

Amanda arrived promptly, having got over her guilt at including Gwendolen in the list of suspects, and was admitted by Moffat, the ladies' general factotum.

'Off on a spree, are you, with Miss Armstrong-Witworth?' he asked Amanda.

'Er, yes,' she answered doubtfully.

'Don't you worry. Miss Armstrong-Witworth will take good care of you,' he reassured her.

The lady in question appeared from the drawing room.

'Ah, Amanda, I'm ready, Perhaps you could tell me on the way what this is all about. Though, it's only a very short journey.'

Amanda opened the Astra door for Miss Armstrong-Witworth then got in and started it up. Her friend looked over at the rear seat.

'I see young Tempest is with us. I don't think they'll be very happy about having you inside the house,' she said to him. 'Could you content yourself with exploring the grounds, do you think?'

Tempest raised his shoulders in the semblance of a shrug.

Miss Armstrong-Witworth turned back to Amanda. 'So do tell.'

'I think the death of the doctor at the lab is somehow connected to something that happened during the war. Mrs Pagely showed me this.'

Without taking her eyes off the road, Amanda pulled a folded photocopy from her jacket, and handed it to Miss Armstrong-Witworth.

'That man looking out of his door was a carpenter, judging by what's in his hand. I think he was connected somehow to the Mosquito design team at Salisbury Hall. I think he might have been Violet's George, and Violet might be able to tell us more.'

'She's not always terribly lucid, you know,' Miss Armstrong-Witworth warned Amanda.

'No harm in trying. Do you recognise him?'

'Hmm, yes, it is like him, as far as I remember. It was a long time ago. How is this connected to Dr Sidiqi's death?'

'I think someone stole some design schematics. Someone who was in the building that's underneath where the lab is. Toby, the doctor, told me that he was going to explore the ruins that night, the night he was killed. Someone knew that, knows what's under there, and killed him before he could find out, or before he could tell anyone.'

'The design and the building of the prototype was top secret,' agreed Miss Armstrong-Witworth, 'but it must have leaked somehow. There was a spy, you know?'

'A spy?'

'A German spy. He was caught in the area. And it would also explain the bombs being dropped around here.'

'You think they knew about the building of the prototype?' asked Amanda.

'They wouldn't have seen where it was being constructed from the air. The hangar looked just like an ordinary barn. That was the idea, to keep it hidden. This was a pretty rural area, so why bomb it? But if someone had given them some idea of where it might be, not exact coordinates, perhaps, but enough to stand a chance of hitting it, then that would explain why bombs fell on Little Madley. We're a few miles away from the hangar where the prototype was designed and built, but that distance is soon covered in an aeroplane, you know.'

'I see. Yes, of course,' agreed Amanda.

'The left fork here, then it's on the left ... Yes. You can drive straight in. I telephoned and checked that it would be convenient.'

They called in at reception, and were standing at the desk when they heard a familiar voice behind them.

'How nice to see you, Gwendolen,' said Miss Hempling, former proprietress of what was now The Big Tease.

'Winifred! My dear,' responded Miss Armstrong-Witworth with pleasure, holding out her arms. The two old friends greeted one another warmly.

'And Amanda. How lovely!'

'Hello, Miss Hempling.'

'Who are you here to see?'

'Violet,' said Miss Armstrong-Witworth.

'Oh, Violet,' said Miss Hempling sadly. 'I think she'll soon be going ahead of us, if you know what I mean. But she'll be pleased to see you, Gwendolen. We get a lot of visitors here, you know. I'm sure I get more than when I lived in the village! Come this way. I'm sure they won't mind if I show you in.'

They were walking along a thickly carpeted hallway, when a tall, fair, comely young woman, with a kindly, good-natured air of efficiency, met up with them.

'Oh, Megan, that's good. I was just taking my friends,

Gwendolen and Amanda here, to see Violet. Perhaps you want to take them there now. I was just on my way to beat young Harold at backgammon again,' Miss Hempling said mischievously.

'You do that,' encouraged Megan cheerfully.

'I'll leave you with Megan, She's from Australia, you know. Isn't that nice? And she's a darling.' Miss Hempling hurried off to her tournament with the hapless 78-year-old Harold.

'Hello, ladies,' Megan greeted them. 'I've seen you before, heven't I, Gwindolen?'

'Oh yes, I've popped in to see Violet from time to time.'

'She appreciates it, I know thet. I'm afraid our Violet's not long for this world. We can just make her comfortable. I think she'll be pleased to hev a bit of company, but try not to tire her out.'

'Of course,' responded Gwendolen, warmly.

Megan showed them into a well-lit, comfortable room and left them to it. A lady, white wispy-haired and looking small as a child, lay in the bed. Gwendolen gestured to a seat by the wall for Amanda, and drew up a chair at the bedside for herself. She sat down and took the lady's hand.

'Hello, Violet, it's Gwendolen.'

Violet's clouded blue eyes gradually focused on the face near her, and recognition dawned.

'Gwennie, … you've come to see me.'

'That's right, Violet. You know who I am, don't you,' said Gwendolen.

'Oh yes, Gwennie. How are things at the house?'

'Very good.'

'I remember the old parties,' said Violet happily.

'We had such good times, didn't we?' agreed Gwendolen.

'The masks and the dancing, … it was lovely.'

'And Georgie,' Gwendolen added gently.

'Oh, my Georgie ….' Violet's eyes filled with tears. 'He was such a sweet boy ….'

'He was lovely.'

'He was half Canadian, did you know that, Gwennie?'

'Yes, Violet, you told me.'

'They'd been working with wood for generations. He was so proud of that, you know?'

'You used to meet him …,' gently prompted Gwendolen.

'We used to meet in the pub ….'

'The Apple Cart,' Gwendolen reminded her friend.

Violet laughed softly. 'The Apple Cart, … funny name …. Yes … meet … in that nice room with the fire ….'

'You remember the last time you met?' asked Gwendolen.

'Oh yes. I'll never forget it, not as long I live,' Violet said sadly. 'I met him in the bar …. He was already there, … he had something on his mind …. I could always tell when he had something on his mind, you know, Gwennie? Yes, you know what it's like when you're that close to someone …. He was telling me … and then the siren went ….'

Gwendolen nodded. Violet continued.

'I thought he was right behind me. It was dark and raining …. I didn't see that he wasn't right behind me …. He never came. We were all down the shelter and the bombs falling, … he never came ….'

'What was he telling you, … in the pub, Violet?'

'He didn't want me mixed up in it, … said it was a bad business ….'

'Miss Armstrong-Witworth,' whispered Amanda. Gwendolen looked round at her young friend.

'Did she see *every*one else from Little Madley apart from George in the shelter that night? Was anyone else *missing*?' Gwendolen nodded and turned back to the bed.

'Violet, … remember the siren went off and you ran through the rain and the dark to the shelter …'

'Yes, we were all piling in.'

'Were you *all* there? *Every*one from Little Madley?'

'Oh, yes,' Violet answered vaguely.

'Was everyone from Little Madley in there?'

'Yes … in the end ….'

'Someone came late?' asked Gwendolen.

'Yes ….' Violet's face grew troubled. 'That man … staying at The Apple Cart ….'

'He was visiting? Do you know where he was from?'

'He was … muttering ….'

'What about, Violet?'

'No …. Oh, I wish I could see my George again, Gwen …. What I wouldn't give to see my Georgie. I do sometimes, … I see him clear as day …. Oh, I'm so tired …. Do you mind if just close my eyes for a bit ….'

'That's all right, Violet. I'll come back another time, when you're rested.'

'Thank you, Gwennie.'

Miss Armstrong-Witworth bent and kissed the soft wrinkled cheek, and beckoned Amanda out of the room.

'Did you get what you wanted, Amanda?'

'Yes. Thank you.'

'Well, it seems that I was right,' remarked Miss Armstrong-Witworth with satisfaction.

'About what?' asked Amanda.

'It was long before I had my training as an agent, and it was only in retrospect, when I thought about it, that I suspected.'

'A spy in your midst?'

'Staying at the pub,' confirmed Gwendolen. 'After all, why would he be *there* and not staying with his family up the road? He was an engineer of some kind, I believe.'

'You think he got hold of some of the Mosquito plans? But how? And if he did, maybe he meant to hand them to the German who parachuted in?'

'But he couldn't, because the German was captured,' said Gwendolen.

'Maybe he hid them in the pub. Georgie got wise to it but was killed in the bombing raid before he could report it. That explains the history. But what is the connection with Toby's murder? And I do think it was murder.'

Gwendolen asked, 'Who, today, would stand to be affected by old plans in the ruins?'

'No one at the Centre is old enough to have been the spy,' Amanda said.

'What about their offspring or grandchildren?' suggested Miss Armstrong-Witworth. 'Reputation. Treason is a terrible stain. A stain upon the person, the village, the family. The sins of the fathers …'

'Really?' asked Amanda. 'In this day and age?'

'Oh yes, my dear. To some people, reputation is everything. And if such a person's parent had been selling secrets, more than one, they would have had money after the war; not a great deal but an unexplained amount.'

'If we could identify this man at The Apple Cart, it might lead us to Toby's killer.'

Miss Armstrong-Witworth said calmly, 'Leave that to Cynthia and me.'

Amanda stopped outside The Grange and pulled out her phone. 'Look at these, please, Gwendolen. I scanned them into my computer. This is a photo of the design team.'

'Ah yes.'

'And this is a photo of Lost Madley with the pub. You can see the rooms above and the proprietor, I think it is, outside. I'm sending these to your phone and email in case they're of any help.'

'All right, dear. We'll be your backroom boys! As soon as we have anything, you'll hear from us.'

'Thank you. There's just one more thing. Violet said that she and George used to meet in a room with a fire. Not the bar then?'

'No, the room was off the bar.'

'Miss — Gwendolen, what was the layout of the pub? Can you remember.'

'Oh yes. The door was on the left of the front of the building. You went in through that to the bar, the saloon. The bar where the drinks were served was opposite the entrance. If you followed the bar along to the right, you'd come to the door to the passageway that went out to the lavatories and the door to the cellar. But if you followed the line of the bar to the right-hand wall of the pub part, then you'd come to the room with the fire and the games, dominos and cards and so on.'

'Could that room be under the end of the Centre now?'

'Yes, I believe it could.'

'But the pub bit, the bar, that would be *next* to the Centre? Still exposed, well, at least, the top bit of the rubble?'

'Yes, I think that would be right.'

'Thank you, Gwendolen, you've been a great help.'

'Good. Well, off you go. Now be careful, Amanda,' Gwendolen cautioned her. 'You've been asking questions and talking to people, haven't you? Even one person ... it'll be all around the village, and whoever it is that's responsible for the doctor's death will know. You may not be safe, or the person may make a run for it. You probably don't have much time. Whatever you're planning, you need to do it quickly.'

'I understand, Gwendolen.'

The former spy got out of the car and waved as she entered The Grange. The clouds were directly above now and thickening. Amanda drove home. Tempest dashed in past her legs as soon as she opened the front door. Senara and Perran were in the hallway to greet her.

'You've been doing very well, dear,' said Granny, leading the way into the kitchen.

'Thank you,' said Amanda, as she filled the kettle. 'But I'm stuck now. Georgie — George has the answers. I need to interview him. I have to discover the connection between now and then. I *have* to get back to the lab. I've tried asking to get in, I've tried magic, and I've tried Trelawney ...'

A phone rang. A mobile phone. Amanda looked around. It was the ringtone of her grandmother's phone. She went to the bureau in the corner where the grandparents' paperwork was kept. She'd stashed their mobiles there too.

Amanda dug until she found it. It had been called by her own phone.

'OK, that was you, Granny. Very clever. You want me to call someone?'

A second ring tone sounded in the desk. 'Grandpa? All right,' said Amanda, 'I get it: someone on both your phones. This could take ages,' she grumbled taking the two devices to the sofa and sitting down, one in each hand comparing the contact lists. Tempest jumped up beside her, and wriggled under her arm and onto her lap.

'You going to help me?' she asked him.

She started with the A's.

'Aunt Amelia?'

'No, dear,' said Granny.

'B's. Dr Bertil Bergstrom?'

'No, Ammy,' Grandpa said, 'keep going.'

'I have to hurry! Miss Armstrong-Witworth told me. C's. Not Claire, I take it. D's?'

Abruptly, Tempest put up a paw, and pushed Perran's phone out of her hand and onto her lap. He swiped the screen with his paw several times, then meowed.

Amanda bent to look without touching it.

'Hogarth, Michael, Chief Inspector?'

Quickly she checked that it was on Senara's phone too. Yes.

'I'd completely forgotten about him. But I barely know him. He used to call from time to the time when I was little .... And then ....'

'He came sometimes when you were out studying at the library or outside,' Granny told her, 'but I'm sure he'll remember you, and know who you are.'

'I don't know.' Amanda felt reticent. 'Then again ... he was kind to me. Yes, I recall now .... You really think he'd help?'

'Trust us,' urged Grandpa.

'OK, I must say, I'd never have thought of him as one of

my "resources". But if you say so ….' Amanda got out her phone and stood up. She blew her nose. It seemed to help before a call she was nervous about making.

'Here goes.'

Chapter 38

❧

THE GETAWAY

Hogarth knew he was there. Getting bolder, if he'd come close enough to alert Alf.

He heard his neighbour's raised voice.

'Estate agent? Loik no estate agent I seen near 'ere, and I censure I knaw them all.'

Hogarth took a discreet look out of the window, at the man in the dark glasses and unseasonably warm jacket.

'New? Well, what office then? … Yas, you'd best be off. And don't you come nyst my neighbour's house agen without an appointment, vitty!'

The man retreated with one more studied look at Hogarth's house. Hogarth went into the garden to convene with Alf.

'D'you 'ear that?' asked his neighbour.

'Yes.'

'I'll give 'im a wor-wop round the 'ead if he comes round 'ere agen.'

'Don't worry, Alf, you won't have to. I'm off to my sister's tonight. Most likely, if I clear off for a bit, they'll lose interest.'

'Aar you, then? Give 'er my best, and don't you go werratting yourself about your house while a gone.'

Hogarth smiled. 'I won't. Thanks, Alf.'

'Enjoy yourself.'

Hogarth knew the stranger would be back and he'd bring others, and they wouldn't just be watching. One he could deal with, even two, but Hogarth knew it was not yet the time for an open confrontation. And as he said to his neighbour, if he disappeared, they'd find some other lead to follow. And he had inkling where they where hoping it would take them.

He phoned his sister.

'Tonight.'

'Right,' she replied. 'Possible tail?'

'Yes.'

'Hold on.' Her keyboard pattered furiously as she checked flights and train times.

Another call showed on his phone. The caller was 'Senara.'

'Can you hold, Vera?'

'Sure.'

Hogarth switched to incoming. 'Hello?'

'Chief Inspector Hogarth?'

He recognised the voice. 'Miss Cadabra, if I'm not mistaken. Unless your grandmother is calling from the Great Beyond.'

'Yes, that's right. Your number was still on her phone. I hope it's OK to call?'

'Of course. What can I do for you?' he asked, amiably.

'It's a bit difficult to explain. Would it be possible for you to come up? I know it's a long way and —'

'It's not that, Miss Cadabra, it's that I'm … I have an idea …. Can you hold?'

'Of course,' said Amanda.

'Vera. Flights from Heathrow or Stanstead?'

Patter patter. 'Heathrow 1.30 am. Seats available.'

'Earliest train from here?' Mike enquired.

Patter patter. 'Can Ken come now?' Vera asked him.

'OK to put you on hold?' Mike checked.

'Course.'

Hogarth picked up his landline phone and dialled his former-colleague-turned-cab-driver. 'Ken? It's Mike.'

'Alright?' asked Ken.

'Yes, can you come now?'

'Where to?'

'Plymouth station.'

'Ten minutes,' offered Ken.

'Make it twenty? I need to finish packing and lock up.'

'No problem. See you in twenty.'

'Vera? Yes, in twenty, I've said to Ken.'

'Good, you'll be in time for the next train from Plymouth to Paddington. Gets in at 6 o'clock.'

'OK, can you hold again?'

'Uhuh,' said his sister patiently.

'Miss Cadabra, how would you like to masquerade as a cabbie?

Taken aback but game, she replied 'OK. Let's see.' She looked out of the window. Claire's car was in the drive, where she always left it when abroad. Amanda was free to borrow it.

'From where to where?' she asked Hogarth.

'Paddington station to Heathrow.'

'Yes, I'll come in my neighbour's car; it's an Audi Sportback. Rather noticeable, I'm afraid; it's lime green. But, at least it doesn't have Cadabra Restoration and Repairs emblazoned along the side in gold letters.'

'That will be fine.'

'Shall I come into the station and hold up a piece of paper with your name on it?' Amanda offered.

'No need. I'll come out and find you.'

'I might have to circle the station,' she warned him.

'That's all right. I'll be wearing dark trousers and shirt with a light jacket. I'll have a medium-sized wheelie bag with me, and I'll be carrying a laptop case.'

'OK,' said Amanda

'6 o'clock.'

'I'll be there,' she promised.

'Good. Thanks. Behave like a cabbie, OK?' Hogarth reminded her.

'Yes.'

'And then we'll have a nice chat, and you can tell me what it's all about,' said Hogarth comfortingly.

'OK. See you then.'

Well! thought Amanda. Whatever is this about? Incognito, Hogarth catching a flight. He must be under some kind of surveillance. And I don't even know where he's going.

'Hello, Vera?'

'Still, here, Mike. Train and flight all booked. Got the emails?'

He checked. 'Yes. Thanks, Vee, you're a star. See you in the wee small hours then.'

'Yes, love.'

'Harry there?'

There was a pause, followed by Vera's affectionate laughter. 'He's gone to the kitchen to make your cheese puffs.'

'I won't be hungry,' said Mike.

'He says you always say that and you always are!' countered his sister.

'He knows best,' Mike conceded.

'That's what I always tell him,' said Vera warmly.

'He's a treasure.'

'So he is. I'm a lucky girl. See you before dawn.'

Hogarth hung up.

Efficiently, he packed the last few necessaries, and put his bags by the door. Next, he washed up the dishes in the sink. Finally, taking out the salt, he went to the back door and closed the gap in the line in front of the low step, intoning something under his breath.

Ken arrived in his black Toyota Prius, and Hogarth handed

his bags over the threshold with his right hand. He came out, closed and locked the front door then released the salt from his left fist, murmuring what, if anyone had heard him, would have sounded like an incantation. He took one look back at the cottage and nodded his head.

Hogarth got into the front passenger seat. Ken moved off, asking, 'Tail?'

'Almost certainly,' replied Hogarth calmly.

'Do you know who they are?'

'I can make an educated guess. Something to do with an old cold case. They're looking for someone. And they think that I can assist them with their enquiries,' said Mike, with irony. 'But I don't think whoever sent them has the resources to have them hanging around. If I buzz off for a bit, I'm hoping it'll all cool down.'

Ken was an ex-copper and knew his business. By the time they reached Plymouth station, he was pretty confident he'd lost whoever might be following them. He handed Hogarth his bags out of the boot.

'Don't you worry, Mike, I'll keep an eye out.'

'I know you will.'

'Take care. Give Vera my love.'

'Will do.'

Ken parked where he could see the station entrance, and in a nonchalant manner stood leaning against the car while he lit a cigarette. It was a year since he'd given up, but it was still a useful ruse for loitering.

After twenty minutes of watching who else entered, he concluded that either he had lost them or they were very, very good.

He sent a text:
Probably all clear.

Chapter 39

༃

Heston

Amanda, dressed in jeans and blazer, checked her Pocket-wand was on board, and headed south to Paddington.

Hogarth waved her down as she rounded the block for the second time and got in. Neither of them showed signs of recognising one another. Hogarth sat in the back passenger seat where he could use her rearview mirror to good effect. It was the height of the rush hour.

'We'll talk once we're on the M4,' the motorway west out of London to its principal airport. 'I'll let you concentrate on the road until then,' said Hogarth.

He guided her, so there was no uncomfortable silence, past Hyde Park, south through Kensington, west along Hammersmith, past Charring Cross Hospital to Chiswick.

At the first traffic lights in Chiswick High road, confident that they were free of watchers, Hogarth got out of the back seat and joined Amanda in the front of the car. Finally, they were joining the M4. It was slow near Kew Gardens, but after that, they gathered speed.

'There now. Well done navigating all of that,' Hogarth commended Amanda.

'Thank you. I don't often come to these parts,' she admitted.

'So. How have you been since the funerals?'

'Fine, thank you.'

'And how's Tempest the Terrible? Misbehaving himself, is he?'

'Same as ever; still thinks most humans are one of nature's most dreadful and embarrassing mistakes!'

About six miles before the airport, Hogarth asked Amanda to pull off the motorway into the Westbound Heston Services. Somewhat unprepossessing, they enjoyed the distinction of having been voted the worst service station in Britain. Nevertheless, the drinks were hot, and they managed to find comfortable seats with a measure of privacy.

'Right. Fire away, Miss Cadabra.'

'Please call me *Amanda*. I remember you used to when I was growing up. You were very kind to me. I haven't forgotten. I still have the clothes.'

'The clothes?'

'The ones you used to bring for my teddy bears.'

'Ah yes, Honey and er … Jam?'

Amanda laughed. 'Marmalade.'

'Yes, well, it was my sister who used to find them, you know,' Hogarth confessed.

'It was a kind thought, knowing I couldn't have much chocolate because of the asthma and finding me another present. Not that you needed to bring me anything. But I did appreciate it.'

'I'm glad. *Amanda*, then.'

'Well. Chief Inspe—'

'I'm retired you know. Call me *Mike*.'

'Oh, I couldn't!' Amanda had been brought up old-school-style to address her elders with respect.

'Let's see. How about Uncle Mike?'

'Yes ... I can manage that. As long as it's not too familiar,' replied Amanda.

'Not at all. I'd be honoured to have you call me Uncle Mike.'

She smiled, more at her ease. 'Uncle Mike, then.'

'So what's it all about?'

'Did Inspector Trelawney tell you? About the murder in the lab?'

'Yes, and how you found the body, and were consulting him about police procedure.'

'Then I expect he told you what I asked him to do?' she queried, with a slight blush.

'Indeed, and that was a bridge too far for him. But tell me about it anyway.'

'Yes, well, you see, while I was in there, in the lab, the day I found the body, I sensed ....' Amanda tailed off, uncertain of how best to express it.

'You saw something? Something you didn't think other people would believe?' Hogarth suggested helpfully.

'Yes, ... or ... or —'

'Would ridicule?' he guessed.

She nodded emphatically.

'Or just dismiss? Or think you were mad?'

'Yes! Yes, exactly!'

'And you think that what you experienced might be material — or should we say immaterial — evidence?'

'Yes. Oh, you do understand?'

'I do. "There are more things in heaven and earth..."'

'... than are dreamed of in our philosophy".' finished Amanda whole-heartedly.

'You didn't feel you could confide this to Inspector Trelawney?' asked Hogarth.

'Hardly!' Amanda exclaimed.

'Perhaps you are right. Or not. Time will tell. Are you going to tell *me* what you saw?'

This time Perran and Senara did not present themselves to guide Amanda. Her instinct was to trust him. She was in this too deep, he was her only hope. Miss Armstrong-Witworth had said she'd gone far enough to have put herself in danger. There was no going back.

Amanda asked tentatively, 'Do you know about … other dimensions?'

'I do. You saw someone from one? What most people would call a ghost?'

'Yes. He thought I was from his time, the 1940s. I could tell the period from the way he was dressed. I think his name is George. There's an elderly lady I know, who had a friend, called Violet, who lived in Little Madley. Violet had a boyfriend of that name. The last time Violet saw George was in the pub, on the night of the bombing.'

'OK,' said Hogarth, encouragingly.

'He was a carpenter who worked on the Mosquito prototype that they were building at Salisbury Hall, just a few miles north of Sunken Madley, in the strictest secrecy. I know this because he asked me if I was working on the Wonder and they called it the Wooden Wonder, you see.'

'Yes.'

'I asked him what had happened in the lab, and George said that he'd seen the same person as the one who'd stolen the plans. I think that those plans were some design specs, drawings for the Mosquito. George also said he'd seen the person at the Hall, and that would be Salisbury Hall, of course.'

'Right,' agreed Hogarth.

Amanda continued, 'The person that George saw in the lab that day, must have looked to him like the same person who stole the plans. What if the documents are still down there? There was a spy caught around that time; a German spy. What if that was the thief's contact, the one they were going to give the plans to? Once the contact was arrested, what could they have done with the plans except hide them?'

'That all sounds logical.'

'But I need to know more. George said he'd meet me tonight. That was two or three days ago, but I figure if it was back in time then "tonight" could be any night. To him, that lab was the part of the pub he was standing in. I can meet George again and get him to meet me in another part of the pub, that's now outside the lab, if ....'

'If only you could go back in time ...,' said Hogarth, quietly.

Amanda stopped breathlessly.

'But you can, can't you Amanda?'

She didn't know what to say, and remained silent.

'In fact, there are a lot of things that you can do, aren't there? Things that would make normal people very uncomfortable indeed.'

Amanda sat quite still, neither confirming nor denying.

Hogarth smiled reassuringly. 'You're safe with me. It's all right. I can see you've been getting bits of help from this person and that person, and whatever resource you can, and well done. You've got this far.'

Finally, Amanda spoke. 'Thank you for recognising that. I did try to find him outside the building, but the police didn't even like me being there. But I just have a feeling that, if I could get back inside that lab, the ghost, George, would show himself. He saw what happened, or he knows what happened or something to do with it.'

'You do realise that the testimony of an individual in another dimension is inadmissible in court?' said Hogarth.

'Yes, but if we knew who killed the doctor and how, then we would know what kind of evidence we're looking for,' responded Amanda.

'That's certainly a reasonable assumption. So you want me to get you a visitor's pass to the lab?'

'Yes, please, Uncle Mike.'

Hogarth nodded, 'I think you deserve your break.'

Chapter 40

 formsa

TRUST AND CIRCUMSPECTION

Hogarth got out his phone and tapped. He sipped his tea while he waited, looking at Amanda.

'Francis? Mike here. Sorry about the after-hours call .... I need a favour. The lab murder. Your turf, right? ... The young lady who discovered the body, Amanda Cadabra, she is an unusually insightful person ... could you possibly get her five minutes in the lab alone? .... Yes, ... and if she could roam around the grounds freely that would be .... ' Hogarth put his hand over the speaker and asked Amanda, 'OK to give him your number?'

Amanda nodded eagerly. She showed him her phone with the digits on the screen.

'Here it comes. I'm texting it. .... OK ... I'm skipping town for a while ... Yes, the weather's warming up down there .... OK, thanks. Over and out.'

He smiled. 'Done. Chief Inspector Francis Maxwell is your man. Here's his number in case things get sticky. Don't flash it around.'

'I won't,' Amanda promised. 'I'll be discreet and deferential to whomever I deal with.'

'Good girl.' Hogarth put away his phone. 'What exactly happened when you tried Trelawney for this?'

'He wouldn't play ball at all. Didn't want to tread on any toes, and, to be fair, I was very vague about my reasons.'

'Ever thought of trusting him?'

'No,' she said straight away.

'Why not?' asked Hogarth.

'He's not like you.'

'Sure about that?'

'He doesn't give credence to any of .... He doesn't believe any of it and never will,' she said with conviction.

'Or maybe he's just not ready to,' Hogarth suggested.

Amanda shrugged helplessly. 'What's the difference, Uncle Mike?'

'Maybe you could encourage him to be ready.'

This was a new thought to Amanda, and not an entirely comfortable one, at that. However, she had to trust her new ally.

'What can I do?' she asked.

'Help him to remember. Help each other.'

'To remember *more*?'

'Yes.'

'Why?'

'For peace of mind for both of you, for one reason,' Hogarth explained.

'I suppose that's a good one,' Amanda conceded.

'For another ... don't we all want to know the truth about what happened to your family?'

Amanda's colour rose. 'Please don't call them that, Uncle Mike. My family is my grandparents and my Aunt Amelia.'

He looked her understandingly. 'Your blood relations, then. Don't you want to know?'

'*Why* would I want to know?' she asked carefully, regarding him intently. 'I don't care about the inheritance.'

Hogarth looked at her seriously, and said slowly, 'Because

whoever went after them … if they thought you could do … useful things … will come after you, Amanda. You've known that for a long time. *Haven't* you?'

Suddenly the service station, the plastic table, the wooden chairs, the autumn dusk fading out of the sky outside the window, and the voices around them faded. It all seemed unreal. The misty world of the mystic, the cunning, the dark and light energy of magic seemed material and immediate.

Amanda looked at him with solemn eyes.

'Yes,' she said.

'But,' Hogarth continued briskly, breaking the sombre mood. 'Forewarned is forearmed, and you are not, have never been and never will be, alone, my dear. And whatever happens, they will not find you through *me*.'

She felt a little relieved.

'I understand your reticence,' he said, 'about going the whole hog with Trelawney, and you're right. He's not ready for your world. He's not even ready to come to terms with all of his own, yet. But trust Trelawney as far as you can. I think he may surprise both of you. I must be going. I have to check in. I won't be gone long: two weeks, perhaps more, perhaps less. I'll let you know.'

'You have to go?'

'How else can I make a heroic re-entrance if I should be needed? To paraphrase my favourite fictional character, look to my coming, at first light, on the fourth week.'

They got up, Hogarth insisted on paying, and they walked to the Audi.

'Once you've dropped me off, go straight home now. No detours through the woods, no stopping to pick flowers or chat with wolves,' Hogarth bade Amanda.

'And trust the Woodcutter!' she returned, mischievously.

Amanda stopped outside the car and hugged him. 'Thank you, Uncle Mike.'

'Oo, a hug. You haven't given me one of those for many a

long year!' he said appreciatively.

'Well, it's my last chance before you go. I can't hug you when I'm playing cabbie.'

'Yes, that would present a rather odd appearance. Bet it would get you lots of gentlemen customers, though!'

Amanda laughed. They got under way. It was a few short miles to Heathrow Airport Terminal 3.

Hogarth said, 'No point in taking chances. When you drop me off, open the boot, and come to the back of the car with me. I'll ask you to go and get a trolley.'

'OK.'

'You bring it back, I'll put the heavy bag on, and you put the laptop on top. I'll give you £35.'

'There's no need!' Amanda protested.

'Just as I would a real cabbie, to preserve the fiction, do you understand?'

'Yes, I see.'

'You can fill up the petrol tank with it for your neighbour.'

'Thank you. I will.'

'Yes, well, you take the money, then get in the car and drive off, without waving or looking at me.'

'Yes, I understand.'

'Take the M25 north anti-clockwise.'

'Yes, I know it,' Amanda confirmed.

'Check around you. I doubt very much that you'll be followed, but just to be sure.'

'OK.'

'Here we are ... turn in here. Now ... we're on.'

They exited the car. Amanda went and fetched the luggage trolley. As Hogarth produced his wallet, she said quietly, 'Are you going to be all right?'

'Of course,' he replied confidently, taking out three ten-pound notes. 'People like us are never without resources.' Hogarth put them into her hand, and he looked into her eyes, '... are we, Amanda Cadabra?' He gave a barely perceptible wink before he turned away, and pushed his trolley towards the glass doors of the terminal.

Mindful of his instructions, Amanda closed the boot, got into the car and drove away, without a backward look, but with a feverishly speculating brain.

Chapter 41

༄

IN THE LAB

Amanda had come off the M25, and was on the road down towards Barnet, when her phone dinged and showed a text. She pulled over. It was from Chief Inspector Maxwell, Hogarth's friend.

Evening shift starts in 20 minutes. Constable on duty doesn't know anything about the case, is just standing guard. Get there asap before he settles in. I've told him to expect you. You're a special forensic consultant. You'll have your 5 minutes in the lab. Show him your driver's licence for identification. That'll be sufficient. Good luck.

Twenty minutes. She put her foot down and drove up to the speed limit.

Amanda stopped in the car park and gathered herself. She got out of the car, and walked, with all the confidence she could muster, towards the reception doors. The young constable spotted her through the glass and opened up.

'Miss Cadabra?'

'Yes,' she said, and showed him her ID.

'This way.'

He led her down the corridor, through the waiting room,

and into the office. 'You have five minutes. I'll be in reception.'

'Thank you, Constable.'

Amanda heard the first then second double doors clung shut. She turned to the place where she'd last seen the ghost.

'George? Georgie? ... I've seen Violet.'

George materialised. 'Is she all right,' he asked anxiously.

'She's coming here tonight.'

'That's right.'

'Only not into this room. She'll meet you in the bar. Can you be in the bar tonight? You said you had some things to tell me, about what happened in here.'

'That's right. It was the same person.'

'The same *man*?'

'That's right.'

Ah, thought Amanda, now at least I have a gender for the killer.

'You saw him at Salisbury Hall?' she asked.

'Yes. I didn't see you there.'

'No. I wasn't there. Why were *you* there, George?'

'For the spruce. They wanted to consult me about using Canadian Spruce for a particular bit. My dad's Canadian. The family have worked with wood for generations,' he said proudly. 'My dad taught me all about it. We went there once for a visit, all the way to Canada. After the war, I reckon I'm gonna marry my girl, and we'll go out there to live .... There won't be much left of this country when it's all over, you know. I want us to start fresh, me and my girl, my Violet.'

'So they consulted you about Canadian spruce? And you went to the Hall for that?'

'Yes, and they said I had just confirmed what they thought, but it was good to get a second opinion.'

'Of course. And this man — the man who stole the plans — you saw him there?'

'That's right. He was a consultant too of some sort ... but he disappeared ... he was acting funny ... he was staying at The

Apple Cart here upstairs in one of the rooms, and that was funny too, see? Violet said it. She said it was funny … anyway, she can tell you herself tonight when she comes. I can point him out to you.'

'Yes, please, do, George. But you said he disappeared.'

'Yeah, I see him come into the pub and disappear. Only I think he goes down to the cellar. Nothing odd about that once in a while, 'cos they all got trunks down there for the people who stay above the pub for a while, like boarders. Only why go down there all the time? Mostly it's only extra winter clothes they put in them trunks, and it's not that cold now, so I say, what's going on? … but I'll tell you tonight.'

'When?'

'Seven o'clock.'

'Seven o'clock in the bar. But what happened here?' asked Amanda. 'The man lying on the floor, all the mess in here?'

'It was terrible. The noise.'

'The man, did he do something to the big machine?'

'That's right. It was the same man,' said George. 'Maybe he wanted to blow up the pub.'

'Was he alone in here?'

'He was with the sleeping man.'

Toby lying dead, Amanda guessed. She prompted, 'The man did something to the machine, and then he left?'

'Yes, but he'll be back. You'll see, tonight at seven.'

'OK,' Amanda had barely time to say before George vanished.

She breathed. It was a lot to take in. She looked around. There was nothing else to see here. Amanda went back to reception.

'Thank you, Constable. I'm going to make some notes, and then I'll be inspecting the area outside later. I may bring an assistant.'

'Very good, ma'am.'

The policeman let Amanda out into the dusk.

Chapter 42

❧

DRESSING UP

It was one thing to parade around in the 16th-century woods, as she had done recently, in 21st-century jeans and jacket, and then walk through the village under the aegis of the local aristocracy. It was quite another matter to wander into a far more egalitarian, 1940s, very local pub, arrayed in trainers and other noticeably modern gear.

No. Amanda would have to get into costume. But what? And more importantly, how?

'Tempest!' Amanda uttered. 'We need Lauren and we need Ingrid.'

Her cat graciously removed himself from her nice warm laptop and gave place to her rapidly tapping fingers. They soon conjured a selection of YouTube clips of Lauren Bacall and Ingrid Bergman, in a range of films noirs from the Second World War years.

'Granny?' called Amanda. Senara obligingly became present.

'Help yourself, dear.'

'Would you like to help me?'

'You need to find your own style,' Granny encouraged her granddaughter.

'My own style? I'm not planning to be there for longer than half an hour!'

Amanda, dust mask in hand, climbed up to the attic to find Granny's hoard of things she had refused to part with over the decades, anything, in fact, that evoked pleasant feelings. Amanda unearthed a navy A-line skirt and a white v-neck blouse. That way, once she returned to the 21st century, she could change into the jeans she was going to put in the car. The skirt had no pockets, so she was going to have to carry her mini-wand either in a stocking top or in an outer layer. It was also a snug fit. Granny was taller and slimmer than Amanda.

Amanda didn't care for the style of the clothes so far, but did take to a trench coat where she could carry her wand, and a fetching dark red fedora. Senara's black peep-toe heels were too large for her. Granny was taller and had bigger feet than Amanda. Another black-heeled pair with laces, stuffed with a couple of insoles, solved the problem. She would change into trainers afterwards. Amanda was about to come back downstairs when she heard Grandpa call: 'Gas mask!'

'Yes! Thank you, Grandpa.' But nowhere among Granny's things could she find that wartime essential.

'Granny!'

Senara was standing beside her, and pointing to a trunk to the left of the one Amanda was searching in.

'I've looked in there already, Granny.'

'You're looking for the wrong thing. There's a black handbag in there.'

'What this one?' asked Amanda, pulling out a deep leather one with the initials SC on it.

'Yes. See? It has a compartment at the bottom for the gas mask.'

'Ahhh,' marvelled Amanda. 'How clever! Thank you,

Granny.'

'And you'll need a proper torch. You can't go flashing your phone app around in 1940!' said Grandpa with amusement. 'There's one in the workshop'll do.' Amanda went to fetch it then returned to the computer.

'Now for the next stage,' she announced to the uninterested Tempest.

She went back to YouTube for inspiration. Then she commenced ladling on the cosmetics: the exaggerated upper lip line, the scarlet lipstick, the defined eyebrows, the false eyelashes, the smouldering eyeshadow, matt powder and puffs of rouge. Granny had clip-on earrings that hurt Amanda's ears, so she had to make do with the largest studs of her own that she could find.

It was hot in her bedroom. 'You're shining dear. More powder,' said Granny, then went off to the living room. The air was thick. Amanda opened a window, but it didn't help. A dense lid of cloud was sitting above.

She tonged her hair into curls and waves. Amanda looked at herself in the mirror, and scarcely knew her reflection.

'Good grief,' she exclaimed, not sure whether to be pleased or aghast at the transformation. 'I think I may have gone a bit overboard. Do I look too vamp?' she asked Tempest.

He projected the emotional equivalent of rolling his eyes.

'You're no help at all sometimes. You know that, don't you?'

Tempest smirked and attended to his own toilette.

Granny entered to check her granddaughter's apparel. She looked at Amanda's legs, and pronounced, 'What have you got on?' Amanda followed her Senara's gaze.

'Erm … tights?'

'Tights hadn't been invented in 1940.'

'Oh.' Amanda went to her top drawer and pulled out a pair of black holdups.

'Nor holdups.'

Amanda went to another drawer and drew out a pair of stockings.

'How about these?'

'Seamed?'

'Erm. I have seamed holdups.'

'No. They won't do, dear.'

'I'm not planning to dance on any tables. Does it really matter?'

'Always be prepared. You'll find a pair of proper nylons in the trunk where you found the handbag.' Granny returned to the living room. Amanda made the trip back up, and soon was correctly attired.

'Right,' she addressed Tempest. 'We're going to go back in time to find out what's down there, and then we're going to have to excavate. Yes, *we*. I'm going to need you find that hole you found then covered up.'

Senara and Grandpa came in. 'You're going to need more help than just him,' Granny pointed out. 'You haven't had practice levitating more than one weight at a time. What if the ceiling comes down? Your spells won't be able to hold it.'

'You're saying I need muscle? And I'll need discretion with it. Trelawney?'

Grandpa nodded. Amanda was doubtful. 'He said *no* last time I asked him to do something. What if he says *no* again?'

'He won't,' said Grandpa with conviction.

Amanda tapped the number on her phone.

'Inspector?'

'Hello.'

'Inspector, are you free? I wonder if you could help me. I've got permission to look at the ruins, and I need a hand, if you're willing.'

Mindful of Hogarth's instructions, and to Amanda's astonishment, he repeated, 'Yes, Miss Cadabra.'

Chapter 43

༒

1940

Amanda parked short of Lost Madley and got out, followed by her grey feline. The light was dimming from the dense blackening clouds.

As she approached, she could see that the time was ripe. The ruins, although close, looked far away and the atmosphere was fizzing; the marks of a time boundary. The magic that Amanda was about to perform was powerful, it would cause a disturbance in the ether. But there was no help for it.

Amanda drew out her wand and, holding it to her heart, looked into the air and made her request of Lady Time,

'*Hiaedama Tidterm, Hiaedama Tidterm, Ime besidgi wou. Agertyn thaon portow, hond agiftia gonus fripsfar faeryn ento than aer deygas.*'

Her vision flickered. Suddenly, before her, was a dramatic change of scene. It was darker. The only light came from the half moon. Blackout. But Amanda could still see the lost village in all its completeness. The long row of neat cottages reached out either side of her and, there, before her, was the tall shape of The

Apple Cart.

The unmistakable voice of Vera Lynn singing *A Nightingale Sang in Berkeley Square* floated across to Amanda. She looked up hoping to see the familiarity of the stars, but there were none. A few raindrops were starting to fall. Amanda pulled the lapels of her trench coat closer and walked the few steps to the building. She opened the pub door, got herself and Tempest inside. He darted under a table and ensconced himself, as she shut out the night, before anyone could shout 'Blackout!'

Amanda stood by the door to get her bearings. The low-lit little bar was sparsely peopled with only two or three desultory drinkers, sitting at the mellow, rectangular, warn wooden tables. Fortunately for her, only one of them had a cigarette. It was strange to be inside a pub seeing the smoke rise, caught in the soft orange glow of a lamp in an opaque globe lampshade. There were photographs of Paris, New York and Rome on the walls, and souvenirs on a shelf over the bar.

'*The moon that lingered over London town,*' sang Vera.

George was propping the bar, dividing his attention between a solo darts match and chatting to the proprietor. She recognised the latter's tall, portly form, bald head and white apron from the photograph in the library book. He was carefully tuning the dial on the wireless, to get Miss Lynn as clear as possible. George's eyes were casually scanning the bar and adjacent spaces. They clocked Amanda.

She walked over to him and spoke softly. 'Hello, George, I'm Violet's friend. Remember me? We agreed to meet tonight about the —'

'That's right. You made it, then. Good.'

Amanda was relieved that he knew who she was. The proprietor spoke up.

''Ello Miss. You far from 'ome?'

'The chain came off my bicycle. Thought I'd stop here for a bit.'

'Course.'

George intervened with introductions. 'She's a friend of Violet's. This is Frank. He owns this place.'

'Ah, I see. Hello Frank,' Amanda said, in a friendly voice.

'What'll be your pleasure, Miss?'

'Tea?' Amanda wanted coffee but couldn't remember if it was available during the war.

'Of course. No sugar. Sorry. What with the rationing, we're outa that.'

'That's quite all right,' she replied politely.

Frank cast an eye over her ensemble. 'You must be from London. Nice 'at like that. Can get all sortsa stuff there still, if you know where to go,' he added with a broad wink.

'Thank you. It was a present.'

'Anything to eat? We got some nice 'am sandwiches, if you fancy that.'

'No, thank you, I'm fine.'

'Right you are, Miss. I see you lookin' at the pictures. Thems from my Missus' dad. 'E used to go travelling. Was well to do, was her family. But she married me just the same. She's away, or she'd tell you all about it 'erself. 'Ave a seat. I'll get your tea.'

Amanda glanced around, and spoke quietly to her companion. 'What's the name of the man you're going to point out to me? Do you know, George?'

'Not yet,' he answered.

'But he's staying here?'

'I reckon so.'

Amanda looked at the bar. 'Is there a register for the rooms upstairs?'

'Yeah, Frank keeps it under the bar.'

Amanda turned towards the proprietor. 'Excuse me, please, Frank.'

'Yes, Miss?'

'Do you have any rooms vacant?'

'It so happens we do have one free, but it's a bit cramped. It's the one where the Missus keeps 'er piano. You're right not wanting to be out and about on a night like this. Let me sort out yer tea first, then we'll see about it.'

George spoke quietly to Amanda. 'That man, he should be back in here in a mo'. Gotta make this quick. Violet'll be here soon. Don't really want her mixed up in this.'

He looked towards the room that adjoined the bar and nodded.

'He's in the back room at the minute. He's got a big black bag. Find an excuse to go in there, and have a gander. He can't leave without passing us, though.'

'What's in there?' Amanda asked.

'Nice fire when it's chilly. Dominos, cards, magazines. Violet likes it. Go and get the dominos.'

Amanda strolled in. The man looked up at her. She recognised the brows and chin that he would bequeath to his future son. He was a much younger version of the man she knew, yes, but … unmistakable. She feigned boredom and indifference. The box of dominos was on one of the tables. Amanda picked them up, then spotted a mirror on one of the walls. She walked to it and checked her makeup, getting another look at him, then walked out.

The proprietor was at the bar with a plain light green cup and saucer. 'Here's your tea. That'll be tuppence, Miss.' Amanda realised she didn't have any of the old currency: shillings and pence. Even her five and ten-pound notes would be strange. She pretended to be searching her pockets, the colour rising in her face and her chest tightening.

'I er …'

The siren blasted through the air, its mournful rise and fall piercing every sound in the pub; the chatter, the orchestra on the radio. The publican pulled the glasses off the counter and clicked off the wireless. The patrons grabbed their bags, coats and hats.

Amanda and George made a show of collecting themselves. Their quarry was still in the back room. Violet ran in,

'Georgie!'

'Violet, go on!' George urged her. 'I've got to do something. I don't want you mixed up in it. It's a bad business. Don't worry, I'll be right with you. Go on.'

She looked anxiously at him then someone pulled her towards the exit

'Quick!' George urged Amanda. 'Into the lavvy.'

As the rest of the gathering headed for the air raid shelter at the end of the lane, the two slipped into the hall beyond the bar and hid behind the door of the ladies lavatory. They left the light off.

'Hope to goodness Violet's gone in the shelter,' George said in her ear

'I'm sure she has,' Amanda affirmed.

She looked at her watch but couldn't see the dial. She counted a minute. The Apple Cart was now in darkness. But not silence. The crunching bang of falling bombs was already sounding. Amanda peered out into the hall, but all she could see was black. She pulled out her torch with mental thanks to Grandpa, cupped her hand around it and switched it on, on its lowest setting.

Cautiously, Amanda leaned out, to see the door under the stairs swinging to. George nodded and they stealthed into the passage. He pointed and whispered, 'Cellar,' and put a finger to his lips. Carefully, he opened the door just wide enough for them to look down and round the steps.

There was the man, weakly spotlighted by his torch, a pool of glowing yellow in the pit of the cellar, kneeling before a trunk as he struggled to fit the key into the lock.

An explosion sounded nearby. Amanda and George instinctively crouched as the building rocked. A second impact followed swiftly. A creaking groan above made Amanda flick her torch beam up. The ceiling above them buckled. He had time only to push Amanda out of the way before it engulfed him, as the weighty piano above thrust throughout the floorboards, through the weakened joists and down on the entrance to the cellar and the hapless Georgie.

Amanda, under debris, on the floor, up against the door of the ladies, was protecting her head with her arms. Beneath the wailing siren, she could just about discern sounds of dislodging rubble and a moan. With her hands over nose and mouth, she stayed stock still, as the man pulled himself up from the space below. He stumbled out empty-handed into the night. She struggled out after him, Tempest now at her ankles. Just in time. The collapse was great. In seconds, The Apple Cart lay razed to the ground. In ruins.

Chapter 44

੭ဆ

THE CELLAR OF SECRETS

Amanda got away into the trees, coughing. It was more than time to get out of the 1940s. She spoke the spell, and the world billowed. Amanda gasped the clear air of the 21st century. She was opposite the end of the research centre, and hurried toward the Astra to change.

Amanda stopped. Bombs? No. The first thunder of the storm that had been building for weeks rumbled in the distance, as Trelawney drew up and got out of his silver Ford Mondeo. The exterior lights of the Centre were falling on her.

He stood, arrested for a moment. She looked unexpectedly …

'Lili Marlene,' he murmured.

'Theme party,' said Amanda, observing his reaction to her appearance. 'Just come from one.' Fairly true.

Trelawney gave a slight shake of the head as if to reset his brain.

'Right. So, we are here because …?'

'There's evidence down there in what was the cellar,' stated

Amanda. 'Evidence of a crime in the past that's linked to a crime in the present.'

'Which was?' asked Trelawney.

'Espionage, treason. I think we'll find documents of a secret plane design that would influence the course of the war: the Mosquito. Whatever's down there, to someone in the present, was worth killing for in order to hide it. That's why Toby Sidiqi was killed. You said the investigating police would need evidence. You could help me get it, if you would be so kind.'

'Right,' Trelawney said and looked at the ruins. 'What's the plan?'

Tempest hove into view, directed a double beam of quelling look at Trelawney and went to the correct place in the rubble. He flicked some of it away to reveal a shattered wooden surface.

'That's a grand piano,' said Amanda, aiming her torch at it. 'OK ....'

'The action of a grand piano is like a harp with an iron frame,' Amanda explained. 'It and the strings will be creating a roof above the cellar below, and holding up the collapsed building on top of it.' Tempest was digging out the crevice. 'If we can just dislodge a few of these minor boulders it should create an entrance.'

'All right, leave this to me,' Trelawney said, mindful of the effect of dust on Amanda's lungs.

'Thank you. Just a moment.' She hurried to the car and came back with a mask for herself and a pair of thick DIY gloves, which she handed to Trelawney.

They both looked up at the sky, hearing a threatening grumble above.

'I think the storm's coming this way,' he said. 'Let's hope it doesn't rain until we're done. We'll have to work fast.'

'Yes, here, I'll help you.' She put on her mask. Soon they had a wider opening, and he could see inside.

'Still pretty cat-sized,' commented Trelawney. 'But enough for me to see the rubble forms a sort of ramp down.

'I'm no six-stone fairy but it's big enough for me to get inside,' said Amanda, standing up and removing her mask.

'For *you*? I can't let you go in there,' Trelawney objected.

'I'll be fine,' Amanda insisted. 'I can hand the swag out to you, and you can help me out.'

'I'm not sure how this is going to look in official circles,' said Trelawney disapprovingly.

'You'll be fêted as a hero, for cracking the Lost Madley Murder case and bringing a felon to justice.'

'Or treading on the London Metropolitan Police Force's toes, and colluding with a civilian in contaminating a crime scene.'

'Well, I offered them the crime scene, if they'd listened to me,' countered Amanda, 'and they didn't want it!'

'All right.'

Amanda had meant to change into jeans and trainers, but the thunder was almost upon them. There was no time. She handed him her hat and torch, put on her mask, sat down and wriggled her legs inside the entrance to the cavity. With catches and scrapes, Amanda got herself into the hole. Trelawney handed her the torch.

'Keep watch' she called up to him. 'Just keep watch. I'll call out when I've got something.'

Amanda wanted Trelawney's attention elsewhere so she could use her wand. She was going to need it. The grand piano was suspended above her on the very edges of the iron frame, on a couple of splintered joists. She had to support it by magic. Amanda took the pencil out of her trench coat pocket.

'*Herda hevan,*' she intoned, softly.

She looked down. Under fallen masonry and floorboards were three steamer trunks, each with a number on it, presumably a room number. Mrs Frank had been an organised woman.

All three were locked. Which room had the man stayed in? There was no way to know, and it was too late to ask Frank. Having only seen the cellar in the dark in 1940, and now amongst the chaos, was disorientating. She would just have to try the first trunk and hope she got lucky.

Amanda knelt before the most accessible of the three. It was a proper lock. With skeleton keys or lockpicks she could have got it undone. That was part of furniture restoration work. But she had neither tool, and the storm was closing in.

'*Agertyn*,' she pronounced. The lock popped. Amanda had to fight the detritus on top of the lid to get it open just enough to reach in and feel around. The contents were just clothes and shoes. She got her hand out, and released the lid and its burden with relief. But she felt something above dislodge. The place was a pile of Jackstraws, each rock and stick of wood precariously balanced.

There came a low bang above. The storm was upon them, and the very ground was taking up its vibrations. Amanda grabbed her wand with both hands, pointing it upwards:

'*Herda hevan, herda hevan.*'

She needed stronger magic to shore up the ceiling and walls. Now Trelawney was calling to her, blast him.

'You all right?' came his anxious voice.

'Yes, yes I'm fine! Just go back and keep watch!'

The ceiling shuffled and lowered as Amanda's concentration wavered. She went to the second chest. Keeping the force of her intent on supporting what hung perilously above, she whispered, '*Agertyn*'. Click. Lift. Search. Again she disturbed the debris for nothing.

Thunder rolled. Rubble, dust and wood were falling. She ducked.

'*Herda hevan*,' she repeated.

Trelawney, seeing the ground shift, wriggled his hands under the piano frame, taking as much weight as he could, and willed the ceiling to stay up just long enough to get her out of there.

Amanda's voice floated up to him. What was she saying? Herder heaven? Strange how it resonated. It began to echo is his head, repeating as his arms and back strained to keep the iron frame from tumbling down into the cellar and onto Amanda.

He heard things falling in the cavity below and called to her.

'I'm fine!' Amanda shouted. 'Just give me another minute!'

Chest three. It had to be in here …. Yes! Under blankets, there was a suitcase and papers. Eureka! She'd have to get the chest open properly. She forced back the lid, and all that leaned on it.

'*Herda* hevan,' she insistently chanted at the failing structure over her head.

Quickly, Amanda took out her phone and recorded the open chest showing the room number. Yes! Files and papers. She quickly opened one folder at random, then another and there it was: notes on the Mosquito, schematics and a codebook. Amanda opened the suitcase to reveal a radio transmitter, headphones and a morse code key. She hid her wand, gathered up the papers and climbed, slipping and turning her ankles on the rubble ramp.

'Here!' she shouted urgently.

Trelawney dropped Amanda's hat, reached in and took the bundle.

'Come out!' he urged her.

'I have to get the radio.'

'There's no time, the whole thing is going to go!' he told her.

She slid back down, magically holding the mess above her head together through every ounce of sheer force of will now.

'*Herda hevan, herda hevan, herda hevan,*' Amanda chanted.

Wheezing even inside her mask, she grabbed the radio and ran for the ramp as the cavity began to collapse, the furthest end of the piano swinging down. Trelawney took the suitcase in one hand and tossed it aside. In one swift move, he grabbed her arms, and jerked her out of the hole as the piano collapsed down. Flailing strings whipped out and caught her shoe, threatening to pull her in. He reached, knocked the shoe off her foot, wrapped his arms around her, and rolled them both clear.

Amanda was coughing helplessly but waved her hand along the lane. The papers were strewn about it. Trelawney ran, catching them in the light of his torch and collecting them. He hastened back to her side.

'Come on, let's get you away from this dust.'

Chapter 45

❧

THE BACKROOM BOYS REPORT

Tucking the documents under one arm, Trelawney fairly carried Amanda to her car and sat her down, sideways, on the edge of the driver's seat.

'I'll get the suitcase,' said Trelawney, and went back into the dust-filled gloom.

The storm, having done its worst with the ruins, banged its way on over Madley Wood. Amanda used her inhaler and had a second look at the files, while she waited. She began to wonder what Trelawney was doing, when he reappeared. He put the radio onto the Astra's back seat, and handed Amanda her hat.

'Thank you.'

Unexpectedly, he knelt beside her. He was holding her shoe, actually her grandmother's vintage heel, scuffed and crushed but still in one piece.

'You rescued my shoe?' she marvelled.

'Once your foot wasn't in it, it was easy to get it free. I fished it up with a long piece of batten and unwound it.'

He fitted it onto her foot and did up the lace.

'There,' said Trelawney with satisfaction. 'But it's going to need some polish.'

'Thank you,' she smiled in amazement. 'You didn't have to do that, you know.'

'All part of the service. I'm afraid your nylons are laddered beyond rescue, however.'

'I'm sure Granny wi— would understand.'

'Well, I hope our efforts were worth it, Miss Cadabra.'

'Look at the papers,' she urged him, handing over a bundle. He flicked through them.

'Yes, well, if the person who secreted these documents was in unlawful possession of them, then this certainly looks like evidence of espionage.'

'Open the suitcase. Put it on the bonnet.'

He lifted it onto the front of the car, and flicked the catches. 'Hmm, what have we here,' he remarked with interest. 'All right. I see. Let's get you home and then work out how to deliver this. Can you get yourself over the gearstick into the passenger seat?'

'Yes, but are you allowed to drive this car?' she asked doubtfully.

'I'm insured to drive any car.'

'What about yours?'

'I'm insured to drive that too,' he replied humorously, holding out his hand for the keys.

Her laugh turned into a cough. She dug them out of her coat and passed them to him.

'I mean, what about leaving your car here,' said Amanda. 'Aren't you going to need it?'

'I'll come back for it while you get cleaned up and put the kettle on.'

'Don't you think we should hand this in straight away?' Amanda asked, looking back at the papers and suitcase, as he drove along the lane.

'Firstly, the person in charge is likely not going to be in until morning, and I think it *should* be handed to the person in charge. And, secondly, *we* are not going to hand this in, *you* are.'

'Don't you want —?'

'No, I don't,' Trelawney interrupted firmly. 'I was acting unofficially, as your assistant, and if you can keep my name out of it altogether, then I would infinitely prefer it.'

'Oh. All right,' she agreed.

Amanda's phone rang.

'Hello, Amanda, it's the Backroom Boys reporting in,' said Gwendolen Armstrong-Witworth. 'We've been speaking to our dear friend who runs the museum, and has kindly opened it up for us, especially. The pub register was salvaged from the wreckage long ago and is one of their exhibits. There was only one guest on the night of the bombing, staying in room number three. He gave his name as James Smith.'

'Thank you. I am going to send you a photo, and I'd like you to tell me if he reminds you of anyone you saw in Little Madley.'

'All right, dear. I'll hold on.'

Amanda searched for the name on Facebook and finally found him on LinkedIn. It looked like a pretty recent photo, too. She pressed 'send'.

'Well …,' came Miss Armstrong-Witworth's hesitant tones, 'it was a long time ago … and this man looks older … but, yes … When I was with Violet in The Apple Cart. Any stranger would stand out. With petrol rationing you got far fewer sightseers, you understand. And he was quite impressive this man. Yes.'

'I think the man staying in the pub was this man's father,' Amanda explained.

'Oh … wait, dear … Cynthia wants to see … ah … of course. I see now. That's what Violet was trying to tell me: *not* that the man "was *muttering*", but that she recognised he came from *Upper Muttring*!'

'And that,' came Miss de Havillande's voice, 'is the same place his son said he comes from!'

'Oh, poor young man,' said Miss Armstrong-Witworth compassionately, 'his parents must have told him. What a thing to live with, knowing that his father was a traitor.'

'No wonder they could afford that house,' said Cynthia. 'Everyone was surprised. Even though it was neither large nor ostentatious.'

'No indeed,' chimed in Miss Armstrong-Witworth, 'spies are not usually well-paid.'

'Although,' continued Cynthia, 'the word was that he'd had an inheritance. Well, that's easy enough to check. I can see if there were any deaths in the family around that time, and I'd bet my last farthing that there weren't!'

Amanda was confused. 'But the man who spied is dead. His son isn't accountable under the law. Why would it be so dreadful, in this day and age?'

'If he's lived with the secret since he was a child,' Gwendolen replied sorrowfully, 'it would have magnified in his mind into something colossal, mark my words. His father must have felt that what was buried beneath The Apple Cart was a time bomb. I wonder what could have driven a respectable engineer to become a seller of secrets.'

'Well, I've got the documents relating to those very secrets,' announced Amanda. 'They were in the cellar, in the old steamer trunk that was allotted to that room.'

'Have you, dear?' marvelled Cynthia. 'Well done!'

'I did have help,' admitted Amanda.

'From your young man?' asked Gwendolen.

'He's not my —The inspector was kind enough to lend me his aid, but he doesn't want his name to be involved.'

'Understood,' said Gwendolen.

Trelawney was parking the car in Amanda's driveway. 'I'll call you later,' she said to Gwendolen. 'Thank you both very much indeed.'

Amanda and the inspector disembarked, he locked her car and handed her the keys.

'I won't be long,' he said, and headed off on foot up Orchard Row.

Chapter 46

∽

HOGARTH CHIMES IN

Amanda found Tempest on the mat, de-dusting his coat.

'Thank you for your help, Tempest,' she said, letting them into the cottage. 'I'd give you a big cuddle, but I'd get you all dusty again, and I know just how you'd feel about that!'

Tempest hurriedly put some distance between them to underscore her point. She put the kettle on then headed for the bathroom. By the time Trelawney was back, she was clean and changed.

Amanda poured the tea, brought in the tray and set it on the coffee table. She sat down on the sofa beside the inspector, opened her laptop, and pulled up the LinkedIn photo she had sent to Miss Armstrong-Witworth.

'I think this is the son of the man who was staying at the Lost Madley pub. Miss Armstrong-Witworth can place his father at the village of Lost Madley around the time of the bombing. There was only one person, according to the pub register, staying there, in Room 3, and as this photo that I took shows, the radio and papers were in the trunk that corresponded to that room.'

'Not watertight, but go on,' responded Trelawney.

Amanda set her laptop aside. 'You got the text from Uncle Mike? I updated him while you got your car.'

'Who?'

'Chief Inspector Hogarth.'

'Uncle Mike? What do you mean *Uncle Mike*? Since when have you been calling him *Uncle Mike*?' asked Trelawney, horrified.

'Oh, I forgot to tell you, but we haven't had any time, I gave him a lift to the airport.'

'From *Cornwall*?'

'No, from Paddington,' Amanda returned placidly.

'Why, for goodness sake?'

'Because I wanted to talk to him.'

Trelawney stared at her in bewilderment.

Amanda continued, 'He was very kind to me when I was little, you know. I'd forgotten all about that but Gra ... gradually I remembered.'

'Really?' he asked curiously.

'Yes, he used to bring little clothes for my teddy bears,' replied Amanda, happily.

'He did, did he?'

'Yes, anyway, I explained to him that I needed some help and ... he helped me.'

'Hold on ....' Trelawney checked his phone. There were a couple of unread messages. One from Hogarth:

Have given AC a bit of help, got her a pass to the CS. Be her knight in shining armour if you can, she might be onto something. Off to sis, back soon. Keep in touch M

Thomas was appeased. He supposed he had saved her, in knightly fashion.

Next message:

Dr was drugged

Trelawney looked up from the screen. 'Yes, I understand now. So ... it was murder then.'

'Yes, he was drugged so he could be left in situ when the centrifuge exploded. That's what I think,' opined Amanda.

'But how did he get past the security man, er —'

'Bill.'

'Yes.'

Their phones dinged in unison. Two heads looked down at their devices.

Crossley refuses to say where he was at time of death. Gibbs was home confirmed by daughter, Streeter in pub

'Crossley!' Amanda exclaimed. 'Yes, he was the one would have sorted out Dr Sidiqi's lab, ordered the equipment!'

Their phone once again proclaimed the arrival of a message.

'What!' cried Amanda. 'Bill MacNair has confessed?' She stood up, knocking the table and sloshing the tea perilously in their mugs. 'I don't *believe* it. That makes a complete nonsense of my theory.'

'There *could* be a link between MacNair and traitor,' said Trelawney, consolingly.

'Surely not an Upper Muttring One,' objected Amanda. 'Bill comes from Scotland. Dammit.' Amanda collapsed onto the sofa. She was reaching for her mug, when their phones dinged again. They looked down.

to falling asleep at reception that night after having accepted a drink with the boss

Amanda jumped up again.

'We're back in business!'

'Yes,' agreed Trelawney, 'MacNair could easily have been drugged too.

Ding!

Testing him now

'Well, Miss Cadabra, I doubt that we can do or know any more until morning, when you can deliver the evidence to the incident room.'

'You're not going, are you? Not when it's all getting so exciting,' protested Amanda.

'I think we've had enough excitement for one evening. I know I have. And I would very much like to get cleaned up.'

'Oh. Oh yes, of course. You're right, Inspector. But do have your tea.'

'Yes. Yes, thank you I will.' He took a sip. 'If you would like to call me and let me know of any progress. By the way, do you know how your "Uncle Mike" comes to be in the know, and getting minute-to-minute updates as we speak, as well as getting you a pass to the crime scene?'

'He's friends with the chief inspector in charge of the case.'

'Of course he is,' grinned Trelawney.

Amanda looked at him earnestly. 'Inspector, I want to thank you. I couldn't have done this without you.'

'You're welcome, Miss Cadabra. I hesitate to say "any time", you understand.'

Amanda laughed. 'I do.'

'But I hope you'll ask me anyway. Knowing that I may say no.'

'Yes, and I'm sorry again that I put you in an awkward position when I asked for your help before.'

'That's quite alright.'

Ding!

'See! I told you it wasn't over yet!' exclaimed Amanda inaccurately. 'Wow, he's been stopped at Dover! With Dr Schofield!' Amanda looked at Trelawney with round eyes. 'Who would have thought?'

'Who is Dr Schofield?'

'She was the first doctor I saw at the Centre. Remember I told you? She was horrible and totally out of her comfort zone, and she used to commute all the way from Dover. Charlotte Streeter told me; She's the acupuncturist. Schofield, she got the job over Toby who was way more suited to it because …'

'Of course,' said the inspector. 'He needed as many people in place working at the Centre that he had some kind of control over. He knew what was down there, from the very beginning …'

The doorbell rang. Amanda looked at Trelawney. 'Who on earth could that be?'

Chapter 47

ॐ

AN UNEXPECTED VISITOR

'Do you want me to get it?' Trelawney offered.

'No, it's OK. I should answer it. This *is* my house, after all.'

Cautiously, Amanda opened the door. There, on the mat, stood Detective Sergeant Baker.

'Sergeant,' she said in astonishment.' Er ... hello.'

'Good evening, Miss Cadabra.'

'You're not here to arrest me, are you?' she asked, worriedly. 'I know I don't have an alibi.'

'No, miss, nothing like that,' he reassured her comfortably.

Relieved, Amanda was suddenly aware that she was keeping her visitor standing at the door. 'Would you like to come in?'

'Thank you.'

She showed him into the living room where the inspector stood up as the sergeant entered.

'Oh,' she said, aware of Trelawney's embarrassing situation. But the sergeant held out his hand, saying, 'Inspector Trelawney, I take it. My CI said I might find you here. He speaks very highly of you, sir. Pleasure to meet you.'

'Thank you … er?'

'Baker, DS Baker, sir. I understand you are here investigating another case in connection with Miss Cadabra's family, and kindly assisted her in extracting some evidence that may pertain to the case of the death at the Centre.'

'Yes, but I'd rather my name was kept out of it. I don't want you to think I've been treading on your toes, Sergeant.'

'Not at all, sir. In fact, Miss Cadabra, the chief inspector said I should come round, and take the evidence off your hands at once. Help the case along, and save you the trouble of bringing it in.'

'That's very kind indeed you, Sergeant,' said Amanda appreciatively. 'Please sit down, and let me make you some tea.'

'Thank you, Miss, that would be very nice. It has proved to be a somewhat busy evening, what with one thing and another.' Amanda went off to the kitchen. 'I understand, sir, you've been kept informed of developments?'

'Yes,' confirmed Trelawney.

'The suspect has been apprehended with possibly an accomplice. We have a warrant to search their places of residence. I believe that may be under way as we speak.'

'You didn't want to be present for that?'

'No, that's all right, sir, my young DC is very capable, and I understand this case may have a history that, it seems, you and Miss Cadabra can help me with, if you would be so kind.'

Amanda came back into the room bearing tea and Hobnobs. Baker greeted the sight with unqualified approval.

'Ahhh, Hobnobs. Now that's just the ticket. Thank you kindly.'

'While you're having your tea, would you like to see what we found?' offered Amanda.

'I would indeed.'

'Can I start at the beginning, please? I'd like to explain how I come to be showing you Exhibits A and B?'

'Please do. In your own time.'

'Well, Lost Madley has always…'

After she had given Detective Sergeant Baker the back-story, Amanda showed him her map of the hamlet and the diagram of the Centre. She leaned over the table. 'See how the end of the Centre overlaps half of the pub. One day, my cat was exploring and found a crack in the ground, and you could see there was a room, a cellar, down there.'

She sat back. 'On the day he was killed, the doctor had said he was going to poke around the ruins. What if he told someone, and they were scared he'd get down there, and find what was still hidden inside? Well, this is what was there.' She picked up the bundle of files and loose sheets from the floor by the sofa. 'These papers.'

Baker flicked through them. 'Hold on … I see why they sent me here instead of on the searches. *I* know what this is. Specialist area of mine, World War II. This is the … yes, the Mosquito. These are the plans —'

'Yes, stolen by the killer's father who was a consultant on at least one occasion at Salisbury Hall.'

'Well, there were a lot of schematics, blueprints and drawings. It's possible that these wouldn't have been missed.'

Amanda leaned down again, picked up the suitcase, and plumped it on the table. Baker's eyes instantly narrowed. 'Wait,' he said. 'I bet a pound to a penny that I know what *this* is. This is how he communicated with his German masters.'

He popped the latches and opened the case almost reverently.

'Oh yes … I know what this is …. You don't see many of these. They didn't make many, you know. Those were the early days.'

'Is it …?'

'Oh, it's German all right. 1939. Have you touched this handle on the morse key?

'No,' said Amanda definitely.

'There's just an outside chance we could get a print off it.

Don't know if it would be any good or useful but… you never know.'

'There's a lady who lives here, who is very elderly, and she remembers this man being in Little Madley at the time. When I showed her the picture of his son, she recognised the likeness. We think his son must have grown up with the terrible burden of knowledge that his father was a traitor to his country. And when he found out about the Centre project —'

'Or maybe it was his idea so he could get access to this stuff.'

'I guess,' agreed Amanda. 'But the most important thing was that he should be in control of the situation. So he tried to influence who the staff would be. People he personally had a hold over.'

'Like Schofield,' commented Baker.

'And like Charlotte Streeter, his niece. And that's why Schofield got the job over Dr Sidiqi when I know from personal experience that she was far less qualified. In fact, I wouldn't be surprised if she wasn't actually the homoeopath she claimed to be either.'

'I've just had a thought, if I may chime in,' said Trelawney.

'Please do, sir.'

'When Miss Cadabra and I were in the Big Tease, er …'

'That's all right sir, I know the place you mean. Very nice sausage rolls.'

Trelawney grinned. 'Thank you, Sergeant. Well, Bill MacNair came in.'

'The security man,' added Baker.

'Yes. He was distraught, naturally. But he recounted an incident at the Centre. He said it was the day that Sidiqi came for his interview. It was also the day that MacNair had been called into Gibbs' office and told that a complaint had been made about him, uncharacteristically, I understand. Later, MacNair was in the café and saw Gibbs and Streeter looking as though they had had an argument. MacNair reported that Streeter said to Gibbs,

"I thought you trusted my judgement." MacNair assumed it was in regard to himself but what if it was in regard to Robin's claim that Sidiqi wasn't the best candidate?'

'Of course,' said Baker. 'Streeter wanted Schofield, and Gibbs wanted Sidiqi for the post.'

'And Bill said,' added Amanda, 'that Damian Gibbs had given him his first job when he came out of the army, so Bill was one of Damian's people not one of his, Robin Streeter's, so Robin tried to get Bill fired, by saying there'd been a complaint about him!' She looked at the two policemen hesitantly, 'It's all just conjecture but what if ....'

'Go on,' encouraged Trelawney.

'Well, what if Streeter heard Sidiqi was going to explore the ruins after dark? So *before* it was dark, Robin acted as though he was leaving, got MacNair to have a drink and drugged him. Knowing that Bill would assume he'd just fallen asleep on the job, and would be too scared to admit it. Then, when Robin got to the lab, he drugged Sidiqi in the same way, then rigged the centrifuge to explode later enough for Robin to be where he could be alibi'd. In the pub or at home with the family. What do you think?'

Baker's mobile rang. He stood up. 'Excuse me .... Baker,' he said into the phone, as he walked into the kitchen for some privacy.

Chapter 48

༦

DR CROSSLEY'S SECRET

Amanda looked at Trelawney, barely able to contain her excitement.

'Clearly, you're enjoying this, Miss Cadabra,' said Trelawney, regarding her with amusement as he leaned back in an armchair.

'Well, of course, I am. I've never been in on anything like this before.'

'I'm so glad,' he said cryptically. 'I see you're deeply affected by the demise of the doctor.'

'Well, naturally I'm sorry that he came to an untimely end. But that's not my fault,' Amanda pointed out 'It's not like he was killed in a fit of jealousy by Samantha Gibbs because he'd had one lunch with me.'

'I expect, naturally, you're sorry about that too. That she has turned out not to be bound for Holloway prison,' he commented.

'What an ungenerous supposition, Inspector,' she replied, with the semblance of outrage.

Baker came out of the kitchen. 'A substance, Somnexepam, was found at the homes of both Schofield and Streeter that corresponds to the substance, traces of which were found in the body. It was an experimental drug, a fast-acting preanaesthetic, being tested at the last place where Dr Schofield was employed.'

'Well!' marvelled Amanda.

'Furthermore, parts of a centrifuge, trace elements of metal, electrical parts and tools were found in the home of Streeter, indicating that it was he who rigged the machine in the lab to explode.'

'Ha!' she exclaimed. 'Oh!' she added, as a thought occurred to her. 'Sergeant, Dr Crossley didn't have an alibi. At least, he wouldn't say where he was. Do *you* know where he was?'

'Yes, miss. We found out by the simple expedient of having him tailed.'

'And?' asked Amanda looking at him with avid curiosity.

'Well, now, miss, we do have to preserve confidentiality, you know.'

Her face fell.

The Sergeant conceded, 'I'll just say this: Mawlten.'

'Mawlten?'

'And whatever you find, you'll keep to yourself.'

'Yes, of course, but …'

'He's a dark horse that Crossley. I'll say no more.'

'All right, er, thank you.'

Sergeant Baker paused and sat back down on the sofa. He dunked a Hobnob in his tea in meditative silence. He looked up at Amanda.

'You know, miss, you took a big risk.'

'I did?'

'Asking questions all over the village when the murderer was still at large. Were you alone at any time between then and when you went to the Centre to have a look-see?'

Amanda thought. She'd gone home to change.

'Yes,' she admitted.

'He could have come after you, in your home. What would you have done then?'

Amanda knew what she would have done. She would have had to use magic. A lot of it, defence spells, against a human. The ripples would have been dramatic. Not a stone thrown into a pool but a hefty great boulder chucked into a lake.

'I take your point, Sergeant,' she said seriously.

'However,' said Baker mitigatingly, 'I commend your good sense in asking the inspector here to assist you at the scene. Mr Streeter might have made sure that you were buried with the evidence.'

'Yes, I see. You're quite right,' she said penitently. 'I will be much more circumspect next time.'

'*Next time?*' responded Baker and Trelawney in unison.

'I mean,' said Amanda carefully,' if circumstances should arise in the future of a similar nature, however unlikely that is, I shall, er … more tea anyone?'

Baker finished off his Hobnob and his drink. 'I think I'll call it a night, if it's all the same to you, Miss Cadabra. It's been a long day, and will be a busy one tomorrow.' He stood up. 'Er … just one more thing before I go,' he said. 'I understand you were given your five minutes alone in the lab. Did you … um … sense anything?

'As a matter of fact, I did, Sergeant.'

'Hm,' said Baker. He didn't ask what, and Amanda wondered why. 'Well, all's well that ends well, is what I say. Good night, sir.'

'Good night, Sergeant,' Trelawney bade him, offering his hand. 'Good work.'

Baker shook it, saying, 'Teamwork, sir, teamwork is what it's all about. And procedure.'

'Indeed, Sergeant,' Trelawney agreed heartily.

'We coppers know that. Perhaps you can explain it to the young lady sometime,' he said, with a knowing look in Amanda's direction. 'Night, all.'

Amanda closed the door.

Trelawney looked at her as she came back into the living room. 'I hope you took all that the sergeant said to heart. He's a wise and experienced man.'

'Yes, Inspector,' Amanda replied meekly.

He was not deceived. 'I mean it. I'm already investigating your relatives' deaths; I don't want to be investigating *yours*,' he said tartly.'

'Yes, Inspector,' she replied seriously. 'I promise to be more careful next — I mean, another time.'

'Good,' he said shortly. Trelawney continued on a more relaxed note, 'Well, if there are any more revelations, let me know. I'm still in Crouch End until Sunday.'

'Thank you, and thank you for driving my car home.'

'Foot not damaged?'

'No, and it was very thoughtful of you to rescue my shoe.'

'My pleasure,' Trelawney replied, gallantly.

'Oh, what do you think the sergeant meant by Mawlten? It's a town, isn't it? In Essex? Or was it police code for something,' Amanda asked earnestly.

'Just a town.'

'Wait …. We have to solve this mystery before you go!' She opened her laptop and Googled. 'Nothing … hold on! YouTube …. Mud racing? Hmm, I don't know why he'd want to hide that … oh … dark horse! The sergeant said he's a dark horse…. Dark horse Mawlten …. Oh my goodness!' Her eyes creased with merriment, and a broad grin lit her face. She looked up at Trelawney.

'Well?' he smiled back in anticipation.

'Look!'

The video played a scene of ten men and women, attired in black with tunics and garters adorned with bells and red and white ribbons. They wore black hats and masks, were dancing with a skipping motion, and periodically clashed short wooden sticks, while a band, similarly clad, accompanied them.

'Well! Who'd have thought! Robert Crossley is a *Morris* dancer!' cried Amanda.

'Indeed,' agreed Trelawney. Amanda studied the screen, discerning the face of the doctor and the red curly hair and features of his wife.

'Here's Mrs Crossley too! But they're very good,' objected Amanda,' and they're carrying on an ancient tradition. Why be so secretive?'

'Well, it *is* sometimes the butt of humour, Miss Cadabra, and he might not have thought it consonant with a man in a serious profession.'

'I suppose ... Oh well, that's *that* puzzle solved.'

'And on that note of success, I shall depart,' said Trelawney. Amanda showed the inspector to the door where they shook hands.

'Goodnight,' she bade him.

'Sleep well.'

He got into his car, and she waved him off as he drove down Orchard Way.

Suddenly Amanda missed Claire. Claire would share her excitement. How she'd love this! '

'I can't wait till she comes home, Tempest,' said Amanda enthusiastically. Then stopped. 'Of course, I'll have to leave out all of the magic bits ... like how I met George and ... went back to 1940 and ... held the cellar ceiling up and ... opened the trunks ... but ... yes ... everything else ... oh and then there was moving the CCTV camera and sending Bill to sleep, and locking the door when I first found the body, and levitating my phone around the crime scene taking video, and then ... oh. Hm.'

Amanda reconsidered. 'Actually, the person I really want to tell. ... is Aunt Amelia.' She smiled. 'Too late at night now but ... yes, Aunt Amelia. She would understand *every*thing.'

Amanda went to the kitchen and poured hot water into her mug to freshen the tea, and got a gingernut biscuit from the tin. She sat on the sofa, and Tempest established himself of her lap. She dunked and sipped and cogitated.

'George. I hope George is at peace now. I think I'd better go and see, as soon as I can.'

Chapter 49

❧

GEORGE AND VIOLET

With all evidence gathered, the crime scene tape was taken down, the police presence departed, the cleaners came in and the Centre reopened.

Amanda called in at reception. The Scotsman was there.

'Bill,' said Amanda with delight.

'Yes, lassie, still here.'

'Are you on days too?'

'Just helpin' oot until they can find a replacement for Gloria.'

'Oh?'

'She, er … left'.

'Ah. So she was one of Mr Streeter's …'

'Quite, miss,' he replied succinctly. 'They're interviewing people to replace Mr Streeter and Dr Sidiqi. It might take a wee while to get things back to normal.'

'Yes, of course. Er … who else?'

'The cleaners, the café staff, the new therapists who actually weren't really therapists, who replaced Melanie and Kathleen who were too intuitive for Mr Streeter's liking, and the acupuncturist,' Bill listed.

'Charlotte wasn't involved, was she?' Amanda asked hopefully. 'She seemed nice and a real therapist.'

'No, I don't think Miss Streeter knew anything about it, but she said she'd rather not stay. I think she felt embarrassed. Mr Gibbs gave her a good reference. But it's another one has to be replaced.' Bill shook his head regretfully then smiled at Amanda. 'Nice of you to pop in, though.'

'I wondered if I might go in to pay my respects, as it were.'

'Dr Sidiqi's lab? Yes, of course. Take as long as you like, miss. The cleaners have been in, it's all tidy.'

'Thank you, Bill.'

Amanda took the familiar route through the double doors along the passage, through the second doors, into the Opal waiting room. And there was the sofa where she'd sat that day, waiting nervously for a second encounter with Dr Schofield and had seen Toby's smiling face around the door for the first time.

She walked into the office, and, with a deep breath, through into the lab. It was bare, just walls, and floor and ... George.

'George? Why are you here?' she asked curiously.

'I'm waiting for Vi. She hasn't come yet. We always meet in here. Vi likes the fire.'

'Violet?'

'Yes. She said she'd come. I can't go without my Violet,' he said anxiously.

Amanda had a thought.

'OK, George, I'll see if I can find her for you.'

'Thanks, er, I don't know your name.'

'Amanda. Amanda Cadabra.'

He grinned. 'You're magic.'

She smiled, nodded, and went out to the car. Amanda pulled her phone from her pocket.

'Gwendolen? Could you come with me again, please, to the residential home?'

'Yes. Now?'

'Please. And do you think you could ask Violet to talk to me for a minute?

'Of course, dear. Give me ten minutes to wash my hands and put on my hat.'

Having driven to The Grange, Amanda opened the passenger door. As she got in, Miss Armstrong-Witworth said, 'What a relief it's all over. Did you assist the police with their enquiries?'

'Yes,' she replied, gladly.

'Well done finding the radio and the papers. His father … it's all such a shame …. Shame that has hung like a pall over the very ruins all these years. Shame: that's what his wife and son felt. And carried it with them all their lives until it drove poor Robin to murder …. Terrible thing.' Gwendolen shook her head. 'So needless.'

They were soon at Pipkin Acres, and seated in Violet's neat, comfortable room again.

'Hello, Violet.'

'Hello, Gwennie,' she answered in a faint voice.

'You know me?'

'I know you Gwennie,' she answered, slightly nodding her delicate little head framed in its fine white hair.

'I've brought someone to see you,' explained Gwendolen. 'A young lady. Her name is Amanda. I think she's got some news for you.'

'Oh, all right,' Violet said weakly, looked doubtful.

Gwendolen nodded to Amanda to take her place at the bedside. Amanda took the frail hand gently.

'Hello, Violet. I've got a message for you … from George.'

'My Georgie?' The clouded eyes brightened. 'You've seen my Georgie?'

'Yes, Violet. He's waiting for you. He's there now, in your favourite room with the fire, waiting for you to come to him.'

'It's been such a long time,' she said sadly.

'But he's never stopped,' said Amanda. 'He's always been there. And now. I think you can go to him. If you want to.'

'I want to …. Who are you?'

'I'm Amanda.'

Violet put up her hand to Amanda's cheek.

'What a lovely girl you are. You've got sparkles all around you … hmm.' She stroked Amanda's hair, and then her eyes closed and her hand relaxed.

Amanda looked up at Gwendolen. 'Is it all right to go now?'

'Of course.'

Quickly, Amanda drove Miss Armstrong-Witworth back, in silence.

'Thank you, Gwendolen.'

'That's all right, dear. Off you go.'

Amanda raced to the Centre and entered reception. 'OK to go to the lab?' she asked Bill.

'Sure.'

She hurried in.

'George, I think Vi ….' But the air beside them was already softly gleaming, as the form of a young woman, a young Violet, as she had been all of those years ago, took shape. Her smooth skin was glowing, her blue eyes were wide and bright under long black lashes, and her dark bronze hair lay in soft rolls on her shoulders. A green dress flowed around her lithe figure, as she ran to him.

'Georgie!'

'My girl!'

The distance between them in time, in years, in space, closed as they embraced.

Amanda looked away and gave them their moment.

Finally, she said to George, 'You can go now, can't you?'

'Yes, we can,' he said, holding Violet's hand. She looked at Amanda curiously, and George said, 'This is Gwen's friend, Vi.'

'Hello, Violet.'

Violet came forward and took Amanda's hand.

'I know you, don't I?'

'Yes, Violet, you do.'

'Yes.' She stroked Amanda's cheek. 'You're a lovely girl.'

'Have a happy life together,' said Amanda.

'Oh, we will,' confirmed George. 'We're going to Canada.'

Violet smiled. 'We'll make a new start.'

Amanda didn't need to perform the spell. A door opened in the wall. George turned to her.

'Thanks for finding my Violet, Amanda.'

'All I had to do was tell her that you were waiting and she came right away,' she said.

'Yes, I did,' agreed the smiling Violet.

Amanda waved. 'Bye.'

'Bye, dear.'

They stepped through, and the door closed, shutting in the light with them.

Chapter 50

୧୨

INVITATION, AND GOLDEN RULES

Amanda went to the café, sat with hot chocolate, and, for the first time in the past chaotic days, felt sad for Toby. Then again, he was probably happy as a king, with a whole new dimension to explore.

Well, she still had a lot of therapy to try but she was glad there was going to be a little gap. She needed time. Time to process all that had happened over the summer.

Suddenly she longed for the workshop. For the normality of restoration. Well, normality for Amanda, and, of course that did involve wielding tools and equipment by spellcraft, and making furniture levitate around the room, but, relatively speaking.

And she had learning to do. Yes, magical weightlifting and practicing to do two things at once that needed concentration. She couldn't afford to be blasé or get stuck in a mystical rut. Especially after all the waves she'd made.

Amanda returned home, and was walking through the hall when her phone rang. She looked at the caller ID: D I. Trelawney.

'Hello, Inspector,' said Amanda, rather pleased.

'Hello, Miss Cadabra. I was just calling to see if you've recovered from all of the excitement surrounding the murder.'

'Yes, thank you. Of course, naturally, everything seems sadly dull by comparison but, truth to tell, I'm enjoying a taste of normality.'

'Good, glad to hear it. By the way, I'd like the tour sometime, if it's still on offer.'

'Of course,' she replied enthusiastically. Inspiration dawned. 'I've just had a brainwave. Why don't you come for Halloween? Bonfire, fireworks, see how the local yokels keep the celebration of All Hallows.'

'That would be delightful. However,' said Trelawney with regret, 'I'm afraid Halloween is a particularly busy time for me.'

'What? Slaving over a hot cauldron all night?'

'I mean for us coppers.'

'Oh? Witches abroad?' Amanda asked teasingly.

'No, more like pranksters and drunks.'

'Ah, I see. Well ... how about if you visit for the Feast of St Ursula of the Orchard? On 17th November. It's a Saturday. It's a local festival, with food and cider.'

'Er ... sounds, er, unique.'

'Oh, it is, believe me.'

'Yes, I would like that very much, Miss Cadabra. I can hardly wait to hear the story behind *that*.'

'It's a good one!'

'Till the 17th then,' said Trelawney.

'Come up for mid-day if you can.'

'I will be at your door on the stroke of twelve,' he affirmed.

'You'll enjoy it, I'm sure. Thank you for calling to see how I am.'

'You're welcome. Goodbye.'

'Bye for now.'

Amanda ended the call. She looked at her phone meditatively. 'Hmm,' she said aloud, evaluating her emotional state. 'I'm pleased. Yes, ... I'm pleased,' Amanda decided .and continued her journey through the kitchen and up the path between the fruit trees, shedding the very last of the plums and late pears.

Granny and Grandpa were in the workshop with Tempest. He was sitting on the workbench having a staring match with Senara. Yellow versus blue. It was the only sense in which they saw eye to eye.

'So,' said Granny, 'what have you learned? Remember your Golden Rules?'

Amanda recited them:

'One: keep my Pocket-wand on me at all times. I do, and yes, I will write to Dr Bergstrom for a spare.

'Two: always use the least powerful spell possible.

'Three: look for potential allies and expect the best from people, but allow them to earn my trust rather than giving it away, however strong the impulse.

'Four: be sensitive to any strange feelings I may experience when casting a spell. Well, I certainly am now.

'And five: always carry a tin of caviar for the purposes of bribery.'

'And what new ones do you have?' asked Granny.

'Six: *don't* drop my Pocket-wand in public!

'Seven: carry two pairs of DIY gloves. I gave mine to Trelawney, and scrabbling away clearing a bigger hole in that rubble did my hands no good.

'Eight: if I have to time-travel, make sure I have the proper currency. Fortunately, I was saved by the air raid siren!

'Nine: I must never be complacent about my magical skills, and must keep expanding them. I can't believe that piano didn't come down on me.'

'You had help, dear.'

'Oh, thank you, Granny and Grandpa.'

'No, *bian*, not from us,' Perran corrected her.

'Who? George?'

'Your inspector.'

'What? He's not my ... Of course, yes, we did say, I'd need

some muscle. Yes, and another time he might not be around. I'd better get practicing my levitation.'

'Is there a number ten?' asked Grandpa.

Amanda suddenly thought of Gwendolen Armstrong-Witworth, former spy on behalf of Her Majesty's Secret Service.

'Yes. Number ten: never make assumptions about people, especially ones you might think of as elderly. Hmm, there's no such thing as "a sweet little old lady".'

'Excellent progress, dear,' said Granny.

'You've done very well, *bian*,' Grandpa praised her.

'So have I passed Magical Sleuthing 201?' she asked, mischievously.

'You have, Ammy. Very well done. But —'

'But I made waves,' she finished. 'And there could be consequences.'

'Just so,' replied Granny calmly. 'You have magic to practice.'

'I know.'

'We'll help you,' said Grandpa, reassuringly.

'So you've seen the happy couple off have you, dear?' asked Granny.

'Yes.' Amanda paused. 'To Canada. George says they're going to Canada. Can they do that? I mean, do you have Canada in your dimension?'

'Of course they can do that. They can go anywhere they like, at any time. You'd be surprised at what we have here.'

'Well, I can see you have tea. And Victoria sandwich and crumpets and scones and clotted cream and jam and —'

'Oh yes, dear,' said Granny with a glimmering smile. 'It's absolute heaven.'

Chapter 51

ༀ

HEIRESS

It was Saturday morning, so blue and gold a day that Amanda was setting off early for her favourite spot with Tempest. In her hand was a picnic basket holding roast beef, mustard and cress sandwiches, ginger beer, and a mini apple pie for her, and some extra meat for him. She opened the front door to Joan, who was about to press the doorbell, once she got her fingers around the wisteria branches.

'Hello, love, look what I've got for you!' said Joan with glee.

Amanda looked at the white padded bag the postlady was holding, and said prosaically, 'Looks like it could be those special brackets I've ordered for the —'

'No!' interrupted Joan. 'It's from Germany! From your young man!'

'What young man?'

'Hugo, of course,' replied Joan, as though stating the obvious.

'How do you know it's from Hugo?' asked Amanda.

'It's on the back, his name and address in Bavaria, from his village.'

'Ah.' Amanda's pulse quickened a little. What could he have sent her?

'There,' said Joan, putting the package into Amanda's hands. 'You take it with you to the priory.'

'How did you know …?' Amanda stopped. Why was she even asking?

'When you take a picnic and a book and Tempest, we all know you're off for a bit of peace, in your little place up there,' Joan answered kindly.

'I see. Thank you, Joan, but, actually,' said Amanda, deciding that she had quite enough to think about for the moment, 'I'll leave it here, and look at it later.' She leaned back into the hall and placed the package on the table to the left of the door.

'Just as you like, dear.'

Amanda drove up Orchard Row, turned left into Hog Lane, then left again into Priory Lane, where she parked. She was just in time to be spotted by Sylvia, off duty from her road duties, as it was the weekend, and there were no schoolchildren to squire across the street.

''Ello, dearie.'

'Hello, Sylvia,' Amanda greeted her pleasantly.

''Ow you recovering after all the excitement? Didn't you do well digging up the spy's suitcase, 'n' all! You won't have to go to testify in court, will you?'

'No, Sylvia. And yes, thank you, I'm enjoying getting back to normal.'

'Well, Jane wants to see you sometime. She's got plans. For the church, I think. She says you're the one to talk to. When you've got time.'

'All right. I'll pop in to see her. Maybe tomorrow.' The rector would definitely be around on a Sunday.

''Ow's your young man?'

'Sorry? Mr Ford —'

'No, no, the other one.'

'Hugo went back to Germany,' she reminded Sylvia.

'No no, and not the one who got himself murdered neither. The nice chap in the suit.'

'Ah. Him. He's *not* my young man.' said Amanda firmly.

'Oh, too bad. Never mind. If you don't fancy 'im, there's a new one coming, 'im and his sister. Oh, look there's Gordon, I must have a word with 'im ...'

Amanda hurried off before anyone else could waylay her. She climbed up to her seat at the top of what was once the night stairs. Here she was away from all the comings and goings and gossip, and yet still able to see her neighbours moving about the village, and through the trees and fields.

She glanced over her shoulder toward Madley Wood, Little Madley, restored to peace, she hoped, with the traitor brought to light. What a summer it had been!

Now deep golds and russets of autumn were all around. Soon it would be time for Guy Fawkes Night; bonfires and fireworks. Fireworks. She'd had enough of that for now. Then it would be November and the Blessing of the Apples and Trelawney's visit.

She stroked Tempest. 'My first real murder. Sad and exciting. Is that wrong? It's like I've ... yes, as Aunt Amelia said, I've crossed the Rubicon.' Granny didn't have to say it: there would be more coming her way. And they hadn't said this either: there was more that she needed to remember. And now she knew she was heiress to sinister Cardiubarn Hall.

The wind blew cold for a moment. She looked to the West, toward Cornwall, and shivered.

The wind dropped. On the other hand, that's where her new Uncle Mike and Trelawney were. So there must be good things about it.

The sun felt warm again.

'It's my birthplace, after all.' She looked down at her village, surrounded by its Wood and its apple orchards. 'But *this* will always be home. I live in the witch's cottage, that's my rightful place. But one day ... '

She looked in her mind's eye across the 400 miles, beyond the Wessex Downs, across the river Tamar and there, on Bodmin Moor, by the Dozmary Pool, to Cardiubarn Hall.

'Yes. One day … I'll be back,' said Amanda Cadabra.

THE END

AUTHOR'S NOTE

Thank you for reading Amanda Cadabra and The Cellar of Secrets. I hope you enjoyed your time in Sunken Madley and it's lost and found annexe.

Whether this was your first visit to the village or your return trip, I would love you to tell me your thoughts about your journey through the book. And if you could write a review, that would be of tremendous help. You can post in on the e-store where you bought the book (if you're not sure how to post a review on Amazon, here is a how-to on my website) or on Facebook, Twitter or your social platform of choice. It would mean a great deal to me.

Best of all would be if you dropped me a line at HollyBell@amandacadabra.com so we can connect in person. If there is a character you especially liked or anything you would like more of, please let me know. Amanda Cadabra Book 3 is in the pipeline, and I want to make sure that all of the things that you liked about the first two books make an appearance for you.

For tidbits on the world of Sunken Madley and to keep up with news of the continuing adventures of our heroes Amanda, Tempest, Granny and Grandpa, Trelawney and Hogarth, visit www.amandacadabra.com, where you can also request to enter the VIP Readers Group or sign up for the newsletter to stay in touch and find out about the next sequel. The VIP Readers is a limited numbers group. Members are invited to receive and review an advance copy of the next book. If you are one of that treasured number, thank you for reading, evaluating and giving your precious feedback.

If Tempest has endeared himself to you and reminds you of your cat or one you know, in any way, you are invited to enter a photograph in The Tempest Competition. Details are at http://amandacadabra.com/the-tempest-competition/

You can also find me on:

Facebook at

h t t p s : / / w w w . f a c e b o o k . c o m / H o l l y -Bell-923956481108549/ (Please come and say hello. It makes my day when a reader does that.)

Twitter at https://twitter.com/holly_b_author

Pinterest https://www.pinterest.co.uk/hollybell2760/

Instagram https://www.instagram.com/hollybellac

Google+ at https://plus.google.com/u/0/110373044289244156044

Goodreads at https://www.goodreads.com/author/show/18387493.Holly_Bell

and Bookbub at https://www.bookbub.com/profile/holly-bell

See you soon.

ABOUT THE AUTHOR

Cat adorer and chocolate lover, Holly Bell is a photographer and video maker when not writing. Whilst being an enthusiastic novel reader, Holly has had lifetime's experience in writing non-fiction.

Holly devoured all of the Agatha Christie books long before she knew that Miss Marple was the godmother of the Cosy Mystery. Her devotion to JRR Tolkien's Lord of the Rings meant that her first literary creation in this area would have to be a cosy paranormal.

Holly lives in the UK and is a mixture of English, Cornish, Welsh and other ingredients. Her favourite animal is called Bobby. He is a black cat. Purely coincidental. Of course.

ACKNOWLEDGEMENTS

Thanks to Pravin Jootun, whose encouragement and support have been unstinting. You are a brother in the truest sense.

Thank you to Philippa Shallcrass for encouraging and reassuring me throughout the writing process, to Flora Gatehouse, for constant support, keen-eyed and intuitive editing and publicity, to Judes Gerstein, my Canadian gem of an advance reader, for noticing issues and offering ideal solutions.

Thanks are also due to the rector of of St Mary the Virgin, Monken Hadley whose fund of information helped me to shape the village of 'Sunken Madley', and to Stephen Tatlow, the Director of Music there and the churchwardens for their kind welcome and delight at being fictionalised.

Praise and thanks go out to my talented and immensely patient illustrator Erik Patricio Lúa (Instagram: tripaciolua) for his beautiful book cover art. Your dedication to the project was truly remarkable. Thanks and admiration are also extended to my map maker Methmeth who skilfully turns my sketches and mockups into exquisite works of art.

I would like to express sincere appreciation to the curator, engineers and other staff at the de Havilland Aircraft Museum, Hertfordshire, for their immense kindness, wealth of information, and support in making the events depicted in the story as feasible as possible. Thank you for the happy hours that I had the privilege of spending in your company and among the vintage aeroplanes themselves. Dear Reader, if you have not yet had the pleasure of a visit, you have a memorable treat in store.

Many thanks to expert Jim Cardoza of Hmsantiquetrunks. com for identifying the correct trunks for the cellar of secrets. I would like to make special mention of Clifford Jack for his inspired suggestion of an eccentric's choice of car, the VW Beetle with the Porche engine, in metallic purple, for which Mrs Irma Uberhausfest, relinquishes her Mercedes.

Thanks to HUF HAUS for generously allowing me the use of images and clips of their beautiful buildings and construction process. Appreciation also is due to Carwow, who kindly supplied three excellent clips of the red Jaguar I PACE. The description of the first appearance of the car in the story would not have been possible to complete without their contribution.

Thank you, in fact, to all those without whose support this book would not have been possible.

Finally, in whatever dimension they are currently inhabiting, thanks go out to my cat who inspired Tempest, and to my grandfather and brother for Perran and Trelawney. Your magic endures.

QUESTIONS FOR READING CLUBS

1. What did you like best about the book?

2. Which character did you like best? Is there one with whom you especially identified?

3. Whom would you like to know more about and why?I

4. If you made a movie of the book, whom would you cast and in what parts? Have you chosen any recasting over Book 1? Would you still have the same actress play, Amanda, for example, as you did in Book 1?

5. Did the book remind you of any others you have read, apart from the first book in the series, either in the same or another genre?

6. Did you think the cover fitted the story? If not, how would you redesign it?

7. How unique is this story?

8. Which characters grew and changed over the course of the story, and which remained the same?

9. What feelings did the book evoke? Which was your favourite group characters, and why?

10. What place in the book would you most like to visit, and why?

11. Was the setting one that felt familiar or relatable to you? Why or why not? If you read the first book, how at home did you feel revisiting the locations?

12.   What did you think of the continuity between the first book and this sequel?

13.   Was the book the right length? If too long, what would you leave out? If too short, what would you add?

14.   How well do you think the title conveyed what the book is about?

15.   If you could ask Holly Bell just one question, what would it be?

16.   How well do you think the author created the world of the story?

17.   Which quotes or scenes did you like the best, and why?

18.   Was the author just telling an entertaining story or trying as well to communicate any other ideas? If so, what do you think they were?

19.   Did the book change how you think or feel about any thing, person or place? Did it help you to understand someone or yourself better?

20.   What do you think the characters will do after the end of the book? Would you want to read the sequel?

THE DE HAVILLAND AIRCRAFT MUSEUM MOSQUITO MISSION QUIZ

1. Where was the Mosquito Prototype designed and built?
A. De Havilland's factory at Hatfield
B. Salisbury Hall
C. Hatfield House

2. What was the de Havilland type number allocated to the aircraft?
A. DH 82
B. DH 94
C. DH 98

3. Where would you find this window on the Prototype Mosquito?
A. In the nose
B. In the fuselage
C. In the cockpit

4. What was the original paint colour of the Prototype?
A. Trainer Yellow
B. Trainer Yellow underside/camouflage upper surfaces
C. Duck egg blue underside/camouflage upper surfaces

5. What was the total number of crew?
A. 1
B. 3
C. 2

6. What was the military code for the prototype?
A. U3040
B. W4050
C. X5030

7. How many machine guns did the Mosquito FBVI have?
A. 2
B. 4
C. 6

8. Who was the pilot of the first flight?
A. Neville Duke
B. Geoffrey de Havilland Jnr
C. Amy Johnson

9. What were the names of the engines that powered
the Mosquito?
A. Gremlins
B. Merlins
C. Perkins

10. What was the nickname of the Mosquito?
A. Wooden Wonder
B. Sky Blazer
C. Flying Finger

11. What were the fuselage and wings made from?
A. Aluminium
B. Wood
C. Steel

12. Who was the chief designer of the Mosquito?
A. Eric Vicar
B. Eric Priest
C. Eric Bishop

13. When did the Prototype return to Salisbury Hall?
A. September 1958
B. October 1957
C. January 1959

14. What was the date of the Prototype's first flight?
A. 1st November 1940
B. 14th November 1940
C. 25th November 1940

15. What was the weight of the biggest bomb carried by the Mosquito?
A. 2000lb
B. 3000lb
C. 4000lb

16. How many Mosquitos were built?
A. 6001
B. 7781
C. 9004

17. What was the biggest gun on the Mosquito?
A. 40mm Machine Gun
B. Molins '6-pounder Class M' 57mm cannon
C. Hispano Mk II Cannon

18. Where would you find these stats on the Prototype Mosquito?
A. On the tail
B. On the fuselage
C. On the wing

19. Who turned 'green and yellow with envy' when describing the Mosquito's performance?
A. Adolf Galland
B. Adolf Hitler
C. Hermann Goering

20. Which countries built the Mosquito?
A. UK and Australia
B. UK and Canada
C. Australia, Canada and UK

The answers to several of these questions can be found in the story. Others can be found on the museum website. For the rest, when you get the chance, visit the De Havilland Aircraft Museum, Salisbury Hall, London Colney, Hertfordshire AL2 1BU. dehavillandmuseum.co.uk. There you can ask for a proper, printed quiz. Then, when you have completed it, take it to the Aeroshop for checking and to collect your prize! The museum closes for the winter and reopens in February.

34195602R00183

Printed in Poland
by Amazon Fulfillment
Poland Sp. z o.o., Wrocław